Praise

"Savvy and whip-smart, ... nary
a false step, *Lucky Wander Boy* is a twenty-first-century's *Fan's
Notes* by way of Philip Dick's *Confessions of a Crap Artist,* with
all their possibilities exploded exponentially. Over ... ver it
takes flight from its own moorings, spanning ... pop
obsessive's private universe, from northern lights, to the
distant ... loves, restless girlfriends and seductive
Asian ... —a
novel not of this moment but the next."

—Steve Erickson, author of *Days of the Black Clock* and
The Sea Came in at Midnight

"*Lucky Wander Boy* is a compelling dive into the twisted
psyche of the video gamer, where old D.B. Weiss has captured
the strange combination of mania and nostalgia classic games
inspire within the collective consciousness of our generation."

—Van Burnham, author of *Supercade: A Visual History of the
Videogame Age*

"I really enjoyed this book. D. B. Weiss treats video games
as a form of modern mythology, a template to understand life.
His passion for games is evident and I'm happy to report that
he represents that science with surprising eloquence."

—Will Wright, creator of *The Sims* and *The Sims 2*

"D. B. Weiss does for video games what Michael Chabon
did for comics in *The Adventures of Kavalier and Clay*: explore
the development of a new medium by telling a beautiful
story. And like Kavalier, Weiss's protagonist Adam's ... is
pursuit of his digital Dulcinea is presented with dazzling
intelligence and mordant humor."

—David Benioff, author of *The 25th Hour*

Lucky Wander Boy

d.b. weiss

A PLUME BOOK

PLUME
Published by the Penguin Group
Penguin Putnam Inc., 375 Hudson Street, New York, New York 10014, U.S.A.
Penguin Books Ltd, 80 Strand, London WC2R 0RL, England
Penguin Books Australia Ltd, 250 Camberwell Road, Camberwell, Victoria 3124,
Australia
Penguin Books Canada Ltd, 10 Alcorn Avenue, Toronto, Ontario, Canada M4V 3B2
Penguin Books (N.Z.) Ltd, Cnr Rosedale and Airborne Roads, Albany, Auckland 1310,
New Zealand

Penguin Books Ltd, Registered Offices: Harmondsworth, Middlesex, England

First published by Plume, a member of Penguin Putnam Inc.

First Printing, March 2003
10 9 8 7 6 5 4 3 2 1

LIBRARY OF CONGRESS CATALOGING-IN-PUBLICATION DATA

Weiss, D. B.
    Lucky Wander Boy / D. B. Weiss.
        p.   cm.
    ISBN 0-452-28394-9
    1. Young men—Fiction.   2. Video games—Fiction.   I. Title.

PS3623.E455 L83   2003
813'.6—dc21

                                            2002029283

Printed in the United States of America
Set in Bembo
Designed by Erin Benach

PUBLISHER'S NOTE
This is a work of fiction. Names, characters, places, and incidents are either the products
of the author's imagination or are used fictitiously, and any resemblance to actual persons, living or dead, business establishments, events, or locales is entirely coincidental.

dedication

For my parents

acknowledgments

Many thanks to my readers: Mark Bomback, David Friedman, Anthony Miller, Peter Craig, Maximilian Schlaks and Andrea Troyer; my agent, Ian Kleinert; my editor, Kelly Notaras; my brother, Rick Weiss; and Dan Rush and Jeff Lipsky for the jacket photos.

Also thanks to Tony Barnstone, Tema Bomback, Gretchen Bruggeman, Van Burnham, Alicia Gordon, Leonard Hermann, J. C. Herz, Trena Keating, Steven Kent, Tony Malone, Scott McCloud, Amanda Patten, Kit Reed and Jason Stone.

Lucky Wander Boy

I cannot be what I am
so I become money, quarter by quarter,
and live as long as I can live.

—Tony Barnstone,
"Why I Play Video Games"

p a r t   i

LUCKY

Like great pain, however, true silence is a thing men and women are not built to endure for long; their minds instinctively fill the latter as they retreat from the former.

—Dafei Ji, *Leng Tch'e*

wakawakawakawaka

● ●

It started with the *Catalogue of Obsolete Entertainments*. All things start somewhere. My thing started there.

I only told one person about the *Catalogue*, ever, and that was well after Lucky Wander Boy had become a factor, or *the* factor, changing everything. I did not tell Anya—the very notion would have been alien to her, as in "from a distant planet," and she was a stranger in a strange land as it was. She would have resented my project as yet another example of the American senselessness she was beginning to see everywhere she looked.

She'd already started trailing specks of resentment into our apartment by Wednesday, September 5, 1999. This 9/5 happened to come exactly 95 days after Anya and I first arrived in Los Angeles together. More importantly, it was the twentieth anniversary of the day Namco game designer Toru Iwatani went out for pizza with some friends in Tokyo, took the first slice from the pie, and forged Pac-Man in the crucible of his mind. An auspicious time for beginnings, in retrospect—and though the concept of the *Catalogue* had been germinating in the damp of my mind for some time, it was on this day that its first shoots pushed through to demand my attention and action.

I was in the second bedroom, which I had commandeered as my "office" back when I'd been paying the bulk of the rent, though those days and that money were long gone. After an hour of diligent online searching, I had found the Clyde's Revenge hack of Pac-Man, the version (or inversion) of the game that lets you play as a ghost while Pac-Men chase you around the screen. The sounds were the same as the original—the electronic swing of the opening theme, the background siren swirl, the downward spiral glissando of death. When Anya heard them coming from my small powered speakers, she closed my office door, flopped onto the living room couch and watched the E! Entertainment Network at peak volume. Through the closed office door, I heard *Mysteries & Scandals* host A. J. Benza pose a wry, rhetorical question about the downside of fame ("Ain't it a bitch?").

I kept playing, switching to the I'm Going Berserk! hack, which allowed the Pac-Man to gobble dots unpursued, and was thus less a game than a meditative exercise. As I maneuvered the Pac-Man through the tunnel on the left side of the screen to emerge from the tunnel on the right side, then back through the right-hand tunnel to the left and so forth in an attempt to remain off-screen indefinitely, I felt the distinct stirrings of a major thought, but the noise from the TV kept it vague and cloudy, prevented it from coalescing.

In an attempt to coax this thought into being, I turned up the volume a bit, causing Anya to turn up her volume, which I would not have thought possible, leading our downstairs neighbor, whose name I did not know, to thump on the ceiling as A. J. Benza explored the mystery surrounding the death of movie producer Paul Bern, whose ghost was seen by Sharon Tate two years before her murder in the same Benedict Canyon cottage where Bern bought a bullet in the brain on *September 5*, 1932.

When the commercial break came, the TV went silent, and Anya opened the office door.

"Wakawakawakawaka!" she said, and left the apartment. It struck me as an extreme reaction, not to mention fruitless; the only places within a five-minute walk were a halfway house for deaf alcoholics, the Elks Club Lodge, and the Kyoto Dreams massage parlor. After the sound of her footsteps faded, however, a rare quiet settled over our four rooms, a rich silence in which my thought could solidify and grow until it wrapped itself around the idea of the *Catalogue of Obsolete Entertainments*. The hardest thing about a massive project, outside of finishing it, was starting it, and I knew I might never get a better chance. I quit the videogame emulator and started up my word processor. It was time to begin.

CATALOGUE OF OBSOLETE ENTERTAINMENTS
by Adam Pennyman

GAME: PAC-MAN
Format: Coin-Op Arcade Machine
Manufacturer: Midway license of Japanese Namco property
Year: 1980
CPU: Z80 3.072000 MHz
Sound: Namco mono (1 channel)
Screen resolution: 288 × 224 pixels

The most universally recognized of the arcade machines, Pac-Man's central icon is the player's avatar, his on-screen representation: the game's eponymous, voracious yellow three-quarter circle. By removing a simple pizza slice, Namco game designer Toru Iwatani breathed life into the simplest geometric form, turning it into a snapping mouth, lovable... but hungry, always hungry, all the time chomping with want just like the player it represents. The Pac-Man must eat its way through the 240 dots and four Power Pill energizer dots that line his blue, bilaterally symmetrical maze, while dodging (or, when under the fleeting influence of a Power Pill, eating) the game's antagonists, the four Pac-Man ghosts.[1]

The Pac-Man's insatiable hunger for the dots and Power Pills that fill the corridors of his maze-worlds suggests weighty parallels, such as the ravenous hunger for More Life that Darwin saw in all species, any one of which would overpopulate and overrun the earth if not for the predatory ghosts of natural selection. Also, we are reminded of Marx's "need of a constantly expanding market" that "chases the bourgeoisie over the entire surface of the globe" (*Communist Manifesto*) with the "vocation to approach, by quantitative increase, as near as possible to absolute wealth" (*Capital*), casting the Pac-Man in the

---

[1] Pinky, Blinky, Inky and Clyde are undeniably cute, cuter than the Pac-Man himself; the first time the author played the game as a fat ten-year-old boy with microwave pizza grease on his fingers at Ed's Convenience Mart in Woodhill Grove, Illinois, his virgin Pac-Man lasted all of ten seconds as he instinctively moved to connect with them, somehow trying to assimilate their cuteness and their all-seeing eyes into his blind yellow proxy.

role of corporate antihero in a utopian fantasy where the agents protesting his unfettered domination of the maze-world actually defeat him in the end. Obvious metaphors, lurking just beneath the surface of the game.

Suspiciously obvious. These kinds of interpretations belie the poverty of imagination that has become all too typical of practitioners of the interpretive arts. If Pac-Man and the games that followed in its wake mean anything to us, if they are central switching stations through which thousands of our most important memories are routed, it is our duty to dig deeper.

To us, the Pac-Man's lives appear short, cheap, and relatively inconsequential once we discover the overwhelming importance of sex and money. But if we perform a thought experiment and try to occupy a Pac-Man's subjectivity, we will realize that these three short spans are not so short to him. We must allow that each dot eaten takes on a meaning for the Pac-Man that we can barely fathom.

I suggest that if we, through force of imagination, were to dilate time to experience it as the Pac-Man does, and increase the resolution to allow us to read as much into each pixel as the Pac-Man must, we would not see the identical dots as identical at all. When the microscopic differences in each pixel are made large, each dot will possess a snowflake's uniqueness, and the acquisition of each—no, the *experience* of each—will bring the Pac-Man a very specific and distinct joy or sorrow. The dots all rack up points equally, of course; in retrospect, however, some are revealed as wrong choices, links in a chain of wrong choices that trace out a wrong path leading to a withering demise beneath the adorable and utterly unforgiving eyes of Blinky, Inky, Pinky or Clyde. As anyone who ever played the game seriously must know, the order in which the dots are experienced is of great importance. For each labyrinth, there are rigid and precise patterns through the maze—i.e., specific sequences of dot acquisition—that, if followed with a samurai's unwavering, arrow-into-hell certainty, allow the knowing Pac-Man to ascend from level to level with Zen ease and deliberateness.

An often-overlooked, seemingly minor feature of the game has implications which, once unraveled, are more radical than anything heretofore discussed. In the middle of each maze, on the left and right sides of the labyrinth, there are two identical tunnels that lead off the borders of the screen. These tunnels are connected, with the left tunnel leading to the right, and the right to the left. In itself, this disappearing off one side of the screen to reappear on the opposite side broke no new ground. In Atari's Asteroids, for instance, a player's ship can do as much.

When an Asteroids ship leaves the screen, however, it reappears on the other side *instantaneously*; thus, the three-dimensional space described by Asteroids' two-dimensional screen is a *continuous*, perfect sphere. In Pac-Man, this is not the case at all. When a Pac-Man disappears into one of the off-screen mid-maze tunnels, there is a lag of about a half second before he reemerges on the other side. Assuming his speed remains constant, we can extrapolate some other-dimensional space of approximately six dots' length that the Pac-Man must traverse each time he goes through the off-screen tunnel. Were it not for the pursuing ghosts, he could remain in this off-screen space indefinitely.

In its evocation of an unseen world beyond the rectangle of the seen screen, Pac-Man forces us to reckon with a space that is real, yet never experienced directly, empirically. An area where no points can be earned, yet one crucial to the successful completion of the higher-level screens. The truly tapped-in player never forgets the off-screen tunnels, like a religious man with one mental foot planted firmly in the hereafter.

Pac-Man is the world's first metaphysical video game. Like a black hole's event horizon, the impassable barrier of its CRT screen hides a richness we can speculate about but never experience directly. What happens in its unseen regions? Perhaps the laws that reign there are not the brutal laws of the maze. Perhaps the tunnels move through an endless Valhalla of energizer dots with no ghosts in sight, tantalizingly close, if only we could break free.

There is a world beneath the glass that we can never know.

kashas

● ●

In the spring of 1999, several years out of college, I found myself out of work, fired from my job as script researcher on a movie entitled *Viking!* It did not bother me much, being let go. The movie was guaranteed straight-to-video. I had been fired from better jobs.

Shortly after my dismissal—effective immediately upon notification, with a severance package of one *Viking!* T-shirt and two refrigerator magnets—I inadvertently came upon a job prospect on the Internet, which was ironic, as I had been pretending to search for one while catching up on movie reviews and current events. On my favorite Chicago weekly's website, I read a brief article about an American video production company called Cattle Raid Productions, located in Warsaw, Poland. The company was run by a fellow Chicago migrant named Derek Palabi, whose older brother owned several blocks of real estate in Warsaw's city center. I had no particular reason to leave Los Angeles, but I had no particular reason to stay, either. I'd heard things were happening in Poland (though I didn't know what, and the article wasn't much help in this regard), and this Palabi seemed easygoing enough. I sent Cattle Raid a query letter and CV. There was an immediate Chicago connection—Derek and I had a few acquaintances in common from my hometown of Woodhill Grove—and he found my graphic-design resume impressive. He offered me a job via e-mail, and agreed to cover my transportation costs. So that summer I drifted across the Atlantic, where I had many novel experiences.

My first night on the town in Warsaw, at a tacky nightclub where the velvet ropes were made of tatty blue vinyl, I entered to find a laser light show on the wall, lots of women dressed in revealing homemade evening wear, and lots of paunchy, thin-haired men speaking loud English to them. I watched a beautiful girl with delicate features and shampoo-ad black hair wink artlessly at the guy behind me, and then turned to find that there was no guy behind me. She dragged me onto the dance floor, and we danced to a 160 bpm dance remix of "Love Me Do" while she felt my back and chest the way a jockey rubs a horse's flanks. I was defenseless; neither my employer nor my coworkers had told me about the way things were in this nightclub, in this city, in this part of the world. Letting newcomers find out on their own was an initiation of sorts, a benign form of hazing. When the song was over, this beautiful girl gave me a business card describing herself—in English—as a "Fashion Designer of Intimate Apparel." Her name was Kasha.

Many American men came to Poland primarily for the Kashas. These men could be seen at all the hot spots about town, stomping through the maze of this oft-stomped-through land in their business suits, snapping up as many gorgeous Polish girls as they could. Yes, gorgeous. My own preconceptions, which tended toward babushkaed cleaning ladies and the shell-shocked faces I saw in a History Channel documentary about the Nazi bombing of Warsaw, were blasted to pieces in the first hour of that first night out. Judging purely in terms of raw material, making allowances for Polish lack of polish and access to high fashion, Warsaw is on par with Paris and Milan for beauty per capita, which, given the country's history and the proportion of its young/bright/able population that has been put to the Prussian/German/Russian sword/gun/bomb over the past 250 years, is a miracle on par with the loaves and the fishes.

I was eventually warned, however, that many of these Kashas were in the market for American men and American citizenship, which they saw as antidotes to poverty, abusive relationships and general hopelessness. I was told to keep my wits about me, which I did, drifting from Kasha to Kasha too quickly for emotion to take root. It was very exciting and new to me, all that movement, and I enjoyed the ride. My behavior was not as cruel as it might seem, in the final analysis—not nearly as cruel as following my natural inclination to stop pushing my luck and grab on to one of them like a life raft. Besides, they were perceptive, and with each Kasha the moment inevitably came: I put my arm around her to smile rakishly, and a tiny chuffing laugh escaped through her nose, and right away I knew that she'd seen the cheap sparkle of fraud in my eye. She knew I was only acting this way because I was American and earned about six times as much as the average Polish Urban Professional, and that I could never play these lothario games at home.

Not that there was anything wrong with me, specifically. I had no obvious deformations. For all my adult life I'd been slim, I kept my beard very neat, I had all my hair. My nose was thin but not overly so, my teeth were small but straight, my wardrobe was strictly casual but always clean. I was on the right side of regular, and with the proper lighting and a few minutes' effort, I could actually make myself look rakish in a mirror, show myself the face I wanted the world to see. But that face never showed up in photographs, and whenever I tried to put it on for girls, they only laughed. There were times I wished I could freeze the mirror and wear it as a mask.

I did all right in Warsaw, though, better than I'd thought possible for myself, far too well to bother with Kasha the Receptionist at Cattle Raid Productions. She was an inventive seamstress with a flawless body who made all her own clothes (though she apparently could not afford fabric thick enough to be fully opaque), the kind of girl I'd never stand a chance with back home. But the word got around that she was high maintenance, too much trouble to be worth an expat's time. She was Tower Records; the other Kashas were Napster before that fucker from Metallica went and ruined it.

I believe Jeffrey Adelman had designs on her, however. He was the other graphic designer at Cattle Raid Productions, originally from Rye, New York. With furtive pride, he once explained to me that she dug him because of the whole Jewish, "Oppressed Other" angle he was playing with her, capitalizing on a long history of Polish anti-Semitism. He admitted appropriating the trick from the black guys he'd known who scored dozens of suburban white chicks at his Eastern liberal arts college, and often wore a knit Rasta cap in secret tribute to them. I didn't have the heart to tell him I'd never mentioned being Jewish to any of my Kashas. There was no harm in his being proud about a thing like that, in thinking he'd found a clever shortcut. Jeffrey was a good graphic designer and a hard worker; he only left his computer to eat lunch and stalk the wild marijuana that grew outside the office, laying the least impotent plants on the roof to dry. We worked in the same room on identical, tricked-out Macintosh G3s. One day, watching me work, he asked:

"Adam, dude . . . you're not really a graphic designer, are you?"

"No," I admitted. "I've got the Photoshop manual back at my apartment."

"How far have you gotten?"

"Chapter three."

Jeffrey's mouth sagged into a frown of understanding, and he bobbed his head. "That's cool. I hear you."

"Don't tell Derek, huh?"

"Pfff. As if."

One Thursday at work, Jeffrey called me over to his laptop with a fluttering hand. "Pennyman. Come check this out."

On his screen was a window titled "MAME."

"What is it?" I asked.

"MAME," he said, homonymous to "maim." "Multiple Arcade Machine Emulator. Observe."

Mirroring the movement of his finger on the track pad, the on-screen arrow shot over to highlight the file FROGGER.ZIP, which was bricked into an array of other files with ZIP suffixes. I felt a faint stirring in my gut. He clicked twice, slid the laptop in front of me, and I crossed over.

I became a small green frog jumping headlong into busy traffic. Not an imitation or a version of the arcade game—it *was* Frogger, the frog, the logs, the cars, the red-shelled turtles and purple ladyfrog, all down to the last pixel. I hopped from street to median to river, the taps of my fingers keyed to the frog-twitching axons in my brain, as if I had never left the Peacock Palace arcade in Wood-hill Grove, Illinois, where I had last played Frogger more than fifteen years ago.

Hundreds of times I had stepped into the palpable darkness that stretched Peacock's three rooms to the limits of possibility, stumbling through the football players and freaks and blacks and gearheads and dropouts and nobody specials and Mexicans and no-good trust-fund rebels, half of them higher than hell judging from my future experience, their blood-engorged eyeballs flashing mote reflections of five dozen CRT screens. I remembered edging past bellicose Rob Nixon, who once hit a kid in the face with a lead pipe, driven forward by something stronger than fear. I remembered closing my eyes and letting five dozen simple sound palettes blend together into an all-out electric jungle womb racket, as I crouched (in my head) in the twittering undergrowth, going Jungle Hunt native, listening to what the womb was trying to tell me, cracking the coded signals that hid in the noise. Though neglected, the memories were pristine, as if they'd been kept in a safe box and set aside to await my return from years of wandering.

The Peacock Palace had long ago burned down and been pounded to rubble and paved over with a strip mall that tried to hide its true nature beneath stately red brick, and I had not played video games with any regularity for years. A quarter here, a quarter there. I didn't much like the new games, which was usually all they had. Along with dirt bikes, Dungeons and Dragons, fireworks and martial arts weapons, they had been relegated to the callow slag heap of youth. The effect MAME Frogger had on me could not have been predicted by anyone, least of all myself.

As I died my last death beneath the wheels of a squat race car, I heard the descending bass bloom of doom that accompanied a death-by-traffic, that marvelous microcomposition: BYYEWwwww . . . *perfectly* reproduced. My own imperfect reproduction of that sound had served as my personal failure leitmotif for as long as I could remember, but the intervening years had all but buried its origins. Though my game was over, I continued to stare at the screen with dreamlike fascination.

"What else do you have?" I managed to ask. He paused Frogger and called up a list:

Araknoid	Galaga	Pengo
Asteroids	Galaxian	Pooyan
Battle Zone	Gauntlet	Popeye
Berzerk	GhostsNGblns	PuckMan
Boot Hill!	Gorf	Punch-Out!!
Burger Time	Journey	Q★bert
Carnival	Joust	Qix
Centipede	Jr. Pac-Man	Rally X
Congo Bongo	Jungle Hunt	Robotron
Crazy Climber	Jungle King	Sea Wolf
Crystal Castles	Kaos	Sinistar
DefenderDemon's	Lode Runner	SpaceInvaders
World	MarbleMdnss	Star Wars
Dig Dug	Mario Bros.	Street Fighter
Discs of Tron	Mr. Do!	Tapper
Donkey Kong	Mr. Do's Castle	Tempest
Donkey Kong 3	Ms. Pac-Man	Tron
Double Dragon	Pac-Land	Tutankham
Elevator Action	Pac-Man	Warlords
EmpireStrksBk	Pac-Man Plus	YosakuDnbee
Frenzy	Pac-Mania	Zaxxon
Frogger	Paperboy	Zoo Keeper

"Where did you get this program? How much did it cost?"

"It didn't cost anything, yo. I got it on the Internet, it's open source."

"Define open source."

"It means it's free, man! It's illegal to sell it. Pretty soon everything's gonna be free. Games'll be free, music'll be free, movies'll be free, no one'll be able to charge anyone for anything. I've got emulators for Atari, Colecovision, Commodore 64, Apple IIe, Intellivision—Come to think of it, I had to pay for that one—"

"I am looking like whore?" Kasha the Receptionist clomped in on chintzy elevator shoes, adjusting her gauze dress.

"Shut up," I said, surprised to find my throat choked up. "We're busy."

I would not let her cheapen this moment. I would not accept it. She swore at me in Polish and clomped out. I returned my attention to the frozen Frogger screen.

"They got it just right. It looks the same as the original."

"It *is* the original," Jeffrey said. "All of them—Frogger, Space Invaders, Tempest, Dig Dug—they're all the original."

"The arcade games came in very large wooden boxes. These come in a small plastic box."

"Look, the game wasn't in the box. The *game* was the *running* of the *code*, man, zeroes and ones, zeroes and ones, the *configuration* of the numbers. Now, take MAME, it's an emulator—some guy named Nicola Salmoria figured out how to get a modern computer to imitate the original arcade game CPUs. You 'dump' the original game programs—the ROMs—from the original arcade machine's circuit boards, download them onto your PC, the MAME software treats all the zeroes and ones the same way the arcade machine hardware did, and *boo*-ya—you got Tempest, Frogger, whatever. It's all in the *running* of the *config*, dig?"

"This emulation, it's a great thing, Jeffrey."

"No shit!"

For some reason, I wanted him to understand the intensity of my reaction, which was ridiculous, as I did not understand it myself, not at all. I am still coming to terms with the repercussions. It went far beyond simple nostalgia. A few years ago, visiting my parents' house, I'd rummaged around in my old closet for a pair of nunchucks and flipped them around for a few minutes with no real emotional aftermath whatever. But when Jeffrey slid that laptop over, I fell into the screen, and in a very real way I never quite climbed out again.

"I mean it, Jeffrey. This is a *great* thing. Thank you for making me aware of it. You mind if I play for a while?"

"Sure," he said. "I'll go, ah, smooth things over with Kasha." He made an absurd clucking sound with his mouth and left.

On his laptop, I found the Intellivision emulator, opened the ROMs folder, scanned his list of games and found Microsurgeon.

I felt my heart pound in my chest. I clicked on it twice.

I played his laptop's battery to death.

CATALOGUE OF OBSOLETE ENTERTAINMENTS
GAME: MICROSURGEON
Format: Intellivision home videogame system (Mattel)
Manufacturer: Imagic (#7604)
Year: 1982
CPU: General Instruments CP-1610 (16-bit)
Screen resolution: 192 × 160 pixels

Perhaps the most innovative game from one of the most innovative third-party producers. Inspired by the film *Fantastic Voyage*, Microsurgeon puts the player in a robot probe and injects him into one of a number of critically ill bodies. Steering through colorful circulatory and lymphatic labyrinths, the player wends his way from brain to heart to lungs to liver and downward, dodging and defeating all manner of real-world horrors: tumors, tar deposits, viruses, bacteria, tapeworms. His weapons are also numerous, and based on real therapies: ultrasonic rays, antibiotics and aspirin. Each region of the body has a variable status rating (good, fair, serious, critical, terminal), which the player must monitor as he eliminates this wide array of pathologies, all while staying inside the safe systemic conduits to avoid alerting the lymphocytes to his presence, and watching his power levels to make sure he does not die himself in his attempt to save the patient. Though the realistic cross section of the patient's head was too unnerving to make the game a best-seller, popularity has little correlation with merit; Microsurgeon showed and showed well that video games can traverse the entire range of imagined experience, and resonate effectively with the wider world of which they are a part.

the microsurgeon winner:
a dead grandma story

● ● ● ● ● ● ● ● ● ● ● ● ● ● ● ● ● ● ●

Microsurgeon was the last Intellivision game I ever owned; my grandfather bought it for me a few weeks before my grandmother got sick. Her illness came as no surprise, given her three-pack-a-day habit. She would stay up until three or four in the morning, smoking and reading in bed, while my grandfather, an early riser, slept soundly in the living room of their Lake Michigan condo. I'd often heard my mother theorize that her parents, with their divergent lifestyles, would never have stayed together had they gotten married in the age of no-fault divorce. Yet I believe they were happy. It never occurred to them to measure their lives together against some glossy ideal.

After her chronic cough became more persistent, the doctors took X rays and found spots in both her lungs. Further inquiries revealed that the cancer had recently metastasized to her brain, though it had not yet gotten a firm foothold there. They started her on aggressive chemotherapy, and the rest of her body deteriorated along with her tumor cells. There is no need to catalogue the details of this deterioration—you have seen it for yourself, or you will. I have nothing to add to your current or future memories, no light to shed on them, no meaning or hope to extract. Her sickness was a constant whisper in our house, even when it was not being talked about. In the living room at night, you could hear my mother's murmuring remorse that she'd done nothing to stop my grandmother's smoking, or her own for that matter, and the hallway walls would carry her cries of helpless rage through my closed bedroom door.

It took me a while to get around to playing Microsurgeon; I was still infatuated with Astrosmash. When I finally did get to it, I was taken aback by its complexity. Power, brains, antibiotics, tumors, lymph ducts, tapeworms; it was a lot to think about all at once. But I kept at it, fueled by morbid, obsessive tendencies, and finally got the hang of the game with patient #23, a relatively easy save compared to some of the others. She began the game with lungs in critical condition, brain in serious condition, and everything else good or fair. I saved her, barely, doing the absolute minimum necessary to get her brain and lungs up to good or fair while preventing any of the other fair systems from falling ill, and made it out through her eye socket just before my power ran out.

The following day, my mother took my grandmother to Presbyterian St. Luke's Hospital for a checkup, where the doctor told her that the chemo was working. Her cancer had not retreated, but it had not advanced either. My mother seemed hopeful, which lifted my father's spirits, and mine. Making the connections I could hardly expect anyone else to make, I retreated to the basement for more Microsurgeon, hitting Reset on the Intellivision until it delivered patient #23. As I got better at the game, I was able to bring all of #23's systems up to good condition, and once a body region was in good shape, it stayed that way and never got bad again. In Microsurgeon, health was forever. Once, when my mother came down to check on me as I sat cross-legged on my orange vinyl cushion, I told her what I was doing.

"I'm killing Grammy's tumor cells," I said.

Thinking I was being metaphorical, she kissed me on the head.

I refused to go to summer camp that year. I had work to do. My resolve was such that my parents saw little point in denying me what might be my last summer in my grandmother's company. One day on the patio of her condo, after swearing her to secrecy, I told my grandmother what I was doing with the game on her behalf, explaining the whole thing to her in my disjointed way. She squeezed me weakly to her side and looked out over Lake Michigan, the wind sending ripples through the top of her terry-cloth turban. I think she believed me.

"Thank you," she said as she lit up a cigarette.

She would occasionally smoke in my presence, having exacted from me a standing promise not to tell anyone. Though I knew this was not a thing for her to be doing, I never asked her to stop; it only made me work harder at Microsurgeon. Even after all systems were good, I continued to blast away at pathogens, paying special attention to lung and brain tumors. I would not leave the body of patient #23 until all traces of disease had been eradicated.

In spite of her stolen cigarette moments, my grandmother's cancer began to recede. The doctors, my parents, her friends—none of them could conceal their surprise. I had to fake mine. She began to venture out, holding on to my grandfather's arm as he led her to their usual table at Barnum & Bagel deli. We even took her to a movie, *An Officer and a Gentleman*, I think it was. It nearly bored me to death, but she didn't cough once.

Then, a week before school started, the Intellivision broke.

Its bronzed top panels would often get very hot after a few hours' continuous play, but I ignored the warning signs. Four hours into a Microsurgeon session, some piece of circuitry inside the console apparently melted down, and it would not play a single game. Nearly breathless, I took the machine into the furnace room, opened the toolbox and began to unscrew the bottom to see if I could solve the problem myself. I might have had a chance—I owned a soldering iron and I knew how to use it from the few Heath Kit home electronics projects I'd done—but my mother walked in while I was dismantling the machine and made me put it back together again, prey to irrational fears of my electrocution.

The mustached man at Archon TV & Electronics was out of new Intellivisions. He suggested I consider a Colecovision system, the Next Big Thing that had hit stores that summer. Misunderstanding the source of my disproportionate distress, my mother offered to buy me one on the spot, but I was adamant: I needed an Intellivision. I needed *this* Intellivision. The property or aura in this machine that had yoked my grandmother's fate to that of patient #23 might be absent from a new one, and I could not risk that. Intellivision might have been verging on obsolescence, but I had to protect what was truly valuable against the encroaching demands of absolute modernity. The Archon salesman shrugged and told me he'd have to send it back to Mattel Electronics. It turns out Mattel Electronics was on its last legs and therefore probably not a good place to send anything important, but I was unaware of this at the time.

While I waited for Mattel to complete the repairs, my grandmother's health deteriorated in step with the weather. She stopped going out, and the smell of death blew into her dim bedroom from upwind in time. I do not know how I recognized it, but I did, and with it came the first taste of the helplessness that had seasoned my mother's life for months. I could not look my grandmother in the eye.

My parents stopped taking me to see her, and got her a full-time nurse from Belize. Soon, they got the nurse a bottle of morphine sulfate and an eyedropper. At home, they tried to maintain an air of normality, but slow death took a grinding toll on everyone, my mother especially. Every phone call raised a sickening mixture of dread and relief that she tried to neutralize with Pepto-Bismol. When Archon TV & Electronics called to tell me my Intellivision was in, however, neither she nor my father was home.

I put on my gym shoes and ran to Archon myself along the Edens Expressway. It was a mile away, nearly enough to render a chubby, sedentary eleven-year-old unconscious, but I made it, paid the man most of the allowance money I'd saved over the past few months, and trudged back home with the Intellivision under my arm.

I was very thirsty, but I went straight to the basement without water and summoned up patient #23. I killed every wrong thing in that body, every tumor cell, every pernicious virus, every spark of the malicious world, I played and played without regard for score or status, and maybe it was a glitch in the programming or maybe it was something else, but the game lasted far longer than it should have. My power readout stopped declining, and the tumors stopped appearing altogether. The game gave up.

Dizzy from thirst, brow salty with dried sweat, I stumbled upstairs with the Microsurgeon cartridge in hand to find my mother and father entering from the garage with my grandfather. Grammy was dead. When they told me, I fainted.

After I came to, drank some water and assured them I was okay, they took me to see my grandmother one last time. She was just a thing now, an object that could no longer pretend to be otherwise because it could no longer tell itself otherwise. Although I had to work up my courage to touch her hand, it was cool to the touch, not at all unpleasant. As her body dropped to room temperature, and my mother cried, and my heavily sedated grandfather slumped listlessly in a chair, I remember exactly what went through my mind. There were three things, in this order:

1) When I was six or seven, back before my fascination with the mysteries of the natural world was bludgeoned to death by a seventh-grade science teacher, even before video games, I would often sit for hours gazing into books on dinosaurs and prehistoric mammals, poring over their lush painterly reenactments of primeval drama, thinking about my own death. Not what would happen to me after I died—I thought about what would happen to everything else. For the first time in years, I revisited the post-Adam scenario. The situation was thus:

I was the linchpin in the machine of forward-moving time, the only thing that kept it together and propelled it through a fierce storm of regression. When I finally drew my last breath, the storm would sweep time up in its back-blowing gusts, causing fern-heavy rain forests to explode through the lawns and concrete and asphalt, toppling the homes and shops and even the skyscrapers downtown. Saber-toothed tigers would come to prowl through those forests, nostrils flaring after a whiff of mastodon blood, and there would be no defense against them. Everything would keep going backward, through the triceratops and anklyosaurus to the trilobite and beyond. There was a gap in my knowledge of a few billion years between the illustrated dinosaur book and the illustrated astronomy book, but I knew where it would all end up: in a featureless freezing vacuum punctuated by swirling masses of superheated gases. These were the changes that my death would precipitate. I shared this information with no one.

2) While thinking about the things I'd known from childhood, my thoughts moved naturally to my secret knowledge of God's true appearance. From the age of three or four, I had known he was not the conventional white-bearded Ineffable, or the burning bush they told us about in Sunday school at Temple Solel, or the guy nailed to the cross downtown at the Art Institute, though I found those depictions of the crucifixion entertaining.

No, God looked exactly like George Reeves, the barrel-chested, beer-gutted, ill-starred star of the 1950s *Superman* TV series, wearing the chunky black glasses of his Clark Kent incarnation. He wore a green-and-yellow court jester's costume, the kind with little bells on the ends of its three-pointed hat, and rode a donkey so small that God had to hunch over and lift his legs to rest on its mane so they wouldn't drag along the ground. The poor donkey was a third of his size. It was one small donkey. Though I no longer believe in God per se, I still know this image carries some deeper truth.

3) I thought about the Microsurgeon cartridge in my pocket. I knew its effect had been real. I still know it. For no good reason I could ever fathom, it had become a fulcrum point between opposing sides of the screen where leverage could be exerted from one side to the other. If the Intellivision had been fixed sooner—a week, a day, an hour—I could have saved her.

they meet

● ● ● ● ● ● ● ● ● ● ● ● ● ● ● ● ● ● ●

Sitting in an unsteady chair at my two-person kitchen table in my apartment on Chocimska 23 in Warsaw, I plugged the phone jack into my laptop and searched for the videogame emulators to which Jeffrey had introduced me earlier in the day. The Intellivision emulator was only available on a CD-ROM that you had to order, but I found the MAME website easily, and the program was free as Jeffrey had promised. On the Frequently Asked Questions page, I found the following mission statement:

> Even though MAME allows people to enjoy the long-lost arcade games and even some newer ones, the main purpose of the project is to document the hardware (and software) of the arcade games. There are already many dead arcade boards, whose function has been brought to life in MAME. Being able to play the games is just a nice side-effect.

I liked the sound of this. It made me feel a sense of vocation. By copying these games onto my own hard drive, I would become an anonymous participant in a communal project of great significance, like one of those medieval Irish monks whose thankless thousands of hours' scribe work saved the works of classical civilization from destruction at the hands of the invading barbarians.

I downloaded the MAME program itself. With the intermittent service of Polish land lines, it took all night; I'd often get 80 or 90 percent of the download before the connection was severed, suggesting sentient malice. As I monitored this process, I took occasional puffs of the weed I'd borrowed from Jeffrey when he left the room, and considered that each game ROM I downloaded onto my laptop would be one more perfect instantiation of a specific piece of history that would cease to exist without the efforts of people like me, raised from a frangible circuit-board tomb and granted an indefinite continuation of existence through boundless reproduction.

I would pass this history from computer to computer as I kept a half step ahead of obsolescence, and someday I would pass it on to my children (if I had children) before the future games du jour dug their flashy claws into them, and they could pass them to my grandchildren as my grandfather had passed me the large gift-wrapped box that contained my first Intellivision. It hadn't made sense to him, as he stood behind me with arms folded in our carpet-walled basement, watching me plug in the Skiing cartridge for the first time. When I pushed Reset and held it for a moment after the game was finished, I saw his reflection shaking its head in the black screen, and heard him suck one of his canines clean, in lieu of the pipe his doctor had forbidden him to smoke.

"Whatsit, dots and beeps, you push the button and it moves around?" he said. "That's foolishness. That's nothin'."

As I finished off the plug of weed, it occurred to me that he'd been right, in a sense. At the most basic level, what I was interested in was nothing—not the innumerable plastic wedge-shaped cartridges he and my parents would buy me at $40+ a pop, not the computer code on the chips inside those cartridges, not even the numbers that the code boiled down to, but ghosts of numbers, flickering states of circuitry imagined as numbers as we were all flickering patterns of neurons imagined by themselves as thoughts. And when you thought about it that way and were relatively stoned, it was impossible not to fall into the infinite regress cliché, because soon there would be a computer that could perfectly emulate my computer perfectly emulating a Frogger machine, and someday (maybe long after I was dead, but someday) there would be a computer that could perfectly emulate *me* using the computer that could perfectly emulate my dinosaur laptop perfectly emulating the eternal return scenario of that poor little frog. It was all configs, all down the line, like the world on the back of a giant turtle in *The King and I*, which was on the back of an even larger turtle and so on, and that was a kind of immortality, wasn't it? And not just for the games. I reasoned: If I were to die 60 seconds from now, but a complete representation of the state of my neurons 59.999 seconds from now, my *config*, were perfectly reproduced in some über-computer one thousand years from now and allowed to continue interacting with a perfectly reproduced representation of the state of my laptop trying valiantly to suck MAME version 2.1 through a perfect representation of the Polish phone system, would the one-thousand-year pause in my config's activity matter? And what if our life is someone else's game? Etc. Etc.

By the time I managed to get the entire MAME program, the squat woman in apartment four had started beating her rugs in the building's central courtyard, which meant it was 4 A.M., and either Tuesday, Thursday or Friday. It was too late to start looking for the ROMs themselves. Plugging my ears with a dirty pair of foam earplugs, I fell into bed, determined to catch a few hours' sleep despite the rug beating and the intermittent spikes of pain in my lower back. I would take my laptop to work and Jeffrey would show me how to set up the emulator, and lead me to the sites that stored the game ROMs (the MAME site would not harbor them for copyright reasons), and by tonight I would have it all.

The doorbell woke me through the earplugs, cutting through my sleep more insistently than the rug beating or the alarm clock I'd slept through, because no one ever rang my doorbell except the walrus-mustached landlord, and I'd paid him last week. I did not know who it could be, because I'd forgotten about the cleaning lady. I'd called her a week ago, after I woke up one morning to find a message I'd drunkenly written to myself in the dust on my nightstand: "CLEANING LADY."

"Hello? I am Anya? Cleaning?"

She wore no babushka; her curly black hair was held back by a little pink ribbon. Somewhere between nineteen and twenty-three, she was very petite. Her breasts were natural and large, very large, almost irreconcilable with her tiny, thin-wristed, pixie-assed frame. I'd have been unable to stop staring at them if her green eyes were not somehow more compelling in their refusal to meet my own, bouncing between my face and the floor as the corners of her rosy doll mouth turned bashfully upward. Although she was lugging a bucket full of bleach-soaked sponges, she gave off a faint floral scent.

So far I had avoided falling for any of the Kashas, no matter how beautiful, but I was so groggy, and Anya was so demure and quiet and perfect that I faltered. Had I smoked less schwag weed, gotten more sleep and showered before she came, I might have remembered that Kasha the Receptionist had given me her number, that she and Anya Budna had grown up in the same neighborhood and were childhood friends. Had I remembered this, I might have thought twice. As it was, thanks to MAME, in the precise config I was in when I answered that door, those green eyes swallowed me. The ground that allowed us to grow together also contained the seed of the weed that would tear us apart. Very Hegelian.

Two days after our first encounter, I called in sick to work and Anya took me to Praga, the suburb on the unfashionable side of the Vistula River where she and Kasha had grown up. She showed me dilapidated buildings that reminded me of the Cabrini Green Housing Projects in Chicago, truncating abruptly in odd places, ending in stark, faceless brick and plaster facades. I saw a great deal of graffiti, a Warholian repletion of dick motifs, and a well-rendered hairy butt with a cigarette jutting from its crumpled asshole. She showed me an exhaust-blackened monument to the Russian heroes who died for the liberation of the Polish homeland—heroes, she informed me, who in fact waited on the Praga side of the Vistula for the Nazis to finish scorching the earth before crossing the river and "liberating" Warsaw proper. Only fifty-four years (1945–1999) and the heroic faces on the monument had already worn away into featurelessness. (Or did they start out that way? Hard to tell with the Soviets.) I saw a store advertising Pierre Cardin but selling only nameless vodka and ice cream. I saw mismatched sweatsuits. I saw a used-up soccer stadium with a Chinese/Russian bazaar scattered around its walls, its grass half gone, its seats splintered like matchsticks. Michael Jackson played there once, years ago. The majority of those who could not afford tickets went anyway to see the effluvia of the spectacle, to watch the colored lights spill out over the stadium's rim and feel the seventy-thousand-watt sound system in their bellies.

In the bar where we stopped to get a Zubrowka vodka before going back, I saw an old arcade machine: Mr. Do. I recognized the telltale diagonal blue stripes of the second level right away, being newly resensitized to the presence of such things. An old man fed one-zloty coins into it, drinking from a flask balanced next to the joystick. I thought about the path this machine had taken from the Universal factory (in Las Vegas, it turns out) to this its final destination. I briefly considered telling the man about MAME, but decided against it. When he saw me looking at the machine, he motioned me over.

This guy, *he* looked like one of the shell-shocked faces I saw in the History Channel documentary. Neither his wool sweater nor his tweed coat with one wounded elbow were woven finely enough to seal in the alcohol vapor that exuded from his pores. Oddly enough, it made him smell clean, sterilized, or perhaps embalmed. He spoke to me rapidly, either not catching or not minding my obvious incomprehension. Marathon chains of consonants with no vowel relief, compound sounds my ears were not used to hearing together. The middle four letters of "fi*sh chi*ps" popped up a lot. Using arm motions, he made it clear he wanted me to play the game with him.

"Mr. Do," I said, nodding.

"Mice Tar Dough, Mice Tar Dough!" he said, followed by more fi*sh-chi*pping. He put two coins in the machine and would not let me pay him back. Careful not to knock over his flask, I went first. Though I had not played the game in ages, I remembered it well—the innovative extra-man incentives, the eschewing of the traditional Pac-Man-style intermission for an entr'acte statistics display—and the smattering of Mr. Do strategy I managed to pull from dormancy impressed him. He slapped me on the back and shouted something after I killed a red dinosaur with each of the six apples of the first screen, and I returned the gesture when he made it to the third board on his first man, even trying to repeat the encouraging syllables he'd barked in response to my feat. He offered me a swig from his flask, and I accepted. It did not taste entirely unlike vodka. When I winced and coughed, the old man cheered, and the bartender did as well, and Anya clapped four tolerant claps. The old man won. I did not let him win, I am proud to say; I tried my best to beat him, but despite the erratic moves his shaky joystick hand sometimes made without his approval, he knew the game well, and appeared to have a genuinely intuitive feel for it.

Anya and I went back to the other side of town on an overstuffed tram, and I took her to a Moroccan restaurant for dinner. She had never been there before. She did not eat out much. Trying to impress her, I reminded her how I'd almost gone native back there in her old neighborhood. She did not know what that phrase meant, so I explained it to her some other way. Dropping her gaze away from mine until it came to rest on the basket of pita slices, she shook her head almost imperceptibly.

"What? You saw me, I was speaking Polish to him!"

"He not speaking Polish."

"Beg pardon?"

"Not Polish. He talk nothing, nonsense, crazy." She fluttered her lower lip with her fingers and made gibberish sounds. Furrowing my brow, I looked down at my plate.

"BYYEWwww," I said under my breath—the descending bass bloom, my personal defeat theme—and took a bite from a pita slice swiped with hummus made with far too much garlic.

When I looked up at her and met her eyes, a deep laugh that couldn't escape from her pursed lips snorted up through her nose, triggering the same in me. I spit a half-masticated mouthful halfway across the room, nearly hitting the shiny black boots of a guy in a black suit with heavily moussed blond hair. He burned with a silent demand for satisfaction, but I could not address the challenge because I could not stop laughing. It was right there, I think, coughing, laughing, wiping my mouth with my sleeve and touching Anya's hand, it was there that it suddenly occurred to me I was in love with her.

Three weeks later, I was fired for lying about my graphic design experience. I think Jeffrey may have turned me in. Kasha liked being mistreated; she began paying more attention to me after I was rude to her, complicating his exploitation of the Jew angle, and I think he wanted me out of the way. I returned to Los Angeles, and Anya Budna went with me. The entire plane ride back to L.A., I had to keep reminding myself that the beautiful girl in the next seat was with me.

CATALOGUE OF OBSOLETE ENTERTAINMENTS
GAME: DONKEY KONG
Format: Coin-Op Arcade Machine
Manufacturer: Nintendo of America
Year: 1981
CPU: Z80 3.072000 MHz
    I8035 400KHz
Sound: 1 × DAC + samples
Screen resolution: 256 × 224 pixels

The brainchild of Nintendo Corporation's Shigeru Miyamoto that finally knocked Pac-Man from its throne, Donkey Kong spread like a virus, with more than 65,000 machines appearing in the USA its first year alone—an excellent showing for a company that got its start making playing cards for fin de siècle Yakuza gangsters, a group from which Nintendo would borrow many business tactics a century later. Notable for his ability to get gamers excited about something besides killing things or blowing them up, Miyamoto would go on to innovate further, from the hidden treasures of Super Mario Brothers to the cinematic camera angles of the Zelda games (after the author's time, it must be said), but whatever the sales figures, none of these has ever matched his maiden effort in cultural ubiquity.

Donkey Kong's phenomenal success can be attributed in large part to its concessions to realism relative to the megahits like Pac-Man and Defender that ushered in the Golden Age, swinging back toward the concreteness of the driving/sports/war games so prominent in the Antediluvian Age that preceded it. Donkey Kong moves away from abstract or space opera locales to a more recognizable setting: a variegated construction site. Its antagonist, protagonist and victim are all recognizable representations of creatures more prosaic than Pac-Men or space ships: Man, Woman, Monkey.

The first Girders board first appears with its six maroon-purple horizontal girders in perfect parallel. The cosmos of the screen is in order. Then Kong comes, the girl under his arm, a comic menace; the xs representing his teeth reminded many Original Gamers of their own braces, leading them to sympathize with him for the second following his arrival.[1] Donkey Kong then destroys the order, shattering the geometric tranquility of the clean right angles, skewing the once-straight girders with six forceful stomps, and closing with a grimace, lest anyone doubt the mayhem was intentional.

Enter Mario, an after-the-fact name borrowed from the Seattle man who rented warehouse space to the Nintendo Corporation of America and given to the original Japanese "Jumpman." He appears at the bottom of the screen next to a blue "OIL" drum. Kong has deposited Mario's girl, Pauline, on a platform at the top of the screen, where he holds her captive. The game was programmed in Japan, so naturally Pauline is Caucasian with long red braids, an iconic embodiment of chaste womanhood in her floor-length dress. She waits helplessly, dancing a little two-step of despair and silently crying for Mario's "HELP" with comic-book words that hang above her head. So the player starts Mario running.

It is difficult to ignore the similarities between Donkey Kong (the creature) and the demiurge of the Gnostic heresies. The Gnostic sects—pre-Christian, early Christian, Jewish Kabbalist—shared a belief in the fundamentally corrupt nature of this physical world and the despotic God or demiurge who ruled over it, the one they knew as Ialtabaoth and we know as Jehovah. In a power grab, this demiurge usurped the purely spiritual creation of the true God, as we learn in the *Apocryphon of John* from the second century A.D.:

> It took great power from [its mother, the female principle of the true God], retreated from her, and moved out of the place where it had been born. Taking possession of another place, it made for itself other eternal realms . . . and it became stupefied in its *madness*,[2] which still is with it.

---

[1] Identifying with Donkey Kong, admiring the Pac-Man ghosts—a servile, masochistic pattern presents itself, a digital Stockholm Syndrome.

[2] Miyamoto used the word "Donkey" to describe his update of Willard O'Brien's building-climbing ape because his Japanese-English dictionary had translated it as "stubborn, wily and goofy." To the author's grandfather—and thus, one might reasonably assume, to other members of his

After imprisoning the true creator and occupying her harmonious creation, Donkey Kong defiles it, knocking it out of whack, making it as imperfect as the material world we are compelled to live in. But this is not enough; he must also fill the usurped creation with emanations of his own malice. The fourth-century *Hypostasis of the Archons* tells us that the demiurge "contemplated creating offspring of itself" after seeing its new dominion, and did so shortly thereafter: "It engendered for itself authorities... the second is called Harmas, the eye of fire...." (*Apocryphon*). And so Donkey Kong sends down a spark of his evil in the form of a blue barrel that ignites the fuel drum behind Mario, giving birth to sprites[3] of living flame that will continue to scourge Mario throughout all four levels of the game.

As in the Gnostic cosmology, a Lone Chosen One is sent forth to put things right. He is not one of the "angelic beings about whom none of the races of humankind knows anything" mentioned in *The Revelation of Adam*, but like Jesus Christ, he is a carpenter, and as in all twentieth-century popular expressions of the Gnostic cosmology,[4] this Savior figure is our own point of identification. We jump a barrel in his shoes. We become "Sha'ar Elohim" or "portals of God," that we might foil the Great Ape ourselves, and deliver the embodiment of (female) innocence into a better world where the girders are straight and the Factories produce something other than deadly mudpies. As in the Lurianic school of Kabbalistic mysticism, we will participate in *tikkun*, the healing of the divine vessels. We will fix what has been broken.

The problem with Donkey Kong: You can never fix what has been broken. You can never make the crooked girders go straight. On August 20, 2000, when Tim Sczerby scored 879,200 points on Donkey Kong (thought to be the highest score theoretically possible), the game killed him off on Level 22 without explanation or apology, and

---

generation—"goofy" was a synonym for "crazy," "insane," "*mad.*" E.g.: When said grandfather's older brother Harry returned from WWI, he came back "goofy," and shot himself in the head not long afterward.

[3] In addition to the computer science usage of "sprite," where it denotes a small bitmap image used in video games and is often synonymous with "icon," the word has an older meaning: "A spirit; a soul; a shade; also, an apparition" (*Webster's Unabridged Dictionary*, 1913).

[4] *The Matrix, The X-Files, Buffy the Vampire Slayer*, et al.

he *still* did not make the crooked girders go straight. And you can never maintain your grasp on Pauline. When you succeed in reaching the top of the screen and climb the platform to free her from the Monkey God's prison, he takes her away, and on the Rivets screen, even after you send him plummeting to the ground level headfirst, the reunion with Pauline doesn't last. Why?

Because she is not a girl at all. She is the *idea* of a girl pretending to be a girl, distorting impressionable Mario's reality with the old bait and switch, and inasmuch as the Monkey God is also a distorter of the straight and real, she and the ape are in cahoots. Even more: The ape is a part of the girl, and the girl a part of the ape. They are facets of the same deception—which is to say, the fallen world, the one we live in.

the mario illusion

· ·

When I took Anya back to live with me in Los Angeles, I was operating under the Mario Illusion. To me, she was a beautiful idea of womanhood, no floor-length dresses to be sure, but a more carnal modern abstraction, a finely tuned balance of contemporary virgin and whore tropes. Shy and unsure, yet possessing a native intelligence she wore with more grace than most similarly bright American women I knew—all she needed, I was sure, was to be removed from the cage of her native land and brought to America, which would surely compare favorably to her *idea* of America, the place she thought and talked so much about. My illusions were powerful ones, and held fast for several weeks of hand-holding, constant rutting and fearless (if ungrammatical) talk of the future, as if the good times had traveled ahead and were waiting for us there.

Ultimately though, the idea of America for Anya, like the idea of Anya for me, was damaged in the collision with the thing itself. America's enchantment lay in its remoteness, and nearness to a world of strip malls and surface smiles and what seemed to her an almost willful stupidity ("I am a waitress, and I read books! This man, executive movie man in fucking suit, he does not!") bred a creeping contempt for it. Our rutting fell off. Her enthusiasm for my best-laid plans waned. I began to feel deceived.

A sense of justice damped my indignation, however. As she appeared to be in cahoots with the destroyer ape from my perspective, from her perspective the equal and opposite situation likely held. She had entrusted her hope and confidence to this foreign savior with charming facial hair who seemed so surefooted and promising when seen at a distance, ascending the girders and ladders . . . but the whole thing was a good-cop/bad-cop routine between him and the monkey, a con to entrap her. When the savior came close, the truth about him became clear. He was not rich, not in his world. He was not even a graphic designer (yes, I had lied to her too), and thus could not get a job as one. When his money ran out, he did not get a job at all; he retreated into an "office" where no work was done, and glutted himself on electric dots and beeps and childish foolishness. He talked about his friends, but she had yet to meet one. There was something suspicious about their one-word names—Sexy, Goldie, Skinny—and she often (correctly) surmised that these friends were actually his largely fictional *ideas* of friends, mythic figures carved from an idealized past with which he had long lost contact. His prospects were as limited in his world as hers were in Warsaw, if not more so; at least in Warsaw, there were always more American men.

By the time she realized all this, though, she was stranded on the ape's platform, too high from her home ground to jump, and before she knew it the ape had her in its clutches. When she craned over her shoulder and courageously looked it in the eye, she no doubt saw my face looking back at her, and just like in the game, a jagged rent tore through the center of her poor, off-pink heart.

As I watched this happen over days and weeks, and thought about the responsibility I bore for the countless irreplaceable hours I had stolen from her life because it seemed like a good idea at the time; as I watched her receding from me into herself as if mirroring my own withdrawal from her; as our unfolding estrangement from each other led me to daily strain underdeveloped portions of my brain, trying to figure out how to make it stop; it was about this time that the necessity of a truly in-depth catalogue and analysis of the Golden Age video games from 1978 to 1984 became clear to me, clear enough to warrant action by 9/5/99.

The games themselves would live on thanks to MAME and other such emulation programs, but due to their diversionary status and their laudable but deceptive simplicity, they would likely be taken at mere face value—and to live only in fleeting moments of others' wistful nostalgia is not to live at all. It was important that someone begin to peel back the layers of meaning beneath their colorful surfaces, because they were a crucial strata in the bedrock on which a generation was built. Hollywood movies are considered important enough that, in many circles, interminable discussions and serious commentaries on them are acceptable. As a place where America has been distilled and redistilled to the point of toxicity, Las Vegas has been subjected to numerous sociological, psychological, literary and critical incursions. Yet in 1981, the videogame industry's $5 billion take was more than Hollywood and Vegas combined—and so much of it was taken one quarter at a time.

Billions of quarters, back when a quarter was worth 39¢. And the home video games were to computers what pornography was to VCRs; in modern gearhead parlance, they were the Killer App. They facilitated the evolution of the microchips that have grown like happy bacteria in the Earth's petri dish and continue to do so, each year becoming faster, cheaper, smaller and more numerous, seething into all spaces between us and inside us.

Can we afford not to see our world their way?

a monster of selfishness

. . . .

"You are . . . you are a *monster* of *selfishness*!" Anya screamed, and I smiled, and she snarled at the smile and ran to the bedroom. I tried to explain, but she slammed the door.

What I did to earn this title:

The *Catalogue of Obsolete Entertainments* was coming along nicely, accumulating the critical mass of insight necessary to strike through the mask of "entertainment" and reach the truths hidden behind it. I was proud of my work, I'm not ashamed to say. This little bit from the Tempest entry, for example:

> If horror films can be seen as the nightmares of our culture, it makes sense to view video games as our lucid dreams, the ones in which we are given the luxury of taking arms against the transfigured, pixellated seas of our troubles and doing battle with the creatures that wait for us in their depths.

My comparison of Berzerk to *The Castle* by Franz Kafka was unique, I think, as was my take on the dialectic between purpose and aimlessness in Sinistar. Despite my own newfound sense of purpose, however, when I scrolled through a Print Preview of the *Catalogue* and examined it with an honest eye, its aimlessness struck me. Something was missing—and I'm not talking about a game plan, a sales strategy. I honestly hadn't given that any thought. The end was a long way off, and the work was an end in itself. I had no desire to convert it to a means by sullying it with questions of marketability or potential audience. Still, it seemed shapeless, somehow. The high I got from working on it reminded me of something I'd heard a crack user say in a Discovery Channel documentary on addiction: "It feels so good . . . but it's always incomplete. There's still this big hole right in the middle of it."

Taking a break from the Frogger entry to read through some posts on alt.games.video.classic, I came across the following message thread:

Subject: LWB info   From: T. Bush
Am currently in the market for information pertaining to the obscure 1983 game Lucky Wander Boy. Please contact.

Subject: Re: LWB info   From: Clio
i heard a rumor that the japanese chick who designed the old game lucky wander boy is going to be interviewed on zd-tv tonight at 8pm pst .just a rumor.

Lucky Wander Boy.

Seeing the name, saying the name, I felt its five syllables drop into my midst and expand, as if on cue.

It had been sealed off from the sludge of my consciousness for so long—but then, years of the mundane can so easily stomp out the wondrous and strange. Though intense, my encounter with Lucky Wander Boy was brief. I do not hold on to passions forever; I tend to let them fade.

Take my passion for modern Japanese literature. Five years ago it flared up like a flu, and subsided almost as quickly. All that remained of my obsession with Mishima, Abe, Tanizaki, Öe and Murakami was the following quote from Mishima's *Way of the Samurai*, printed out in twenty-four-point font and taped on my wall between a Billy Dee Williams watercolor postcard and a recently acquired Pac-Man clock:

One may choose a course of action, but one may not always choose the time. The moment of decision looms in the distance and then overtakes you. Then is to live not to prepare for that moment of decision?

I had never given too much thought to my reasons for taping this particular quote to my wall. It leapt out at me, but never told me why. If pressed, I probably would have admitted that it represented some vague hope on my part that someday something of note would happen to me, somehow. But I had no idea what this something might be, and had never sensed that my Moment of Decision was anywhere in the vicinity. Its existence had been purely a matter of faith, until now. But Lucky Wander Boy had summoned it, and I now saw my Moment peeking over the horizon, too far away to reveal any particulars, but present, waiting to come to me, or for me to come to it. If I squinted my eyes, I could just make it out, right there, just over the Pac-Man wall clock, which read 7:59 P.M.

I ran into the living room and flipped to channel 63, ZD-TV, the all-tech-all-the-time channel. In my defense, I did not even notice Anya sitting there on the couch until she began to yell at me. It seems she had been watching a show about celebrity homes, and taking notes about how we might make our own apartment a bit more like William Zabka's, though our apartment was considerably smaller.

Why Anya's anger was already primed:

After a month of cultural acclimatization and language study, she began looking for a job, and after a month of looking, she had found only one that paid enough: waitress at Warsaw Gardens, a Polish restaurant on Fifth Street in Santa Monica not far from our apartment. The nightmarish ignominy of turning her back on her homeland and running almost six thousand miles only to end up in a facsimile of the same had solidified her occasional fits of choleric discontent into a permanent foul mood, and the studied quaintness of the restaurant's exposed beams, creaky wood floors, threadbare linens and shabby carpeting only taunted her with how little they had to do with the Warsaw she knew. To make matters worse, her boss insisted she speak Polish to Leelee Sobieski when she was eating at Warsaw Gardens with her manager, agent and publicist, not knowing that Ms. Sobieski was born and raised in New York City. Rather than admit his mistake, her boss enshrined it as a new policy, requiring her to speak Polish loudly at all times in the restaurant even though no other employee could speak it back to her. She had hoped to improve her English on the job, and saw this new rule as a major setback.

Why I smiled:

It was not a cruel smile like the one James Bond smiles in the Fleming books. No, it was a tender smile, a solicitous, loving, proud smile, because I knew how intensively she had been working on her English in spite of the Polish Only rule at work and her disenchantment with the real America, studying all relevant sources of vernacular with the diligence of a true student, though she'd never had the opportunity to go to college. I'd read one of her *Vogue* magazines on the toilet, so I knew that "monster of selfishness" was a phrase she'd lifted from Elite Modeling Agency head John Casablancas, who had used it to describe a former client, the supermodel Gisele. My girlfriend was turning theory into practice; the rate at which she was going native both impressed and gladdened me. In videogame parlance, she was successfully porting herself to the American platform. I was sure that in no time at all we'd be able to have a regular conversation, and I looked forward to the small talk. I was sure it would help close the gulf that was opening between us, and smooth over our differences.

The commercial break ended on ZD-TV. What was done was done. I sat down to watch, saving my penance for afterward.

The irony of it all:

The rumor that Clio of alt.games.video.classic had heard was just that. The designer of Lucky Wander Boy did not appear on ZD-TV at all. When the show returned, all I got was a profile on the CEO of some Los Angeles digital entertainment company, a guy named Kurt Krickstein with tight, black curls garnishing the sides of his balding head, and a lazy *L* that would drive any speech pathologist crazy. He made it clear that he and his company were not, emphatically *not* Hollywood. Hollywood was peopled by middleman "weasels" who served no function and increased operating costs. He was a media revolutionary, standing at the crossroads of movies, video games and the Internet, planning to oversee a "convergence" of all three, and the subsequent globalization of this final consummation. He was all about Cool. Hip. Edgy. His childhood features had remained with him, but in the translation to early middle age they had become cartoonish, as grotesque in their own subtle way as the latex F/X creatures in the background behind him. I knew it was hip to like cartoons, but I did not think it was hip to be one. Perhaps it was edgy. I did not know enough to judge. I did not like the looks of him, and turned the TV off after thirty seconds. When I brought the remote control into the bedroom and held it out as a peace offering, Anya took it in with forlorn green eyes, then turned away.

Before starting to write a *Catalogue* entry, I usually began by logging in at least two or three hours of emulator play to reacquaint myself with the game in question. With Lucky Wander Boy, however, this was not possible, as I could find no ROM dump for it anywhere on the Internet, though I was a seasoned tracker and spent several hours looking. Undeterred, with the cheerful foolhardiness of a sailor who boards the *Pequod* without giving a thought to Captain Ahab, I decided to begin the Lucky Wander Boy entry from memory, and augment it with snippets of information gleaned or inferred from various disparate sources as I went on. There wasn't much. Lucky Wander Boy was different from the rest. It was near-virgin territory.

CATALOGUE OF OBSOLETE ENTERTAINMENTS
GAME: LUCKY WANDER BOY
Format: Coin-Op Arcade Machine
Manufacturer: Uzumaki Corporation; licensed to Midway
Year: 1983
CPU: (3 ×) Z80X 9.232323 MHz
    M6802 895.000KHz (sound)
    Z80 5.000000 MHz (sound)
    M6502 1.5 Mhz (vector)
Sound: (2 ×) AY-8910 2.00000 MHz
    (2) TMS5520 640.000 MHz
Screen resolution: 800 × 600 pixels

The only unstudied, quotidian element of Lucky Wander Boy[1] is the hasty English translation of its name and instructions, and one can hardly blame game designer Araki Itachi for this. In certain circles, much has been made of her being the only female game designer of note in early-'80s Japan, and perhaps its only major female entrepreneur as well, but this holds less interest than the revolutionary nature of her Great Work, or its tragic history. We will note the likelihood that her gender played a part in Lucky Wander Boy's unfortunate fate at a time when the term "Feminist" was used in Japan primarily to describe labor-saving kitchen appliances, and move on.

Before beginning with the game itself, it will be worthwhile to answer a question a few lone enthusiasts have asked on alt.games.video.classic, namely: "Why can't I find a MAME ROM for LWB? :-(Doesn't anybody have it?"

This is not, as one might assume, a function of the game's scarcity, although nearly all the Lucky Wander Boy machines made were converted into other games after their return to the Bally-Midway factory, and the few that were not were quickly snapped up by the kinds of collectors who can afford to pay upwards of $65,000 for an old

---

[1] The author has heard told that the on-screen titles of several machines actually read "Lucky Wonder Boy" or (of course) "Fucky Wand Boy," although he has never seen either of these hacks himself.

coin-op machine, which is to say the kinds of collectors who are very rich and often very proprietary about their collections. The truth is that Lucky Wander Boy is one of a small handful of arcade games that neither MAME nor any similar extant program can emulate. The reason for this lies in the nature of the emulation programs themselves.

An arcade emulator like MAME can run such a staggering variety of games because the seemingly endless list of titles runs on a comparatively limited number of hardware platforms, utilizing perhaps two or three dozen different kinds of CPUs (Central Processing Units, microprocessors). Most Classic games, for instance, had either the Z80, the M6502 or the M6809 processors throbbing in their chests at a pulse of a few million beats per second. The Z80 was the king of them all, being as it was the lineal descendant of the world's first microprocessor, the Intel 4004, by way of the Intel 4040 and the Intel 8080.

Therefore, MAME is by necessity modular, containing many subemulators, one for each CPU (and indeed for each major hardware component) at use in any given game that MAME can emulate. Juergen Buchmueller (author of the Z80 and M6502 emulators) and L. C. Benschop and John Butler (authors of the M6809 emulator) are second-order unsung heroes, having made the work of unsung hero Nicola Salmoria (author of MAME itself) possible.

Now, the Z80X processors selected by Uzumaki hardware engineer Kobo Öe for use in Lucky Wander Boy came from a small test batch made by Zilog Corporation in Campbell, California. The manner in which they were acquired by Uzumaki is not known. In a subsequent cost-benefit analysis ordered by Zilog's CFO, the Z80X's marginal increase in clock speed over the Z80H (an increase of only 1.232323 MHz) did not prove enough to justify a full production run, and the chip was discontinued, soon to be made obsolete with the introduction of the Z180 (18.432 MHz). Lucky Wander Boy was the only game ever programmed on Z80X, indeed the only practical use made of the Z80X whatever. The programming of a Z80X subemulator for MAME or some other emulator would require a very skilled programmer who happens to be a serious Lucky Wander Boy enthusiast *and* have access to a Z80X chip or its detailed technical specifications, and evidently such a person does not exist, or if he does, has not had the time to complete the task.

In other words, Lucky Wander Boy is one of the few Classic arcade games one can only experience if one has access to an actual, original machine, and thereby maintains an aura of uniqueness rare in this age of mechanical reproduction. Though originally sold as a commodity like any other, the combination of obsolescence and scarcity makes the game extremely difficult to commodify.

In 1979, Ms. Itachi left a promising job at Nintendo Corporation to start her own shop. Information regarding her departure is scarce, but given the uniqueness of her personal vision, it should come as no surprise that she would find Nintendo's conformist ethos and the authoritarian personality of president Hiroshi Yamauchi intolerable. She took the proto-multigame diversity of Nintendo's Donkey Kong to heart, however, and incorporated it not only into the structure of her game—which, despite staggering technological advances has never been surpassed in its intricacy—but into the very hardware, as evinced by the above processor list. Lucky Wander Boy's ingenious parallel processing scheme, created by Yamantaka Fukuda and expat Korean programmer Tak Yoon Han, was a necessary precondition for the game's existence. At the time, the only microchips that could simultaneously handle both the game's complex multigame structure and its cutting-edge graphics were being usurped by the United States Department of Defense, and far too expensive for commercial use. As it stood, Lucky Wander Boy's surfeit of processing power and use of the Z80X chip meant that each unit cost half again as much as a typical arcade machine to manufacture, to say nothing of game development expenses.

Ms. Itachi began work on the game from the very first day she established Uzumaki in Kyoto—the same time Toru Iwatani was developing "Puck-Man" over at Namco in Tokyo, which came out three years before Lucky Wander Boy. Iwatani's achievements deserve nothing but respect and admiration, but when looking at Lucky Wander Boy alongside Pac-Man, one can't help but wonder whether Ms. Itachi received her game design training at Hangar 18. In 1982, on advance word about an "Untitled Arcade Machine" project that, to quote the Uzumaki press release, "is giving to a player shivers of excitingness when she see many levels of wandering boyish hero," Midway bought the American rights to Lucky Wander Boy sight unseen, perhaps overconfident in their acquisitions instincts after snagging the U.S. rights to Galaxian and Pac-Man. When the game's complex design specifications finally reached Midway's assembly plant in Chicago, they dampened the company's enthusiasm considerably, and the American production run was scaled back by 50 percent until the profitability of Lucky Wander Boy could be established on the ground.

Its impenetrable cabinet art did little to boost confidence: Both sides of the cabinet featured an identical three-foot-high portrait of a young man, assumed by most to be the title character, against a stark black background. The more-or-less traditional *anime* cartoon stylistics of the boy's facial features[2] stood in contradiction to the expression they formed, or refused to form. The Lucky Wander Boy's face conveyed absolutely no emotion at all. He stared from both sides of the cabinet like a blank, blond Janus, although after you played the game for a few hundred hours, the face underwent a subtle transformation, or you did, and you began to see not blankness, but searching. On the game's marquee, from left to right, were a gargoyle, an apple and a screwdriver. To the best of the author's knowledge, the first two never appear in Lucky Wander Boy, and the last only appears in Stage II of the game, along with sundry other items, after the player has progressed beyond the deceptive ordinariness of the first three screens.

The late arrival of the program itself was another key source of anxiety. Uzumaki withheld the game code until five days before the machines were scheduled to ship, citing last-minute pretesting and debugging. Anxiety matured into panic in Chicago. Midway CEO Sheldon Borehatch decided that a laughable or nonfunctional game was worse than no game at all, and chose to postpone most shipments in

---

[2]If possible, the eyes were even larger than the Japanese cartoon standard, and the mouth smaller. His blond buzz-cut was many years ahead of its time.

favor of a small-scale initial distribution of 100 machines to limit his liability. Midway's records indicate that Chicago, Atlanta, Los Angeles and Milwaukee were chosen as the American test markets for Lucky Wander Boy, with further shipments planned once the game had proved itself able to pay its way. The program finally arrived in Chicago on an audiocassette in the pocket of a pleasant but unapologetic white-gloved Japanese courier who spoke no English beyond "Hello," "Thank you" and "sugar and cream, please," and carried an alloy briefcase that he did not open.

There was no time for the traditional beta testing. Only by working overtime did Mark Ian, Midway's hardware specialist, manage to upload the code to all one hundred Lucky Wander Boy motherboards and run the basic ROM and RAM (character, scrolling, VRAM, etc.) tests before the machines had to be loaded onto trucks and shipped out to the test markets. When Ian turned the machine on, flipped the Coin Receipt lever and hit the "1 Player button," he heard a five-note fanfare, and saw what looked like "a decent platform game, with good graphics and sound—didn't see what the goddamn fuss was about, or what all that hardware was for." He signed off on the machines, one of which was installed in the far corner of the far room of Peacock Palace arcade in the author's hometown of Woodhill Grove, Illnois, before the next day's sun had set.

(Continued)

penny pincher

● ●

A few days after the Monster of Selfishness incident, still feeling a bit guilty about my insensitivity, I acquiesced to Anya's pleas to take her "out of the house and into the public world," to dinner and a movie. At her request, we ate at a Japanese restaurant on the Third Street Promenade in Santa Monica mentioned in a recent *People* magazine article in connection with a celebrity couple. When she ordered, the sandy-haired waiter, who was almost as pretty as she was, told her she had a great accent, and asked her if she had ever done any acting. She said she was "considering seriously it," and smiled at me because I was taking her out to atone for my sins, and thus could not question her acting ambitions at all, much less in front of someone as pretty as our waiter. He told her she had a very unique kind of beauty, and I looked at my hand to make sure I had not become transparent. The attention made Anya happy for the rest of the meal, though, which made me happy as well, except during those moments when the waiter filled and refilled her water glass, which was never more than a quarter empty to begin with.

We finished with time to burn, I paid the check, and we strolled over to the bookstore three doors down to browse for a few minutes before the movie. While waiting for a latte in the bookstore's cafe, I flipped through a typographically adventurous novel I'd snagged off a pyramid display and pretended to consider buying it, or perhaps I was considering buying it and pretending to consider reading it, when somebody punched me in the arm hard enough to make me drop the book. My first guess was punishment for ignoring Anya, but she was over by the magazine rack flipping through the new *Vogue*.

"Adam Pennyman."

The red hair no longer roamed free in an unruly Afro, and the pudgy teddy-bear body was now an amusement park grand-prize teddy-bear body, but there was no mistaking "Sexy" Sammy Benjamin's freckled Cupid cheeks, which had always deflected suspicion for his numerous misdeeds, and the radiant, slightly devious grin I hadn't seen since high school. On his arm was a tall girl of Giacomettian slenderness, with thin filament hair, and sharp eye makeup and lip liner. In case anyone wondered, she wore a T-shirt hand-stenciled with the word "SUPERMODEL" and festooned with rhinestones.

"Sexy Sammy!" I punched him back, but I don't think I hit hard enough. He introduced the girl as Tuesday. She smiled, mouthed a soundless "Hi" and pulled Sexy in close. *She* was claiming ownership of *him*.

"Since when are you out here?" I asked.

"I've been out here for five years! When did *you* get here?"

"I've been here a few months. Three—no, almost four." Explaining that, except for my brief Polish hiatus, which had ended about eight months ago, I had been in L.A. ever since college would have put both of us in an awkward position, forcing an acknowledgment of the distance that had come between us. We had been best friends in grade school. Anya came over to see whom I was talking to, unused to seeing me talking to anybody. I hoped she wouldn't blow my cover.

"This is my girlfriend, Anya."

Pleasantries were exchanged.

"He has told me about you," Anya said to Sexy.

"Really?" Sexy said, then arched his eyebrow. "Wait a minute—that's no Chicago accent."

She smiled at him with that rosy doll's mouth and I gnashed my molars. That was the way she'd smiled at *me* the morning when she first arrived at my apartment on Chocimska 23, and again later that day, when it served as an invitation to close the gap between us, kiss her and begin to unbutton her shirt. I'd seen the smile since then, of course, but not recently, and here Sexy was getting it after one line. The continuing dividends on those cheeks and the huggable teddy-bear frame. Their level of eye contact made me uncomfortable. I tried establishing the same with his girl Tuesday, but she held my gaze for less than a second before her eyes snapped back toward Sexy.

"I am Polish," Anya said.

"We met in Warsaw, when I was on vacation," I explained.

"I hear it's really nice there," Tuesday said.

Sexy slugged me again. "You work fast, Penny Pincher."

This was a nickname of mine growing up, one of the better ones, I'm afraid. It was unrelated to any stinginess; I was reasonably reckless with whatever money I got my hands on. We simply had an aversion to calling anybody by their given name. Life was mundane enough without the name they gave you.

Anya did have the common sense to hide her confusion about the whole "vacation" business, but she chose not to use it.

"Why do you say 'vacation'? What 'vacation'?"

I rapidly changed the subject to draw attention away from Anya's confusion, and her breasts, which interested Sexy. "What are you doing with yourself?" I asked him.

"Producing—movies and Internet shows. I've been working for a company called Portal Entertainment and Development. You always dug video games, Pennyman—you must have seen the *Eviscerator* movie." I had not. "That was us. One hundred and fifty-five domestic, and counting."

"Yeah," I said, "I thought it was pretty great. Liked the special effects, loved the girl."

"Sela?" He rolled his eyes with lust. "Don't even start."

Tuesday slapped his shoulder and walked away. He didn't look to see where she was going and didn't miss a beat. "Listen . . . what are you doing now?"

"I'm a writer."

"No shit. You know what? I always knew you would be. Those

stories you wrote, what was it, in fifth grade? We'd stand up and read them out loud, and yours always cracked everybody up. There was that one about the rocket ship that was fighting these evil aliens, and two of the three crew members died, but they finally made it to the surface of the alien planet, and then huge letters appeared in the sky and said GAME OVER—INSERT COIN. That was some wild shit for fifth grade."

An exaggerated shrug of humility as I tried to remember what he was talking about, to ascertain if it had any basis in reality. I dimly recalled writing something back then and reading it aloud, but I seem to remember it was called "Roll Out the Red Toilet Paper for Brad Kern," Brad Kern being a fellow classmate who punched me in the face shortly after the reading. Was my muffin being buttered?

"What are you working on now?" Sexy asked.

"I'm between jobs. I've got a few projects going." Like many in this city, I spoke a subtle and refined language of euphemism. It was rare for any of us to look shame in the face.

The guy in the apron called my latte. Sexy gave me his business card.

"Call me. I've got something for you. We're expanding, we need writers."

Here some assertiveness on my part was called for. I was not actively in the market for a job at the time, and could thus afford to be choosy.

"Yeah? What are you guys working on over there?"

"A million things. We're doing the third *Eviscerator* movie, privately financed, we've got lots of websites, and just this month we've acquired the film rights to a half dozen videogame properties. There's Demonic, the first-person shooter, and Skate Punk, and Galaxy 500 Racer, and this great, weird old video game called Lucky Wander Boy, and Hollywood Rampage—"

Anya, Sexy and the chain bookstore promptly disappeared, and the Moment of Decision took a stride in my direction, allowing me to see its head and broad-shouldered body; my Moment of Decision appeared to be a "he." The space between us was featureless and empty, the kind of overexposed whiteness that causes snow blindness, like the white phase of Lucky Wander Boy's second stage. I could make out no landmarks, but my mind's ear heard familiar words roll over the null-space before me, despite all my years of bowing to false idols. Not my Moment, but a female voice with a heavy Japanese inflection, saying:

"I am waiting for you, Adam Pennyman!"

"Why do you not tell him about your work in Poland?" Anya asked after Sexy left.

"It's complicated."

"Why do you tell him you are a writer? What do you write?"

I wisely and easily avoided the minor temptation to tell her about the *Catalogue*.

"It worked, didn't it?"

She looked at her watch and smacked the *Vogue* against her thigh, seething.

"Yes, it worked so well. We just missed the movie."

first contact

●　●　●　●　●　●　●　●　●　●　●　●　●　●　●　●　●　●　●　●

I was at Peacock Palace on the day Lucky Wander Boy arrived—at Sexy Sammy Benjamin's eleventh birthday party, it happens. Sexy's parents had not rented out the arcade for our exclusive use, which was just as well, as it would have ruined the atmosphere. They did provide us with unlimited game tokens, and set up an impressive spread of food on a picnic table. The imposing presence of Mr. Benjamin, arms folded over his *Soldier of Fortune* magazine golf shirt, saw to it that the food was ours and ours alone. To this day, I remember Sexy's birthday parties fondly. His parents were gracious hosts. Unlike many of my peers, he invited girls as well as boys, but immersion in the games was ample excuse not to talk to them if you did not speak their language. The games could even serve as feeble translators, allowing you to carry on a conversation with a female on a limited range of topics.

Lucky Wander Boy attracted some attention at first, as any new game did among the regulars. We were eager, as the instructions put it, "to traveling West for finding Lucky objects, and inward to Lucky Haven Zone goal!" or at the very least figure out what this meant. There were never fewer than four quarters in the on-deck line atop the game's control panel, and none of Sexy's partygoers got to play it more than twice, with the exception of Sexy himself, who got three turns. The game's five-note opening fanfare taunted me as I waited for my turns, dancing on the fringes of familiarity, though it was not until months later that I recognized it as a melodic permutation of the five-note *Close Encounters* theme.

All of us—indeed everyone who played—cleared the first board on their first man. It seemed nearly impossible to die on the first board. The Lucky Wander Boy moved three times as fast as his four antagonists, the Sebiros, who inched along like the zombies in *Night of the Living Dead.* The board's eight horizontal platforms were as straight as those on the first Donkey Kong board before Kong stomped them askew, but they were not representations of a building site, or any recognizable real-world space. Their colors were in constant flux, black to red to blue to green in a mood ring swirl, and impressive background graphics gave the impression that Lucky Wander Boy was running along the edge of an improbably deep bookshelf, or a file cabinet with the drawers taken out. Three lift shafts carried the player up and down between the platforms. The Jump! button did as advertised, the Drop! button allowed the player to fall through the floor to the platform below, and the Warp Skip! button sent him hurtling into the screen toward the convergence point of whatever platform level he was on, then back to the plane of play on a different level, determined at random, but always out of harm's reach. The only way a player could conceivably lose a man on the first board would be if, lulled into overconfidence, he glanced away from the screen long enough to confuse his man with one of the Sebiros. It was easy to do, as they were absolutely identical to Lucky Wander Boy, except they had black, blue, purple or red hair instead of the hero's blond, and wore what looked like gray business suits instead of the hero's blue-gray space captain jumpsuit.

All the Lucky Wander Boy had to do to clear the first board was to avoid the Sebiros and collect the items that appeared at random on the screen, which close inspection revealed to be handcuffs and very short pencils. When he collected enough of them—between five and ten, determined at random—a fourth lift shaft appeared at the top of the screen to carry him up to the next level. As he entered the shaft, five Japanese kanji bounced down upon his head, and a synthesized female voice would shout down their translation, in Japanese-inflected English, "I am waiting for you, Lucky Wander Boy!" The speech synthesis was cutting edge for the time, far ahead of Q*Bert's gobbledygook pseudoprofanities.

At first glance, the second board was identical to the first. The moment Lucky Wander Boy grabbed his first pencil, however, a new species of Sebiro appeared less than a body's length from him to the left, one twice his size with a bird's beak on his human head. This Mega-Sebiro was faster than Lucky Wander Boy, and whether or not he immediately caught the hero depended entirely on whether the Mega-Sebiro first turned left or right. In the coming weeks, I would hear of numerous tricks or cheats to make the Mega-Sebiro turn left every time, away from the Lucky Wander Boy, but none of them worked. The Mega-Sebiro's behavior was entirely random, beyond the sphere of human influence. On this second board, the Lucky Wander Boy could not jump high enough to vault the other Sebiros the way he could on the first board, and the Drop! button only worked on the first, third and fourth platforms. The receding background shifted gradually, each level swaying out of sync with the others, one listing right, another bending left, the top level's far end coming closer then pulling farther away. Anyone who stared at the screen for more than a minute began to suffer from a form of electric seasickness, and you *had* to stare at the screen and keep that Mega-Sebiro under close surveillance to have a prayer in hell of reaching the next level, for he could Warp Skip! too, and his Warp Skip!s always put him on the same level as you. Sexy actually had to quit one of his games and walk away clutching his stomach, although that might have been the pizza and popcorn.

This level defeated us handily, all of us save one. Rob Nixon was four years older than us, and a Peacock's regular. Legend had it that the pockets on one side of his army jacket were reserved for drugs, and the other side for weapons. I had about as much interest in spending time with this Nixon as my Democrat father did with the other one, but Peacock's was public property, and convergent desires had made him a member of our party. Cursing, ignoring the No Smoking signs and trying unsuccessfully to run his fingers all the way through his tangled hair, Nixon made it to the third board one time. He didn't last long, but it was enough for me to figure out the screen's basics.

The tentacles of randomness had been extended to envelop the very physics of the game world. The variables in the equations that determined the parabolas of Lucky Wander Boy's Jump!s, the rate of his Drop!s, the number of seconds before the horrible Photo-Sebiro came out with his zoot suit and a camera where his head should be—all were subject to the whims of random-number-generating subroutines, themselves modified by other random-number-generating subroutines. The beleaguered hero could always Warp Skip! away, of course, but he was also forcibly Warp Skipped! at random intervals, usually to the bottom of the screen. All the Sebiros moved quickly, and had been further differentiated from the Lucky Wander Boy by the identical sinister grins that had been pixel-carved into each of their faces.

After about twenty seconds, Photo-Sebiro caught up with Nixon's Lucky Wander Boy and flashed him into oblivion. The flash burned a vertical white rectangle into my retinas for a minute or more. Indeed, a common complaint from most of the venues that kept the machine for more than a few weeks was singularly rapid monitor burnout.

"Fuck you, you fuckin' punk-ass fuck! It's not fuckin' fair! Cheating bitch!" Nixon smacked the machine and we all backed off, but I smiled inside.

Of course it was unfair. That was obviously the point. With the upright cabinet came certain expectations, and this game took a deadpan delight in flaunting them, laughing at the Rob Nixons of the world, wiping its silicon ass on their hard-earned joystick chops. Nixon gave the machine a few more slaps, prompting Dave Lombardo—late fifties, proprietor of Peacock Palace—to come and throw him out.

Overall, Dave was pleased with the new game, which was inspiring the kind of consumer behavior that allowed him to pay his mortgage and feed his children, but he was nowhere near as pleased as I was. I felt a glee akin to what I would feel the first time I saw

Duck Soup and realized that this movie *knew* it was a movie, or saw page twelve of issue #19 of *Animal Man*, where the title character gawked at me wide-eyed from a splash page and said, "I CAN SEE YOU!"—but the joy of Lucky Wander Boy was more pristine, because it came first. Back then, I harbored an inchoate version of a suspicion I still harbor today: that the intrinsic value of a thing is directly proportional to its initial incomprehensibility, and that things worth knowing often cloak themselves in hall-of-mirrors absurdity to scare off dabblers and those seeking choice small-talk nuggets. What Nixon saw as cheating, I saw as an invitation to confront, to decode a game that did not just progress but *unfolded*, brimming with occult detail, promising a revelation for which Pac-Man's mysterious off-screen tunnels were just a coming attraction.

There at Sexy's party, in my second and last game, I had an experience that I almost hesitate to mention. It lost its substance for me over the course of many years, sliding away to the hazy zone between true recollection and vivid dreams, like the recurring one I had about seeing a killer whale in Lake Michigan. But I know what I heard.

At the end of the first board of Stage I, when I'd collected the requisite eight handcuffs and pencils and entered the lift shaft to the next level, the same five kanji bounced down upon my head, and the same synthesized female voice spoke her eleven syllables of Japanese-inflected English, but what she said, what she said *to me* with unmistakable clarity was:

"I am waiting for you, Adam Pennyman!"

I spun around to see if anyone had noticed, but I could tell they had not. Both my name and the name of the game had five syllables, so the cadence of the utterance had been exactly the same, and this beautiful impossibility had slipped right by them. As I prepared for the rigors of the next screen, I tried to work out a rationalization:

Other games had hidden secrets. Four years before Lucky Wander Boy, Adventure for the Atari 2600 introduced the first such "Easter Egg," when disgruntled programmer Warren Robinett gave himself an unauthorized credit by causing his name to appear on the screen when the player entered a secret room, like some mad monk signing his name to an illuminated manuscript to set himself apart from his anonymous fellow toilers. In Mr. Do, you could turn one of the cherries into a rose by moving halfway over it without actually eating it, and repeating this action on all four sides of the cherry—a ritual circumambulation. And there were other games with other tricks. . . .

None of which had any bearing on what had just happened. Vast, shadowy conspiracies involving impossible technologies, an intelligence coded into the machine itself, waiting for . . . me? No. I knew enough about computers and had slogged through enough of *Gödel, Escher, Bach* to know that this was currently impossible for a CRAY-1, much less an arcade cabinet. However improbable, magic was the only explanation that remained. A ghost in the machine, living just off screen right, something hovering above the code. If a pentagram or a crystal could serve as a magical conductor, why not a microchip? It happened to Clint Howard in *Evilspeak*.

Hearing the machine call my name was the second of two uncanny videogame experiences in my life to that point, the Microsurgeon episode being the first. It called me, and I came. By the time I left Sexy's party, I had decided to become a disciple of this game. I would live in its puzzle and remain there long after my friends had drifted on to a newer but lesser sensation.

I would study its habits.

I would find the sense beneath its apparent absurdity, and understand.

Or such was my intention. As I said, Dave Lombardo was a fan of Lucky Wander Boy at first. This was before a few gamers, myself in particular, became familiar enough with the game to clear Stage I—namely, the first three levels—with relative consistency. Like ninety-nine other arcade owners in Chicago, Atlanta, Los Angeles and Milwaukee, Dave fell out of love with Lucky Wander Boy after seeing Stage II, which was extremely problematic.

not hollywood

● ● ● ● ● ● ● ● ● ● ● ● ● ● ● ● ● ● ● ●

On my first day at work at Portal Entertainment and Development, before being shown to my desk, given a tour or offered a bottle of water, I was taken to the boss's office by his stock, leggy blonde assistant and introduced.

"Heyyyy, bud! Kurt Krickstein! Glad to meet you."

The name and the lazy *L* and the tight dwindling curls and the hot-pink pastel T-shirt with a breast pocket were all vaguely familiar, but the memory did not gel until he stopped his pacing through sundry models of fantastic creatures and lurid airbrushed production art, put his arm around a foam-and-latex creature F/X grotesquerie and said, "First thing you have to know: this is *not* Hollywood. *We* are not Hollywood. Hollywood is all about weasels who don't do any work and take all the credit, and we have a strict No Weasel policy. Whatever you know or think you know about Hollywood, flush it all down the toilet. It doesn't apply here. 'Kay, bud?"

I had seen him before. On ZD-TV, when a rumor had led me to hope for someone else.

I sat in a plush chair, at the end of a coffee table. which, if forced to make a wild, game-show guess, I'd have said was Meiji Restoration Japanese, probably built around the time the Nintendo Corporation was founded. Sexy sat on the leather couch next to a man about to be introduced to me as Tom Lyme, Vice President of Internet Affairs and my immediate superior. I glanced at Sexy upon hearing this. I don't know why, but I'd assumed I was going to be working for him. Having an old friend for a boss might make some people uncomfortable, but not me; the Sexy I remembered had too big a heart to ever fire me, and I'd been looking forward to unheard-of job security. I could not catch Sexy's eye, however, because he was looking at Krickstein with rapt attention. Whether this was sincere or just a strategy to avoid meeting my gaze I could not tell, though I hoped for the latter.

"So Sammy tells us you're going to be writing copy for the portal-entertainment.com network of websites," Lyme said.

"Yes, yes," I said, taking a second to remember that Sammy was Sexy's real name. Whatever he'd told Lyme about my job description, he hadn't said anything to me. I did not know what Portal did exactly, and I did not know what I would be doing for them.

Krickstein's mottled brown-and-white mutt Curly opened the office door by herself, rearing up on her hind legs and pulling down on the handle with her front paws. Krickstein snapped her to his side and tousled her head roughly while Lyme continued the interview.

"And of course, you're probably a screenwriter too, right?"

"No," I said.

"TV?"

"No."

Confusion from Lyme. "Oh . . . books, then? Stories?"

"I read them sometimes."

"So what do you write?"

I tried to project meekness. "I was hoping to leave that up to you."

Krickstein and Lyme made passing eye contact. They would not have to waste their time reading my material. I had none of my own material, and because such material did not exist, I would not steal time from Portal to work on it. They would never find themselves obliged to pretend to listen to me as I pitched them my bright ideas. I represented the minimum potential annoyance. Krickstein smirked almost imperceptibly, and I felt my position strengthen slightly.

"You know about *Eviscerator*, right?" Krickstein said. "Lyme, give him a bible."

Lyme dropped a thick stack of paper bound between glossy purple covers on the coffee table in front of me. Krickstein hefted a samurai battle-axe from the movie in question, a very authentic weapon outfitted with sharpened alloy blades by an overindustrious propmaster, and paced as he expounded upon the phenomenal success of the first *Eviscerator* movie. Based on the popular and controversial videogame series, it was the foundation on which Portal Entertainment and Development had been built. Two years ago, Portal expanded into the Internet, which was the future of entertainment, and now ran www.portal-entertainment.com, a network of celebrity fan sites, movie fan sites, online games and Flash-animated "web shows." "I want you to imagine you're being hired by Fox in 1985," Krickstein said, "and I'm Barry Diller." The success of the first *Eviscerator* movie allowed him to generate more than enough capital to operate www.portal-entertainment.com while similar sites were beginning to run low on cash. The second *Eviscerator* movie (*Eviscerator II: The Exsanguination*) was the studio's fault, having fallen prey to the nibblings of dozens of Hollywood middleman weasels; the third was in preproduction, and being financed privately by a venture capital organization called D,S&A. "It's going to explode. Hang on tight, because it's going to shoot everyone in this building right into the stratosphere."

"It will be *huge* with the eight-to-seventeens," Sexy added, and I nodded knowingly.

Axe in hands, Krickstein posed before a man-sized laminated standee of the Portal logo. The same design occupied the upper-left-hand corner of the business card Sexy had given me in the bookstore coffee shop last week, and I'd dismissed it as an abstract little smudge. At this scale, I recognized the stylized silhouette of a muscular man with an automatic weapon in one hand and a Playmate-proportioned woman in the other. Krickstein gestured theatrically to the slogan beneath the logo, and read it aloud:

"*'Don't Ask Why—Fun Is Fun!'* That's what Portal is, that's what we do here. We're all about the things we all loved as kids, okay: chicks, cars, guns, martial arts, cool movies, hot babes, blowing shit up. You get the vibe. We're edgy, we're hip, we're *not* Hollywood, and you have to be too. Ya got that?"

After the mission statement briefing, Sexy led me into the high-vaulted warehouse space in back, dubbed the Plant by the thirty or so lower-level Portal employees who worked there, to set it apart from the offices up front. The exposed insulation foam on the ceiling made it look like the set for a low-budget caveman feature. The Plant was kept in a state of permanent darkness to shield the screens of the graphic designers and animators from glare, and to cultivate a sense of arcane technological processes in the minds of visiting investors. Surrounded by fanged demons and weapons glistening with fake blood trickles, I felt like Dante in the only part of the *Divine Comedy* sensationalistic enough for me to finish, and thought about how enthralled I'd have been by all this twenty years ago. Sexy took me through a cubicle maze to my corner desk—not a provisional corner created by tweed dividers, but an actual, non-negotiable corner. The desk was identical to all the other desks in the Plant, but this one was mine. Flanking it on the left, sixty-plus black IBM monoliths hummed on their L-shaped shelving unit, LEDs flashing inscrutably, the guts of Portal's Internet operations.

Sexy seemed to have forgotten about Anya, for which I was grateful. As there had been no mention of it in Krickstein's office, I casually broached the only reason I had pursued this job in the first place, wrapping my keen interest in a cloak of mild curiosity.

"Say, where are you guys on that Lucky Wander Boy movie project?" I asked as I tried out my ergonomic chair. "Do you have a script yet? I'd love to take a look at it."

"Lucky Wander Boy . . . sure, sure," Sexy said, "we'll get you involved in that ASAP. Kurt just wants to try you out on some other stuff first, some web stuff."

"You want me to write these animated 'web shows,' huh?"

"Not just yet. At first, you'll be writing the copy for the web shows' sites. And we might have you write Amber Anthony's bio.

We just got her fan site." He winked, as if this was a secret perk he was offering me under the table. "Eventually, we'll get you a toon of your own."

He introduced me to my neighbors, Shay, the chief (and only) programmer, and Linda, who was one of the graphic designers. Shay's outer shell—the forearm tattoos, the tongue stud, the combat boots and combative demeanor—lent itself well to the current fashions in double-platinum bands; only his gift for back-end coding had saved him from that fate, and delivered him into a $600-a-week job without benefits. Linda wore work pants and work boots, and had gone so far as to roll a pack of cigarettes into the sleeve of her T-shirt. Sexy then introduced me to Tamar, a web producer and my immediate-immediate superior, subordinate to my regular-immediate superior Lyme, but still senior to myself. She was two inches taller than I, and wore red leather pants. After shaking my hand firmly, she said with an Israeli accent, "I have a lot for you to do. A *lot*." She double-slapped her leathers and pointed a gun-finger at me; though Israeli, she had indeed seen *Happy Days*. A tubby artist named Ted happened to be walking by, and introduced himself without prompting. He struck me as a genuinely nice guy.

Then Sexy took me to the Plant's main attraction. Buried in a corner by the water cooler, a free Eviscerator machine ran through its silent sales-pitch loop. Demonstrations of the game's one-on-one martial arts fights against exotic backdrops alternated with screens displaying its name and backstory, which had something to do with Ibn Alhrazed and his alien cohorts trying to enslave the people of Earth and turn them into aliens themselves.

"Here it is," Sexy said. "Whenever you're not working, feel free."

"Cool, very cool. Say, any plans to get a Lucky Wander Boy machine?"

"Looking into it. They're not easy to come by. Expensive." He stepped to the Eviscerator machine. "How about it? Feel lucky, punk?"

"What's it, like Double Dragon?"

"More or less—but it's not us against them. It's you against me," he said, grinning.

"You can't play it alone?" I asked.

"Yeah, you can. Then it's you against one character after another, until you reach Ibn Alhrazed."

"Ibn Alhrazed."

"Mmm-hmm," Sexy said. "The Big Boss."

"Anybody ever beat him?"

"Nobody here."

I took my place next to him and manned the controls. There were too many of them, five buttons in addition to the joystick. Gratuitous. I resolved not to even try to make sense of them, but to yank and slap at random. Sexy chose to play a tough female mercenary with a ponytail. My sense of balance dictated that, since Sexy was around six feet two inches, 240 pounds, and thus had a good four inches and sixty to seventy pounds on me, I ought to choose an on-screen avatar that looked like it could stomp his little mercenary chick. Thinking of the Mishima quote on my wall, I picked the freakishly large Spectral Samurai character.

Side by side, we pummeled and kicked each other. I managed to tear Sexy's mercenary's head off once, and more than once she cut my samurai's belly open and pulled out his entrails with both hands as a disembodied voice bellowed *"Evisceration!!!"* It was just like old times, standing in the dark, eyes fixed, unblinking, dozens of CRT screens glowing behind us. I didn't tell him how little I liked this game or any of its ilk. He'd set me up with a generous salary, and besides, it would have spoiled the moment.

CATALOGUE OF OBSOLETE ENTERTAINMENTS
GAME: DOUBLE DRAGON
Format: Coin-Op Arcade Machine
Manufacturer: Taito
Year: 1987
CPU: M6309 3.579 MHz
  HD63701 2.000 MHz
  M6309 3.579 MHz (sound)
Sound: 1 × YM-2151a 3.579 MHz
  2 × ADPCM
Screen resolution: 240 × 224 pixels

Technically, Double Dragon lies outside the chronological confines of the *Catalogue*—yet it was the author's personal point of departure from the world of video games, and showcases as well as any game the features and trends that mark the end of the Classical period.

With his blond high-piled hair, the avatar we are asked to play in Double Dragon resembles no one so much as William Zabka of *Karate Kid* and *Back to School* fame. Write it off to idiosyncrasy, but the notion that this ür-bully is supposed to be both the hero of the story and our on-screen representative strikes the author as preposterous, all past identification with Donkey Kong and Pac-Man ghosts aside.

  More important—and this speaks to the central problem with Double Dragon—are the issues of surface versus structure, and inclusion versus exclusion. Double Dragon is the first major step down the road to a high-gloss realism that masks a shift from what Marshall McLuhan would call a "cool" medium to a "hot" one: "Any hot medium allows of less participation than a cool one.... the hot form excludes, and the cool one includes."[1] Strip away this realism and the

---

[1]From *Understanding Media* (London: Routledge, 1994; 1st pub., 1964). Hot media: movies, photographs, the phonetic alphabets. Cool media: television (circa 1964), cartoons, telephones, hieroglyphics. Picture a seesaw, with Pong seated on one side, some future first person shooter indistinguishable from high-definition video seated on the other, and Donkey Kong straddling the fulcrum.

game boils down to beating the hell out of people, a fair-enough fantasy pastime....

But in cool games (Tempest, Raiders of the Lost Ark, Lucky Wander Boy), graphic minimalism goes hand-in-hand with the absorptive, World Unto Itself quality that makes these games special, and indeed, a measure of this quality extends to all the Classic games, however basic in conception. When we play these games, the sketchy visual detail forces us to fill in the blanks, and in so doing we bind ourselves to the game world. Even more, we participate in its creation, we are a *linchpin*, a cocreator, crucial to the existence of the game world as it is meant to be experienced. Without our participation the Classic game is nothing, it devolves into exactly what the gloss-junky detractors see—and they see it precisely because they refuse to put forth the mental effort required to round out the vision.

They prefer games like Double Dragon, games that do all the work, premasticating the images, chopping them fine—but in allowing this to be done for them, they go from *being* to *watching*, as the degree of detail starts to make identification with the character impossible. In his McLuhan-inspired book *Understanding Comics*, comic artist and theorist Scott McCloud makes a deceptively simple observation: "The more cartoony a face is...the more people it could be said to describe."

In Double Dragon, I cannot be the ass-kicking Zabka; he has big biceps, and I do not; he wears a sleeveless blue track suit, and I will not. I am left out, and I feel left out enough as it is, thanks.

A Pac-Man, however, is just a mouth.

I have a mouth. You have a mouth. We all have a mouth.

And the *world* of Double Dragon is a world of car ads and wanted posters and brick buildings, not the iconic *idea* of a building we see in Donkey Kong, but recognizable individuated buildings.[2] The Classic games were Classic because, like classical music or architecture, they

---

[2] "By de-emphasizing the *appearance* of the *physical* world in favor of the *idea* of form, the cartoon places itself in the world of *concepts*. Through traditional realism, the comics artist can portray the world *without*—and through the cartoon, the world *within*." McCloud, *Understanding Comics*.

strove to give life and weight to ideals of order and proportion, to provide a vision of timelessness. In Double Dragon, we can see the cracks in the brick, the mold growing on the drainage pipes, the unmistakable deterioration of the world we live in. We are thrust rudely back into time. When I put a quarter into an arcade machine or call up an emulated game on my computer, I do it to escape the world that is a slave to the time that makes things fall apart. I have never played these games to occupy *my* world.

clio

● ● ● ● ● ● ● ● ● ● ● ● ● ● ● ● ● ● ● ●

All Double Dragon qualms aside, I played the Eviscerator machine
in the Portal Plant quite often, whenever Tamar's eyes were elsewhere; her gaze carried an oppressive weight that made it difficult
for enjoyment to draw breath, and ever since I found out she was a
kickboxer, I couldn't shake the feeling that she was looking down
on me for beating people up through a machine proxy. But Eviscerator passed the time well enough as long as I was willing to sus-
pend my critical faculties, and the arcade cabinet itself had some
ritualistic attraction, like the altar of some sect to which I'd belonged for many clandestine years without once attending a formal service. Its two side panels focused attention that otherwise
dissipated around the edges of a computer monitor. Furthermore,
the Plant was a throwback to times when videogaming skill carried real social weight. The title of Eviscerator Winner, though
they did not call it that or anything else, was a badge of prestige, as
it would have been at Peacock Palace. I began to set my sights on
winning it.

The current titleholder, Shay, did not lose any sleep over me at
first. It wasn't my kind of game, and initially I wasn't very good.
When he challenged me on my first day at Portal, he beat me deci-
sively, though he played with kid gloves, and even took his hands
off the controls from time to time to wave them in my face as he
badgered me with chop-sakey flick taunts: "You look like a samurai, but you fight like a scullery maid, Pen-Yi-Mon!" "Ha ha! Your

kung fu is very weak! Ha ha ha!" I insisted on playing the next game alone, though he repented, and promised to be nice.

In my first one-player game against the machine, I got walloped by the second contender in about twenty seconds (the only thing Eviscerator had in common with Lucky Wander Boy was its no-brainer first screen). Against a lovingly rendered suburban house backdrop, I was cut to pieces by jujitsu serial killer John Wayne Gracie [*sic*] and buried in the backyard.

"BYYEWwww," I said out loud.

"Frogger death sound," a female voice said behind me.

Her eyes were large and round, near *manga* size, her lips thin, her nose upturned Irish. She blinked a bit too frequently and cocked her head while waiting for my response, somehow managing to appear simultaneously knowing and confused, as if her body had been hijacked by an alien who was still getting used to the handling and suspension on this odd, lanky thing.

"Not bad," I said.

"Bwngkabwngkabwngkabwngkabwngka," she said. An extremely faithful approximation, much closer than my own.

"Pac-Man."

"Your turn."

"Tsssschhhhhhrrrrw," I said.

"Defender shot," she said. "Dyeu! Dyeu, dyeu, dyeu, dyudyudydyeu!" It was a small and round sound, like a skipping record of a bleating lamb.

"Asteroids shot," I said. "PCCCCCH . . . chchchchchcht."

"Centipede death, followed by counting of the mushrooms. Pwupup . . . ^{pwupup!} Pwupup . . . ^{pwupupı}"

"Crazy Climber climbing," I said without hesitation, and threw her a curve: "SHHHHHHHHH*SHH*HHH*SHHH*HH-*SHH*HH*SHH*HHHHHH."

"Skiing," she said.

"Platform?"

"Intellivision, of course."

It was all I could do to restrain myself from backing her into the water cooler and pressing my mouth to hers. I'm no man of action, I generally take a wait-and-see approach, but honestly, this time I was close. Luckily, she asked me my name before I could do anything rash.

"I'm Adam. Hi."

"I'm Clio. I'm a graphic designer."

"I pretended to be one of those once."

"Yeah? What're you pretending to be now?"

"A writer."

"Who isn't?"

Instinct told me to tell her about the *Catalogue of Obsolete Entertainments*, but I held off. I have developed the overriding meta-instinct of distrusting all my other instincts. Only a full minute after she walked away did I realize that she was almost certainly the same Clio who had put out the false alarm about Araki Itachi's TV interview on alt.games.video.classic. Had it been a piece of deliberate, mischievous misinformation, or was she one of us, or should I say one of *me*, a Fellow Wanderer? I scrawled a note in the dust of my mind: FIND OUT ABOUT CLIO.

I would have to be circumspect. Enthusiasms were often hidden beneath intricate defenses; like a baby strapped tight into his car seat in the back of an SUV, they were precious cargo, to be protected at all costs. As a promising side avenue, I boldly and impulsively addressed Kurt Krickstein on one of his oversight passes through the Plant and told him how much I'd love to be involved with the Lucky Wander Boy project, in addition to my other duties.

"That's great, great, tell Sammy, I've got some investors coming. 'Kay? Thaaanks, bud!"

In an office that looked like a Comics and Collectables store after an earthquake, Sexy talked on a cell phone so small it could not be seen behind his two fingers.

"—just between you and me, I can't *wait* to get the fuck out—hold on a sec. I'll call you right back." He snapped the phone shut. "Penny Pincher! What can I do for you?"

"Get me involved in Lucky Wander Boy. I want it on top of the other stuff, not instead of it. An added bonus for Portal, absolutely free of charge."

"Definitely, absolutely, no question."

"Also . . . that Clio girl. What's the story with her?"

"Clio *Michael* Camp—good artist, weird chick. Seems kind of fidgety. I don't know her all that well. Why, you wanna fuck her? I could probably arrange it."

Twenty-four hours later, Sexy gave Krickstein his two weeks' notice; he was moving on to greener pastures at Warner Brothers. He'd planned to wrap things up gracefully, but Krickstein kept looking at him as if he were a stain on the couch, referring to him as a weasel in loud whispers intended to be overheard, and later refused to acknowledge his presence altogether. I was therefore not surprised when Sexy decided to cut his two weeks short. His lame-duck status left him unable to help me in the Lucky Wander Boy matter, but he did repeatedly express his sorrow at not being able to take me with him.

On his last day, he came back to the Plant to wish everyone farewell. Having said nothing of a social nature to Sexy in the year she had worked for him, Linda saw no reason to start now; she shook his hand and told him Good-bye with a short, sharp nod. Tamar bid him Shalom with naked envy. Ted told him to Keep In Touch, his eyes wide with the childlike hope that Sexy actually might. Shay shook his hand.

"Out of the sweatshop and into the big show. You extra-extra-large bastard."

Sexy slugged him in the arm, grinned and walked out the back door.

I was stranded.

part ii

WANDER

One can take it on the chin like a whipped dog, or one can bite first. It is clear which of these is preferable.

—Dafei Ji, *Leng Tch'e*

[from beginning of page 19 of entry]…no patterns or cheats to help the player deal with the proliferating randomness and cutthroat difficulty of Stage I's third and final screen. Only through a combination of luck, dedication and an intimate, almost uncanny rapport with the machine did the devotee eventually find himself ascending the lift shaft out of that deadly world, and into the incongruity of the ten-second intermission that followed.

The background disappeared, and Lucky Wander Boy floated toward the foreground until his sprite was twice its Stage I size. From screen left and right, a team of two identical brown, saucer-eyed, roly-poly creatures emerged, and put Lucky at the center of a brief vaudeville routine: the left roly-poly creature kicked him in the ass, Lucky turned around to see who'd just kicked him in the ass, at which point the roly-poly creature on the right would kick him in the ass, and so on for five or six kicks, leaving Lucky looking less like a hero than a tremendous dupe. The last kick was a doozy, sending Lucky straight up to the top of the screen, where he was sucked into a large cartoon sewer pipe that dropped down to meet him. The screen went black.

When images returned, the player found himself emerging from a stumpy outlet that resembled a fire hydrant. He was no longer represented as a tiny sprite of a man, but by a detailed bust of a blond buzz-cut head seen from behind in the lower right quadrant of the screen, with the rest of the body only hinted at by forearms that reached into the frame when he ran, and sometimes by the spindly de Chirico shadow that stretched in front of him. When Lucky turned, the scene turned with him, not allowing the player to see his avatar's face, immersing him in the game world in a way no one had experienced since Battlezone—and the world of Lucky Wander Boy's second stage was far more fully realized than that tank game's sparse vector polygons could ever allow. It was an important precursor to the first-person perspective of Punch Out and the slew of hugely successful shoot-'em-ups that followed in its wake (Doom, Quake, et al.), but is rarely recognized as such because in Lucky Wander Boy's second stage nothing shot or got shot at, hit or got hit.

Instead, Lucky wandered through a calm, beige plain—a welcome sight. The first time I made it to the second stage on the Lucky Wander Boy machine at Peacock Palace after the skin-of-my-teeth escape from the mayhem of the last screen, it looked like a beach to me, and I felt like I'd stumbled onto a vacation.

After a quick look around, I found Stage II to be less beach than desert, shifting patterns in a narrow range of tans, beiges and browns as far as I went in any direction. Still, novelty abounded. The second stage had almost no antagonists whatever. The Sebiros were gone. Nothing attacked you as you trekked across the sands, which were featureless except for sporadic trees with either four or five leaves. Every minute or two, objects would appear for you to pick up: a shovel, a red dress, a hand mirror, a briefcase, a large axe, a screwdriver, a baseball cap.

Sometimes one of the brown roly-poly creatures from the intermission would come, silently shouting "Meku! Meku!" with English letters that came out of its mouth, and do an involved little dance around you. Then it would either give you one of the aforementioned objects, or take one from you. Every once in a while it would take everything you had, but it did not seem to matter, because the things did not *do* anything. They appeared in an inventory strip along the bottom of the screen as you collected them, but no Mortal Kombat-style combinations of joystick pulls and button pushes allowed you to make use of them. They seemed to be empty baggage.

The bright daylight faded to night and back on a regular fifteen-minute cycle. For those who played long enough, the color of the sand began to undergo a similar but slower cyclical transformation, growing lighter and lighter in tiny increments, eventually becoming a uniform white before heading back to beige again in a cycle that took more than an hour. The general consensus among specialists[1] attributes the abstract, white null-space to the influence of *Yellow Submarine*, from

---

[1] Admittedly derived from a scant sample population.

the Jeremy Hilary Boob/Nowhere Man scenes. Given the hermetic nature of the game and its country of origin, however, we might do well to consider the strange novella *Leng Tch'e*,[2] written just before the fall of the Xing Dynasty in China by executioner and poet Dafei Ji, from the perspective of a woman undergoing the brutal Death of a Hundred Cuts for the axe murder of her cruel and faithless husband. A clear parallel exists between the fate of its dismembered female protagonist and the fate of the Lucky Wander Boy machines, mined as they no doubt were for their component parts upon their return to Midway. In *Leng Tch'e*, when the Head Man begins sawing through the narrator's second shoulder, the huge amounts of opium being administered to her to stave off shock begin to transform her consciousness:

> The backdrop of pain transposes from the heard to the seen; it ceases to be a drone, and becomes a whiteness that pervades my vision, though my eyes are closed … It is oddly comforting, this lack of any sensation other than that which was once pain, and is now a whiteness taut like a shadow puppet screen.

And after he removes her breast:

> … the whiteness that once was pain has expanded, dislodging a piece of my twice-lived life from itself, the piece falls away like a discarded puppet and where the puppet's shadow was there is now only the white. . . .

Leng Tch'e first became available in Japan, translated into Japanese by Kyoto monk Kanchingai Ana in 1975, and published in English in 1980. To the best of my knowledge, Dafei Ji's original Chinese has never been published in China; indeed, I am unaware of anyone besides Ana who claims to have seen the original manuscript in its entirety. Upon its publication in Japan, *Leng Tch'e* caused a minor stir,

---

[2]Subject of author's college thesis (unfinished).

providing the fodder for several hours of talk shows, and the fuel for at least one book burning. It is quite possible that Araki Itachi was reading it while designing Lucky Wander Boy, and thereby inspired to include the fade to white in Stage II. I believe that further research in the field will show this to be the case. As a source of influence, Lucky Wander Boy was undoubtedly the Wachowski Brothers' inspiration for the abstract null-space in The Matrix, though the nothingness is even more imposing without the million-mile gun racks.

The second stage was where Lucky Wander Boy earned his name. The whitening desert had no map. After exhaustive observation, I can state with authority that there was no Asteroids-inspired wraparound, no recurring pattern in the layout of the trees to suggest the player was moving around a globe. To be precise, Lucky was on a huge circular plateau, as the player could confirm by walking unstintingly for 235 seconds in any one direction from the point of entry, after which, no matter which direction the player had chosen, a sheer cliff appeared, overlooking a bottomless chasm. The only way Lucky could die in the second stage was to throw himself off this cliff with the Jump! button, arms and legs outstretched, spinning like a propeller as he fell into the darkness, until he contracted to a single pixel of light and was extinguished. Otherwise the machine needed to be reset before someone could start a new game.

Second-stage strategies were numerous. Mumbled tips were passed from player to player in the rare event that one showed up to play Lucky Wander Boy and found another already playing. Detailed tree and object maps were circulated and sometimes sold to the gullible, and none of them worked, for the simple reason that the layout of the trees—the only stationary landmarks—did not remain constant from game to game, or indeed within any single game. Although the player never saw them doing it, the trees moved around behind his back.

By the time I could reach the second stage with any regularity, there were never any quarters in the on-deck line atop the game's control panel. I was alone, but it did not deter me. In fact, what pushed others away is what kept me there, at first. The frenetic, anxiety-dream trial-by-fire of the first stage may have drawn me into

Lucky Wander Boy, but it was the second stage that shut the door behind me, with its near-total absence of death. Outside a game cabinet or TV screen, my first taste of death had come only recently with the death of my grandmother, and I had decided I could do without it. In Lucky Wander Boy, as long as you didn't mind a roly-poly creature occasionally divesting you of your useless possessions, you did not need to worry about being shot, blown up, smashed, burned, eaten, or overrun with germs or tumors. You were free to wander unmolested. To create your own reasons for being there.

I became enamored of the absence of challenges and bought into the game's nomadic spirit, taking comfort in its inscrutability. The more I began to suspect that there was no way to win, the less I thought about winning, and abandoning the compulsion to win was a great relief. Unlike earlier games, I saw Lucky Wander Boy as an accurate analogue to real life, where a similar suspicion of the grand, monolithic importance of winning—or perhaps of my own chances for same— was beginning to foment in my mind.

After a while, though, a feeling of entrapment set in. I could go wherever I liked and do whatever I liked, I could run or Jump! or Warp Skip! or stay still until the arcade closed, but this freedom obscured an ominous possibility: the possibility that, do what I would and try as I might, I would never make it out of this place.

What had I gotten myself into?

There had to be more to it than this.

where it's coming from

● ●

For the first time since we'd left Warsaw, I took Anya dancing, to celebrate my employment. I thought she'd be pleased—my salary was enough that, between the two of us, we were actually crossing the threshold into the middle class.

We went to one of those places that made you wait in line no matter how many people were actually inside, to cultivate a feeling of social urgency in the minds of the waiting, and a sense of exceptionalism in those who knew how to circumvent the line. Maintaining a grip on Anya's pinky, I cast her between two male petitioners arguing their Exceptionalism to the bouncers, insisting that any attempt to relegate them to the ranks of the Waiting would be a horrible mistake. When the bouncers moved the petitioners aside to open the ropes for Anya, she reeled me in behind her, and though they shook their huge heads with disbelief upon seeing me, they were good sports about it.

After a stiff drink at the zinc bar imported from Switzerland, I managed to suppress my impostor complex, and pulled Anya into the fray. We bounced around on the dance floor beneath the strobes and the gumdrop lights, in time with the beat as often as not, and soon the sweat glistened on her cheeks and her exposed shoulder blades. Reinvigorated, she threw off the disappointments of love and life with wild shakes of her arms and uncovered the Anya I'd fallen for. She was beautiful, and alive, and all but topless, and for all that had happened, she was still mine, wasn't she? I should have only had eyes for her.

But I could not help looking elsewhere. If I was quick I could catch them in the act: the guy behind her, the beneficiary of her slow, gyrating pirouettes. The three guys leaning against the zinc bar, looking casual, pointing openly in our direction and laughing amongst themselves. The tall, bald black guy with the perfectly shaped head. They were looking. At her. And she was not looking at me—but she was looking somewhere. The purpose in her darting green eyes belied her dancing abandon. If not me, who? Was she looking at one of them specifically, or at a few of them, or just *looking*, searching, trolling for anyone else? I shot surreptitious glances along her line of sight to see who would turn away quickly.

After a few tries, I locked gazes with (of all people) the pretty, sandy-haired waiter from the restaurant on the Promenade. He did not turn away quickly, or at all; he met my gaze and smiled, because like the Zinc Bar Casuals, he knew that I knew:

It was coming. I didn't know where from, but I knew it was coming.

CATALOGUE OF OBSOLETE ENTERTAINMENTS
GAME: COPYWRITER!
Format: Job
Manufacturer: Portal Entertainment and Development
Year: 2000
CPU: (insufficient knowledge of either physics or economics to state with authority)
Sound: mass polyphonic, 20–20,000 Hz range
Resolution: 11,400 × 11,400

Although the visual and auditory realism of this game are startling and would be even more so if the lights in the Plant were ever turned on, the game itself is relatively simple. Several Producer characters give you, the Copywriter, orders for text that is needed for one of the two dozen websites in the portal-entertainment.com network. Although these Producers are within your Copywriter's line of sight, they always send these orders through e-mail or ICQ instant messenger—such an obvious embodiment of some menacing social trend or other that it is hard to feel menaced by it. Different Producers have different ways of dealing with the inherent ridiculousness of communicating this way, remnants of your basic spitball strategies: Bob Wilson ducks behind his computer after sending you a work order and hopes you won't peek over the lip of his cubicle divider to look him in the eye. Alison Ehrlich turns and flashes you a sincere apologetic grin, and an honest one; she really does hate to impose. Eric Berkeley pretends you and he are not even in the same room, blithely munching Cheetos and wiping his hands on his V-neck sweater. Tamar Tzur stares you down remorselessly as she shoots you the "request" for that two hundred words she needed five minutes before it occurred to her superior, Lyme, to ICQ her with the order to ICQ you RE: 200 words ASAP.

When I e-mailed or ICQed the Producers in return, I always practiced the scrupulous avoidance of the first method.

A sample order:

We're sending out a mailer to all members of the Eviscerator site, 200 words max, 'the slaughter calls, DIS-Member, kill or be killed,' etc etc etc ASAP please thank you

You fill this order, as quickly as possible in the above case, and pass it back to the originating Producer for corrections. Shortly thereafter, the copy is sent back to you with requests for revisions, which you make and send back to the same Producer. After several rounds of same you are given the OK to pass the copy on to one of the graphic designers (Linda, Clio), who incorporates it into the layout of the page they're designing, or occasionally to the programmer (Shay) if it requires coding. All in all, the game is quite similar to the Budweiser-Bally joint venture Tapper or its bowdlerized twin Root Beer Tapper, though harder on your lower back than either.

As with Tapper, Pac-Man or any Classic game, however, mastery of Copywriter! requires elegant and nuanced strategies. My own system was as follows:

On entering the Plant on Monday, I would sit down next to the looming shelves of server towers, power up my computer and open my Netscape Mail Folder Inbox, where my incoming messages (mostly orders for portal-entertainment.com copy) ran from most recent to least recent vertically down the screen. Clicking on the Date header, I flipped the stack and started with the oldest unread or neglected messages, boldfaced to distinguish them from the rest. I often left the Inbox alone for two or three days without penalty.

Success is often a matter of framing a problem. As I saw it, the challenge of Copywriter! was to dispose of as many messages as possible without actually dealing with them. First came the Throwaways. Anything I was CC'ed on was immediately tossed into the Trash; items presented "For Your Information" are unimportant and possibly detrimental, because if you are at all like me, you already have far too much information, more than enough to see you through a seven-year information famine with plenty to spare. This simple discarding often culled the herd by half.

Most of the remaining messages could simply be thrown into a Reply Loop by tagging them with questions such as What do you mean? Clarify please :) or Should we CC John B4 proceeding with this? and returning them to sender. By analyzing each piece of an order, questioning each word and phrase, breaking down each task into subtasks that would themselves be broken down into sub-subtasks and thus increased exponentially, I could dilate any simple assignment into a fine example of Zeno's paradox, endlessly diminishing baby steps toward a finish line that would never be reached before Krickstein pulled the plug on the project in question.

Alternately, I could always pass a task down to one of the exclusively young and female interns who walked pertly and purposefully from cubicle to cubicle, the only Portal employees subordinate to me. I did this only rarely, however. Like superzappers or smart bombs, you had to save them for when you really needed them, or you might really need them and find them gone.

The items that could not be thrown out or Reply Looped or passed down to an intern, I put into the On Deck Folder on my desktop, which I dealt with when I got up-to-date with the e-mail Inbox, or when executive discontent threatened to reach dangerous levels. I arranged its items in order of importance, opening a window on my desktop for each and layering them accordingly. At the top was the To Do stack, every element of which was stamped with a direct order or deadline. Many had been through the hot-potato Reply Loop cycle many times, gifts of those who used me as I used them. After working through these, I put the next third or so of the On Deck Folder that I did not want to or have to deal with immediately in the Repressed Folder, more thoroughly buried in the catalog hierarchy of my hard drive. I dealt with these items only when cornered.

Some things, though, I just didn't want to see, ever, not even in my mind's eye when I casually perused the list of files in my C: drive. They were toxic, undoable, potentially interminable tasks assigned mainly to keep me a bit uneasy and off balance at all times, and went straight to the Shitheap, which was not located anywhere on my hard drive. Shitheap material was printed up, erased from my computer and placed in a folder in my bottom desk drawer, next to the hip flask of Jim Beam I would need on the unforeseeable occasion that I was forced to confront it.

A sample round of Copywriter!:

I was ICQed the following order by Tamar:

Pennyman: I need a SHORT (150-250 character max) description of EVERY Portal site for all-purpose use (ad copy, search engines, etc).

I attempted to initiate a Reply Loop by cutting her order out and pasting it into an e-mail (Reply Loops only work in e-mails; on ICQ the turnover is too fast to allow other tasks to fragment the task you are trying to dispose of). Beneath her order, I wrote:

What is the timeframe on this one? I'm pretty busy. :-o

Ten minutes later, I received my message, cut from the e-mail and pasted back into ICQ with an addendum:

I need it now. *Kurt* wants it ASAP.

I returned the message thread to e-mail, with the question:

Which sites should I do first? Should I go in alphabetical order, or do them in order of heaviest traffic to least traffic—or least to heaviest, to try and boost the numbers of the less popular sites?

One minute later, an ICQ from Tamar:

I don't fucking care! Just do it now!

Peeking around the side of my cubicle, I saw her staring me down remorselessly, and this kicked the order to the top of the To Do stack. Glossing over the four rounds of revisions between Tamar and me, I eventually ended up with twenty-six descriptions. Some samples:

1) Alien Bimbo Range: One of these hot bikini chicks is really a bloodsucking alien—can you find out which one and blow her away before she drains you dry? A cool new online game from Portal!

4) Eviscerator—The Movie: The official site for one of the most popular videogame movies of all time! Only you stand between

Ibn Alhrazed's slavering alien hordes and the helpless nations of Earth! Pics, outtakes, online games. Coming soon—cool inside info on *Eviscerator III*!

8) Taco Stand: "Watch that taco, Paco!" You've always wondered what goes on behind the counter at your local taqueria. Now you can find out, in this hilarious, edgy new web show from Portal Entertainment!

19) Bad Girl!: Come check out a different swimsuit model being spanked every day by Portal CEO Kurt Krickstein himself! "If you want something done right..."

20) Invasion T.M.H. (Trainably Mentally Handicapped): They've got their eyes on world domination, and their pants full of poo! This edgy, hilarious new animated show from Portal gives political correctness the finger! Come check it out...but mind the drool!

24) Amber Anthony homepage: the official web home of Amber Anthony, one of Hollywood's hottest up-and-coming sex goddesses-in-waiting. From erotica to calendars to the UPN hit show *Guardian Angels*, Amber's done it all. Become a member, and watch her do even more!

26) Lucky Wander Boy—The Movie: The most innovative Classic video game of all-time, Araki Itachi's surrealist masterpiece is both a quest game and a deep questioning of the very concept of the quest game, or indeed of quests in general. Now it is on the fast track to becoming a kaleidoscopic Borgesian meta-action movie from Portal Entertainment! Keep up-to-date on preproduction news, and get sneak peeks at pages from the early script drafts on the OFFICIAL website! "I am waiting for you, Lucky Wander Boy!"

Tamar then sent these descriptions to Krickstein, leading to a Meeting, which I was hoping would be a Bonus Round in which the Copywriter got a shot at convincing Krickstein to allow him some involvement with the Lucky Wander Boy film project. My carefully worded Lucky Wander Boy site description had been an opening gambit in this direction. Bonus Rounds were rare and difficult, requiring an expert gauging of the trajectories of Krickstein's many moods and whims. I had yet to complete one successfully.

The Meeting ended up being not a Bonus Round, but a Pac-Man-style intermission set against the backdrop of Krickstein's Office. As with Pac-Man, you do not act or speak during the intermission. You only listen and look, and nod periodically as he skims your work on his laptop.

"This—no. No no no. You've got to *sell* people. They can go anywhere, there are ten million entertainment sites, you've got to make them want to go to Portal and stay there. You've got to write edgy, but fun, so the advertisers . . . take Bad Girl!, that could be seen as fun, or it could be taken the wrong way. Right now it's the wrong way. And you've got to write *inside*, you're writing outside, very outside. Imagine this is a movie trailer for a scary movie and you're writing the voice-over. Right now, *you're* saying, 'This movie is scary, it is so fucking freaky you will not sleep for nights, we dare you to see this horrifying movie.' What you *want* to be saying is, 'Knock. Knock. KNOCK! *You've got three minutes to live.*' You got me? And here, with Amber Anthony . . . '*one* of Hollywood's hottest up-and-coming sex-goddesses-in-waiting'? No! She's *the* hottest up-and-coming sex-goddess-in-waiting! Amp it up, cut to the chase. Write it sexy, from her point of view, what do you call it . . . 'I never could stand the feel of underwear against my bare skin,' like that. And this Lucky Wander Boy stuff, that's all very smart and funny and ha ha ha, but we don't have time for jokes here, okay? This is serious, this has to get done. I don't know, maybe we need somebody with real advertising experience. I don't know. Maybe."

Sitting in front of a green-screen set in the back parking lot, Shay lit two cigarettes and handed one to Linda, as Clio watched us all through the viewfinder of a Hi-8 video camera, pretending to record. Shay shook his clean-shaven head, dismissing the whole scenario out of hand:

"A decent advertising copywriter charges at least twelve hundred dollars a week. You're completely safe," Shay said.

Behind me, I heard the labored whine of the video camera's zoom lens as Clio zoomed in and out.

"How about a half-decent advertising copywriter?" I asked.

Shay shook his head again and Linda seconded, their two heads bobbing back and forth in unison, as if choreographed.

"You're still much cheaper," Shay said.

"A minor expense," Linda added.

I turned to get Clio's opinion. She just grinned and cryptically whistled the bouncy Frogger opening theme.

"What's that supposed to mean?" I asked her.

"What do you mean, 'mean'?" she said. "Does everything have to 'mean' something? What do you think you are, some kind of writer?"

She flicked a penny at me and went back inside.

Sure enough, nothing ever came of the veiled threat. For several months Copywriter! seemed like a decent game that paid well enough. Unlike all other Portal employees, I could walk to work, and thus got to sleep that extra hour the rest of them spent in traffic, an hour that gave them all-too-much time to contemplate just where it was they were going and why. At 8:40 A.M., sometimes as late as 9:10 A.M., I would wake up and tiptoe from the bedroom. Although Anya slept soundly through the slapping of the rugs back in my Warsaw apartment, the sound of my footsteps on creaking floorboards often woke her now, and once she was up she could not or would not go back to sleep. Instead, she would plunk herself down on the couch, comment on how uncomfortable it was and watch me with hawklike head movements until I finished my bagel and juice and left.

Even on those days when I woke her, the brisk three-block walk to work cleared my head. As I left our run-down two-bedroom and strolled through a downscale area of largely upscale Santa Monica, I would pass the Mexican day laborers waiting in their dirty flannels outside the Salvation Army thrift store, spitting, adjusting baseball caps emblazoned with "Camel Lights" and "Vato" among other things. Occasionally I would see someone pull up in a pickup truck or SUV and haggle with one or more of the men over the going rate for a day's heavy lifting. I never heard a figure larger than forty dollars mentioned. Perspective would inevitably settle in by the time I reached the fire hydrant in front of Portal Entertainment—a squat gray stucco building wedged between a body shop and an office equipment wholesaler. Entering the front door, I'd sidestep the front offices entirely by taking the outside hallway to the kitchen, where I'd pour myself a mug of acidic coffee before stepping into the Plant.

Every page of copy I wrote created many hours' programming and design work for Shay, Linda, Clio and the team of artists, leading to a significant bottleneck in the system. Using my computer's onboard calculator, I kept track of actual time spent working and averaged it at just over an hour a day. The rest of the time was spent in idle conversation with Shay and Linda, whose flip bitterness extended to everything that transpired on the Portal premises except their own cigarette breaks, which they took very seriously and with a siege mentality. Clio was more difficult. She was a difficult person to talk to in general, prone to odd silences and unusual facial expressions, and this difficulty was compounded by my own mild social dyslexia. Nevertheless, I made a point of speaking to her at least twice a day (but no more than four times), though often we only exchanged a few words, and she usually put forth little effort to hold up her end of the conversation. She did not run away, or project disgust, or drop any crumbs of encouragement; she just took in whatever I said, let it bounce around in her head for a few seconds, and spit out a pithy reply. Sometimes she reminded me of one of those early conversational A.I. programs like Eliza or Perry, except the programs' responses often made more sense. Whenever I did get a good conversational volley started, I'd begin to ponder whether my conquest of Clio, such as it was, wasn't just a diversionary tactic to prevent me from thinking about Anya, and the waves of guilt that followed would capsize my witty banter before too long.

And yet I persevered despite these obstacles. Although Clio revealed no interest in me, I could tell that the prospect of being interested intrigued her. None of the forces keeping us apart were strong enough to break the bond that had formed between us like a thin silver string connecting us at the navel when we first met. I got the sense that she had seen through my writer ruse, but ignoring the urge to self-justify, I still did not tell her about the *Catalogue*. Both of us were strangely reticent to talk about Lucky Wander Boy as well, circumnavigating the topic as we might the Holocaust, or blow jobs. Several times I dangled bait—"Dodging all the venture capitalist suits Kurt's got running around here, it reminds me of that strange Japanese video game . . . what was it called? . . . ," whistling the opening fanfare—but she didn't bite.

I also toiled diligently on the free Eviscerator machine, developing a strong preference for the Spectral Samurai character I'd played in my very first game. Like many noxious entertainments, the game was addictive once you got over the initial hump of disgust.

It filled me with a private delight for several months, the way I performed my lazy duties and was otherwise left alone to saunter around the office like a Parisian *flâneur,* slowly, casually, proudly displaying that I was not the kind of person who would put up with hurrying or worrying. In conversation, I displayed my superior intelligence by calling attention to the bureaucratic idiocies that surrounded us: the atrocious signal-to-noise ratio in communications up and down the chain of command, the ridiculous refusal to give us keys to the Plant after such a great show had been made of solemnly vouchsafing us the access code to the alarm. I gloated over the fact that even though I turned my brain off every morning at nine and left it off until five, no one knew the difference. Judging on an hourly basis for actual work done, I was nearly being paid the salary of a Beverly Hills psychologist. I often chuckled to myself about that one. Whenever Clio overheard these chuckles, she would laugh too—the only time I ever heard her laugh a real back-brain laugh—as if my bemusement were contagious. She never asked what I was laughing about.

The joke soon wore thin, however, and my joy deflated as I started to question whether superior intelligence could truly be considered an advantage if you kept your brain off all day, and wondered what would happen if I actually left it on. I began to suffer from a visceral sense of the irreplaceable seconds of my life ticking away one at a time like the tiny bits of carcinogenic insulation material no doubt jarred loose from the ceiling with each footstep vibration, falling faintly earthward to rest in my lungs or on the Plant floor. Claustrophobia set in, a weightless, queasy feeling I hadn't felt since I wandered the deserted plains of Lucky Wander Boy's Stage II. I started to suspect that like most video games, no one ever won at Copywriter!, no one ever got to the happy ending. When would my quarter run out? Worse, what if it never did? Was Clio another Pauline in league with another eight-hundred-pound gorilla, luring me into yet another fruitless ascent of yet another set of girders? Anxieties mounted—

Until I remembered something important:

In Lucky Wander Boy, the second stage was not the end.

rumors

● ● ● ● ● ● ● ● ● ● ● ● ● ● ● ● ● ● ● ●

I first heard the rumors when I was thirteen, about the same time the fat around my middle was mercifully beginning to disappear, from a kid in my Sunday-school class whom I knew only by his Sunday-school name, Schlomo. He was very small, probably suffering from some kind of glandular disorder, and his glasses were so thick that the light of the world must have taken an extra second to penetrate them, which would have explained his perpetual, good-natured daze. He wore button-down shirts, and buttoned the top button. When he saw me playing Lucky Wander Boy at Peacock Palace one weekday, he recognized me from class, and sensing my frustration with the interminable desert and the thieving Mekus, he offered some hope.

"There's another stage to that game, you know," Schlomo said. "A third one, after the desert."

"How would you know?" I asked. I wanted very much for him to go away. As it was, my social status was borderline. If someone saw me talking to Schlomo, it wouldn't help matters any.

"I heard it from some guy's cousin."

I huffed, dismissive. He stood beside me for a while longer, waiting for a conversation to develop, but I maintained a charade of deep, silent concentration, and finally saw his reflection disappear from the game screen as he wandered back into the recesses of Peacock Palace.

In the weeks that followed, others came forward with assertions similar to Schlomo's. No one actually claimed to have gotten to

Stage III, but some said they had seen someone else get there, or knew someone who had gotten there, or knew someone who had seen someone else make it.

I remained skeptical until I nearly crossed over myself.

It was at the tail end of a long Lucky Wander Boy session. I was on the way to throw myself over the cliff and quit when I ran across the hand mirror and picked it up. Instead of joining the shovel, the red dress and my other acquired items in the inventory strip on the bottom of the screen as it usually did, the mirror floated before my avatar's eyes, tilting at such an angle that I could just make out the top of Lucky's buzz-cut head. I moved to grab it, but the mirror maintained its distance, drawing me forward. I ran after it, pushing the joystick to the verge of breaking; I had been exactly where I was supposed to be at the precise moment fate had demanded I be there, and now I was going to be vouchsafed a vision. To underscore the biblical nature of the moment, the desert rose up on either side of me like the waters of the Red Sea, the walls of sand flaring out like great wings, and the tips of the wings stretched over my head until I felt like I was riding on the back of a great manta ray. The wings merged above me, forming a tunnel, and then everything crashed into a point of rainbow light in the center of the screen, and then went black—

—because Dave Lombardo had unplugged the machine.

"What's going on?!?" I burned with Old Testament fury, as though my birthright had been snatched from me.

"What's going on is that I've gotta eat, and this thing ain't helping. Gotta make room for one that will. Here—" He gave me two tokens. "Go play some regular games."

He loaded the plywood cabinet onto a dolly and carted it out of the arcade, and I never saw a Lucky Wander Boy machine again.

Many years later, whispers of Stage III persisted on alt.games.video.classic and other backwoods forums, and sometimes I'd peruse them while at work, but they all rang with the otherworldly ping of ancient pottery—miraculously intact after many years, yet long emptied of all contents. The only detail about Stage III that survived was the prospect of its existence.

★ ★ ★

I first heard the rumor from a guy named Brad Kern, a basketball player. Brad was alpha at Woodhill Glen High, where the activities of a few small-to-middling Jews and one tall black guy on the basketball court generated excessive interest. You would not have called us friends, but he approached me congenially enough. If he remembered punching me in the face in grade school, he gave no indication.

"Hey, Adam man, are you and Mandy Cline an item?"

Mandy Cline was the lead singer of the band Putain, the best band at Woodhill Glen High. Word had it they were going to make it big. Marianne Faithfull thin, a bit dirty-looking, a bit unwholesome . . . among my limited circle of friends, she was as much an object of veneration as lust. I told him Mandy Cline and I were not an item. He looked surprised.

"Really. Hmmm. Well, I heard she was into you."

I didn't give the rumor much credence at first, but I heard it from a few other people as well, people on the wrong side of the circumference of Brad's circle, people who did not even know I was listening. Then one night while playing Double Dragon at a Bennigans restaurant, someone next to me said, "Nice shirt," in reference to my R.E.M. *Life's Rich Pageant* tour shirt. I turned to find Mandy Cline standing beside me, bottle-blonde streak in her candy-red hair.

"Thanks," I said.

"Adam, right?"

I nodded.

The restaurant's P.A. called, "Klein party of four, K-L-E-I-N. . . ."

"You ought to quit that kiddie stuff, man, save your quarters to buy Putain's first album. I'll see you around?"

She turned to go.

Quit that kiddie stuff. Quit that kiddie stuff. Quit that kiddie stuff. In the days to come, I heard Mandy's remark in my head, repeated over and over as if she'd taught it to a mynah bird. A disdain for Double Dragon hatched inside me, and like a tapeworm computer virus began to work its way back through my memory to infect my love of all these games with terminal doubts.

It turned out the whole "Mandy Cline is into you" thing was someone's idea of a joke. I never found out who had started it, and I never found out whether Mandy was in on the joke or not. I thought about asking her, but I could never think up precisely the right way to do it, so I disguised my weakness and hesitation as calculation and strategy, and never talked to her again. Whatever the case, the damage was done. My interest in computers, computer programming, and video games most of all crashed and burned, and I replaced them with—

Nothing. Nonathletic enthusiasms were generally frowned upon. In feeble emulation of Putain, some of my friends and I pretended to have a band called Spark the Hooter. It was considered a valid weekend activity; we sat around and made grating noise and drank cheep beer in the drummer's basement because his mother didn't mind, and thereby dulled the pain of being men.

I first heard the rumor from Shay while playing Eviscerator, as his Viking was hacking off my Spectral Samurai's arms with a battle-axe.

"You're not so retarded that you don't know Clio wants you, are you?"

At his right, Linda nodded solemnly, Blow Pop in her mouth. Life is an extension of high school by other means. Unlike Brad Kern, I considered Shay and Linda to be friends. As they both probably had Brad Kerns in their pasts, they were unlikely to play this kind of joke on me, especially since they were telling me something I already suspected to be true. It was a wake-up call, however. I began to think about planning to make my move. This was not Warsaw. Things were complicated here. This would take time, calculation, strategy. I tried not to think about Anya.

I first heard the rumor from Tamar, while honing my Eviscerator skills in a one-player game, practicing some combination moves I'd learned from the Eviscerator fan site while pretending to write new copy for it. I did not see her approach, but the hair on the back of my neck stood up an instant before she spoke.

"Working hard?" she said.

"I was just taking a break," I said. I turned to look her in the eye, even though it meant Miss Thang jumping up and crushing my Spectral Samurai's head like a rotten grapefruit between her biker-short-clad thighs.

"Well, let me tell you something, a lot of people around here are going to be taking very long breaks. *Very* long. Do you understand what I mean, eh? I am not threatening you personally, I cannot fire anybody anyway . . . but there are a lot of companies doing exactly what we are doing. Too many. Not all of them will last, and then there will be a Great Crashing Down. I overheard Kurt and Lyme talking in Kurt's office, Kurt has heard rumors that a lot of the venture capital people are going to retreat, and they discussed maybe 'paring down the payroll.' Just a rumor, but still."

She was probably telling the truth. I was the only copywriter at Portal, however, and I was not aware of anyone else in the building who could write grammatically correct sentences, with the possible exception of Shay, who had very definite ideas about what fell within his job description and what fell without. I was even considering asking for a raise in a few weeks. Why couldn't she just leave me the hell alone?

top of the pyramid

● ●

The visiting venture capitalists of D,S&A had launched an impressive Tet offensive on the food Portal had provided for their visit, but the spread had been enough for twice their number, and a good deal remained in the waiting area after their departure: several sushi rolls, pita, hummus, bagels and cream cheese, a half platter of cold cuts, the Pac-Man remnants of a cheese pizza. I had put cream cheese on a bagel and was feeding it to Krickstein's dog, Curly, when I heard what sounded like the grunt that would follow an unexpected blow to the stomach, spilling over the top wall of Krickstein's office. The walls of the individual offices did not reach the ceiling, leaving a gap that facilitated interoffice communication and created an atmosphere of panaural surveillance that often held the most mundane conversation to a low conspiratorial whisper. Any time I had something to say to anyone in the office portion of Portal, I felt like I ought to run a loud bath before saying it.

"Lyme! Get in here! Look at this!"

At the sound of Krickstein's angry voice, Curly dropped the bagel on the Persian carpet and bolted. Moving as quickly as the dog, Lyme ran past me into Krickstein's office.

"Nobody wants to leave well enough alone!" Krickstein said. "Nobody wants to play their part in the process, everybody wants to be pharaoh, on top of the pyramid. If everybody moved up to the top, then the top would be fat and wide, and the bottom would be narrow and pointy, and the top wouldn't be the fucking top anymore! Get—get—" Staccato snapping, "—whatsisname, the one who always bothers me about this, the Weasel's friend—"

"Pennyman?"

"Pennyman, get him in here."

I did not wait for Lyme, and entered the office of my own initiative. Krickstein adopted a pleasant expression, and leaned on the Eviscerator prop battle-axe.

"Pennyman, bud! We've talked about Lucky Wander Boy before, right? You're a fan."

"Yes, I am." I did not want to sound overly enthusiastic. I was mindful of traps and tricks.

"I want you to look at this."

On his laptop, a single e-mail window sat in the dead center of the screen, and a printer was presently spitting out its contents:

I read script. It is wrong. For first, Lucky is bland haired. Please do again, with emphasis on WANDER. And centralness of screwdriver, making for dismantling of Our Hero. Remember 3 acts, and middle being the longest, and middle also being the WANDER stage. Also, looking at Mr. Finebug's ending, I think, "????" Playing game is mostly essential for scriptwriter. Perhaps find one who is a knower and lover of LUCKY WANDER BOY.
Sincerely,
Araki Itachi; CEO
S.L.S. Inc.
Kiyamachi-dori 32
Kyoto, JAPAN 604
(011) 81-75-433-6252

"There you go," Krickstein said. "Everybody has the right to shoot themselves in the ass."

Lyme shook his head in supportive disbelief. "We never should have given her Meaningful Consultation Rights." He had recently been promoted to Vice President of Internet and Film Production, though I do not believe the promotion was accompanied by a pay raise.

"'Meaningful' my ass. Here's what I want you to do," Krickstein said to me while flipping through the second drawer of a three-drawer hardwood file cabinet. He pulled out a stack of paper held together by two brass brads and slapped it into my open palms. I glanced at the cover:

LUCKY WANDER BOY: THE MOVIE

based on the game by
Araki Itachi

screenplay by
Cheops Feinberg

And for the briefest of moments I had that feeling so rare to me that I was exactly where I was supposed to be at the precise moment fate had demanded I be there. My Moment of Decision bounded toward me, and as if from a vantage point far overhead, I saw myself stepping forward to meet him. The handcuffs of Lucky Wander Boy would shackle us at the wrists, and I would never come unmoored and drift into rootlessness again.

"Excellent," I said, "Great. Now, you want me to—"

"I want you to read it, call her, and convince her that everything in there is exactly the way it should be, that it's going to be the perfect Lucky Wander Boy movie. Amp it up, hype her up on it, it's edgy, it's cool, it's fun. You are the liaison. I'm getting enough trouble from Japanese people with *Eviscerator III*, I've got investors to worry about, I don't have time for this shit."

"We could just let the option on it lapse," Lyme suggested.

"No!" Krickstein said. "Diversity is a very important part of the Portal brand identity. We have a diversified portfolio of intellectual properties, and this one fills our 'weird cult geek bullshit' quota—and it's *mine*, and I didn't get to where I am today by just giving away things that are mine! Maybe Itachi dies tomorrow, she's cool for a month and we can make some money off the licensing."

"License, license, license," Lyme said.

"Go take care of it, Pennyman." Kurt waved me off, and returned his attention to Lyme. "Let's talk about something Japanese that matters: Mount Hiei, monastery deal, Korean demolitions guys—are we going to do this thing or not? We need to do this thing, it's crucial. When can I get to Kyoto and talk to these people?"

As they started talking about explosions, Buddhist monks and first-class plane reservations, I left the office, went back to my desk and began to read the Lucky Wander Boy script immediately. Shay tried to engage me in conversation ("You know what sucks a dead donkey's ass?"), but I waved him off the way I would have if I'd been reading my own draft notice.

FADE IN:

EXT. JUNGLE—NIGHT

TREES. Twisted. Limbs writhing like they're in pain. A
CLEARING. MUD. Fetid, marshy, on the ground. Oozing
with horrible secrets. Eerie JUNGLE SOUNDS. A SICKLE
MOON scars the night sky . . . and DARK CLOUDS annihi-
late it. With no mercy.

And if that weren't bad enough . . . there are also a
few hundred SEBIRO TROOPERS around. In BLACK ARMORED
BODYSUITS. Stony, remorseless faces. Looking like
Hell's damned doormen. Surrounding:

AN AWESOMELY BEAUTIFUL GIRL tied to a POST. Asian.
Sweat glistening on her hot, hairless, near-naked
body. Her name is TIARA. It is lunchtime for *something* . . . and Tiara is the main course.

PHOTO-SEBIRO steps from behind a tree. A thin TELE-
SCOPIC LENS where his left eye should be. *Merged with
his very flesh*.

His LENS EYE FLASHES. A signal. . . .

A team of SEBIRO DRUMMERS start POUNDING. Big, evil,
savage, African-looking drums. . . .

ZOOM ON TIARA'S EYES. If fear was money, she would be
one rich babe. . . .

In the jungle distance, a STIRRING. A RUSTLING. Something   MOVING,   approaching   the   clearing,
something. . . .

Awful.

HI-ANGLE SHOT of Tiara as she screams to the brutal sky:

> TIARA
> HELP ME, LUCKY WANDER BOY!!!

Her SHOUT ECHOES against the brutal sky. . . .

INT. WANDER BOY TEAM PLANE—NIGHT

Ultra-high-tech. The Pentagon would give their left one for a puppy like this. Equipped with totally automated navigation equipment, of course. But someone is steering manually. . . .

LUCKY WANDER BOY. Jet black hair. Darkly handsome, rugged features. If you don't bother him, he won't bother you. If you do, he'll kick your ass on a dime . . . and give you change.

Oh yeah . . . he's also the Chosen One. Humanity's only hope. He knows it. . . .

But he doesn't have to like it.

In back of the plane, the rest of his Wander Boy Team:

DR. MAYA WINDSOR . . . blonde, supernaturally beautiful, the hottest thing to ever make it through M.I.T.'s Biophysics program in one piece. But she's no geeky science stiff . . . whenever she comments on something, you can expect it to be in a cool, sarcastic manner.

SHOUSU UMINZOKU . . . Lucky Wander Boy's trusted friend, and a serious martial arts master in his own

right . . . not to mention a champion race car driver
and veteran sky diver. The bigger the thrill, the more
amped up Shousu is to go and do it!

MEKU . . . the team's cuddly brown sidekick from a
parallel universe, 2 ft tall, full of mischief and
practical jokes . . . but a faithful servant in times
of need. He is the comic relief of the team.

LWB cocks his head. *He hears Tiara.* Somehow, he hears.

> LUCKY WANDER BOY
> She's down there.

> SHOUSU
> But how do you know that, Lucky?

> MAYA
> (sarcastic)
> Yeah . . . are your "Spidey senses" tingling?

> LUCKY WANDER BOY
> I know what I know. I'm taking her down.

> MEKU
> Meku! Meku *Meku* Meku Meku!

With a powerful hand, Lucky takes the plane
down. . . .

EXT. NIGHT SKY—NIGHT

The WANDER BOY TEAM PLANE ROLLS. BANKS.

DIVES!

EXT. JUNGLE—NIGHT

The SEBIRO TROOPERS CHANT in some foreign tongue.
Awaiting the arrival of their unholy god. DRUMS BEAT-
ING. TREES RUSTLING LOUDER.

C.U. OF TIARA, she sees it, she SCREAMS a throat-
shattering scream as

MEGA-SEBIRO emerges into the clearing!

He is enough to stop your heart. Twenty feet high.
Long, metallic SABER TEETH already crusty with dried
blood. His eyes burn with hunger for living flesh.

He is ugliness incarnate.

But he has company.

Lucky and the Team parachute into the clearing in a
perfect diamond formation. Nobody does it better.

Photo-Sebiro LAUGHS wantonly:

> PHOTO-SEBIRO
> So you are the "famous" Lucky Wander Boy.

> SHOUSU
> Yes he is, Photo-Sebiro . . . and he is here
> to send you to Hell!

Lucky steps forward, so cool we can feel the breeze:

> LUCKY WANDER BOY
> And guess what? It's gonna be a one-way
> ticket.

From the wrists of Lucky's BODY SUIT, twin MACHINE GUN HEADS emerge and start to mow the Sebiros down like flies. They try to fire back. . . .

But Maya activates the ONE-WAY FORCE FIELD on her belt. Bullets may be going out, but they ain't comin' in! It's looking good . . . until. . . .

Mega-Sebiro blows them over with a BLISTERING EXPLO- SION OF SCORCHING SOUND from the SONIC DETONATORS in his hands. Throwing them like rag dolls. Thirty feet.

                    MEKU
          MEKU!!!! MEEEEH-KOOOOOO!!!

Lucky and the Team climb back to their feet. . . .

But Mega-Sebiro is already at Tiara's side!!!

                LUCKY WANDER BOY
               Wait, Mega-Sebiro!
            (stepping forward bravely)
         Leave her alone. It's me you want . . . so
           come and get me, you big metal *bitch*!

Mega-Sebiro LAUGHS. Cruel. Horrible. Remorseless. Un- sorry.

                  MEGA-SEBIRO
         No, Lucky Wander Boy . . . it is *her* I
        want . . . or more accurately, the Khazarian
            Crystal that rests next to her pretty
           little heart. Once I have it, there will
          only be one more Crystal standing between
            me and the annihilation of the entire
                       universe!

> (beat)
>
> So say your Good byes!

And with that, he **_plunges his talons into Tiara's chest!_** And emerges with the TROLOGIAN CRYSTAL!

> LUCKY WANDER BOY
>
> Noooooooooooo!!!

Lucky must use his GYMNASTIC FLIPPING ABILITY to reach Mega-Sebiro in time for revenge. . . .

But Mega-Sebiro SPINS like a whining drill and disappears into the earth itself.

Tiara hangs limply on the post. She has used her TANTRIC BODY CONTROL TECHNIQUES to nearly completely stop the bleeding (PG-13). But she cannot repair that kind of damage. No way.

The rest of the Team is stunned.

> MAYA
>
> God _dammit_. . . . God damn him to Hell. . . .

> MEKU
>
> (sadly)
>
> M-m-meku?

Lucky knows there is not much time. He struggles to be strong. For her.

> LUCKY WANDER BOY
>
> Tiara . . . Tiara I . . . we tried to . . . and I
> want you to know. . . .

Maya's eyes fill with tears. Shousu looks away.

But Tiara looks peaceful. She is already on her way.
To the next world. A higher plane. A better place.

> TIARA
>
> I know, Lucky . . . I know. I . . . love . . . y-y-

Tiara breathes her last breath. She is dead.

Lucky clenches his fists and shouts down into the hole
after Mega-Sebiro:

> LUCKY WANDER BOY
>
> God *damn* you . . . *Father*!!!!

finesse

● ●

On my desk (pertinent items): the *Lucky Wander Boy* script. The printout of Araki Itachi's e-mail to Krickstein. The phone.

The first lay across my mousepad, the Lucky Wander Boy name smeared falsely across its title page like rouge on a corpse. Its presence made carrying out my assignment impossible, so I threw it into my bottom desk drawer and slammed the drawer shut. That left the phone and the e-mail. I focused on the latter:

Araki Itachi, CEO
S.L.S. Inc.
Kiyamachi-dori 32
Kyoto, JAPAN 604
(011) 81-75-433-6252

I summoned all my enthusiasm for Ms. Itachi's magnum opus and tried to lock in a smile that would mask my true feelings and season my words with the positivity mandated by Krickstein. Holding the smile, I dialed the number. I will not try to transcribe the voice of the man who answered the phone. When he spoke, it did not sound like the notion of Japanese I had in my head. Something was slightly off, but I could hardly put my finger on it, given that the only Japanese I knew was *domo arigato*. When I asked for Araki Itachi in English, however, he muttered something and left me to listen to Japanese radio ads for three or four minutes; I heard a trio of young girls singing a dinky pop jingle, and what sounded like a Cadillac ad. Eventually, someone picked up.

"Hello," she said with an American accent, in a voice a bit too urbane and articulated. She reminded me of an extremely pleasant, female version of HAL. As I had not yet identified myself, such pleasantness seemed uncalled for.

"Hi, my name is Adam Pennyman, I'm calling from Portal Entertainment in L.A. Could I speak to Araki Itachi, please?"

"Speaking."

I glanced at her e-mail:

For first, Lucky is bland haired. Please do again, with emphasis on WANDER. And centralness of screwdriver, making for dismantling of Our Hero.

"Do not pay attention to that," she said. "It was a calculated stratagem. Non sequiturs are what a man like Mr. Krickstein expects from a Japanese woman's English, and giving Mr. Krickstein what he expects serves my purposes for the moment. If I must deal with him, I do not want him to take me too seriously."

I shook off the shiver that shot through to my extremities. She could have deduced that I would be looking at her e-mail without my telling her. It was not impossible.

"Why *must* you deal with him?" I asked.

"I was cash poor, and I needed the option money for a business venture."

Clearly, I was taking a significant detour from my given assignment, but I made no effort to turn back. "How long does he own Lucky Wander Boy for?"

"As long as he wants—he can renew the option into perpetuity, or until such time as he defaults on the terms of the agreement."

"That seems like a pretty high price for you to pay, if you don't mind my saying."

A single subdued chuckle. "Not at all. Tell me, the man who designed Pac-Man—"

"Toru Iwatani," I interjected in a naked bid for respect, and it worked. I could hear the nod of acknowledgment in her voice:

"—yes, Toru Iwatani. That is correct. Tell me, how much did Mr. Iwatani make off Pac-Man, would you say? Perhaps the most important video game of all time. Give me your best guess."

I had not come across this information in my research for the Pac-Man entry in the *Catalogue*. I picked a conservative, round figure:

"Probably about a million, all told. In 1980 American dollars."

"Well," she said, drawing it out in a way that suggested I'd guessed wrong and served her rhetorical purposes by doing so, "accounts vary. The rumored amount of Mr. Iwatani's 1980 winter bonus was thirty-five hundred dollars. Mr. Nakamura, the president of Namco at the time, estimates it was less than thirty-five hundred dollars. But he probably would have received it regardless, since summer and winter bonuses are—or were—a regular part of the overall employment package in Japan. Mr. Iwatani himself cannot remember receiving any extra 'Pac-Man bonus' at all. He had been hired to create a game. In doing his job well, he had done nothing special."

I felt a surge of indignation. "That's it? He didn't get anything?"

"He did not expect anything. In Japan, the belief in unquestioning, unwavering service to one's master as a virtue in its own right goes back to the very beginning of the samurai tradition. So you can imagine that, as the creator of a video game that was less financially successful than Pac-Man by several orders of magnitude, I might be forced to resort to certain drastic measures for funding. As onerous as the Lucky Wander Boy option arrangement is, the money is mine to do with as I choose. I am beholden to no one. Now, what can I do for you?"

"Oh—right—it's about the script—"

"You are supposed to fob me off, yes? Dissimulate? Dissemble? Finesse? Convince?"

"Yes."

"All right. Go ahead."

"I'd prefer not to, if it's all the same to you."

"Somewhere along the line, though, some dissembling on your part will become necessary, will it not, Mr. Pennyman?"

"Yes, you're right. It will."

I had planned on telling her about my dedication to her game and its central role in my life and work, but I hung up before remembering to do so.

Next time.

I went to deliver a report on the phone call to Krickstein, and found him at the Plant's rear entrance with his assistant, Alicia, who was helping him juggle the simultaneous arrival of a wasp-waisted, cantaloupe-breasted young woman in a knit tube top, and the UPS man, who had a shipment of new IBM server tower upgrades backed up to the door. When it came to hardware, Krickstein believed in the necessity of being absolutely modern.

"Vanessa!" he said to the young woman, clapping his hands, and her cheeks perked up so drastically that her facial structure seemed to reorganize itself, crowding her eyes into tiny mascara smiles that mirrored the one on her mouth. Kurt's version of suavity resonated far more with her than it did with me; they were of the same cartoon tribe. He gave her the "wait one minute" sign with both hands. "I'm going to send you back with Alicia, she's going to show you around, okay, explain to you a little bit about what we do, get you the drink of your choice. Then, as soon as I make sure this million-dollar shipment of equipment is safe and sound, I'll come back and meet you in my office. We'll talk about what your career options are, how you're going to play them to the hilt, how you're going to become the next Amber Anthony, all that good stuff. Sound good?"

She gave a little bounce, riding up on the balls of her feet. "Super!" Alicia took her away.

"Kurt," I said, "I just spoke with Araki Itachi on the phone, and—"

Before I had a chance to finish, someone else entered through the back door; the Mexican day laborer with the Vato baseball hat had seen the UPS truck pull off the street and left his *vatos* behind to follow it. Removing his baseball cap but not the bandana beneath it, he calmly surveyed the scene. Sensing that Krickstein was in charge, he addressed him directly.

"Los computadoras." He pointed at the IBM boxes. "Ayudo con ellos." He flexed his bicep and tapped it with the opposite hand.

For a moment the lone UPS man looked hopeful, but the laborer had picked a bad time to exercise his initiative. Kurt was clearly eager to get back to his office and Vanessa's budding career, and Vato Hat and I had tripled the number of people he had to deal with before doing so. He did not address the laborer. He turned to me, and spoke as if the man were an entrée he did not order.

"What is he doing in here? Get him out of here!"

I dredged the section of my memory labeled "vocabulario" and told Vato Hat: "You should go. Él está enojado."

He nodded thanks. Jerking his head at Krickstein, he said, "¿Él es un puto, no? Él tiene dinero, pero no tiene ninguna alma. Personas como él, creo que alguien los enculame con un tenedor." I nodded almost imperceptibly, resonating with his bitterness through my incomprehension, and he walked out.

"What? What did he say? What did you say to him?"

"I told him you were angry and that he should go. He said he was very sorry, that he hadn't meant to cause any trouble."

Thinking aloud, Krickstein reminded himself to call the police and clear all the day laborers off his block. There must be some kind of loitering law. When the vice president of the Palo Alto venture capital firm D,S&A strolled in the back door a half hour early for his 3:30 meeting, the scene took on a sitcom flavor, though Krickstein did not break character and acknowledge the deferred enjoyment gag at work.

"Everybody's coming in through the out door today!" he said with mock-mock exasperation, and I knew better than to bring up the Itachi phone call, which was just as well, as it gave me some time to figure out the best way to broach the subject with Kurt.

Back at my desk, I searched for a pattern in the Internet servers' flashing LEDs, some secret semaphore that encoded the perfect spin on the matter. When I heard Krickstein approaching, giving the VC an abridged tour of the Plant, I began typing furiously, ignoring the typos.

"What's most attractive to us," the VC VP said, "is the *synergy* at work here at Portal. Your film production arm props up the Internet arm and keeps it on a solid financial footing, and the Internet arm is a perfect platform to market and further develop your film properties. There's a real *convergence* going on here."

"Exactly," Krickstein said. "With us, you're getting a full package, totally self-sufficient . . . and weasel-free, no bullshit Hollywood middlemen gumming up the machine. This is not Hollywood. Whatever you know or think you know about Hollywood, flush it all down the toilet. It doesn't apply here."

He stopped right behind me. I could feel his breath stir a wayward lock of hair on my head, but I did not stop typing. "I'm going to show you some simple math," he said to his guest, "and then I'm going to hand you off to Tom Lyme, our VP of Internet Affairs."

Kurt began rifling through the drawers of my desk, starting with the bottom drawer. I could not react quickly enough to stop him, and once I saw where he was going I could not even bear to look. I could only stare at my screen with highway rabbit eyes and wait for him to find the Jim Beam flask I kept down there in the event of a Shitheap emergency.

"Wait just a minute," he said to the VP. Then to me, in a harsh whisper as he yanked the middle drawer open over the bottom drawer: "You're a writer, where are the fucking pens?"

Twitching involuntarily, I handed him a pen from the center drawer directly in front of me. Then, sensing the opportunity to dispense with me for the day, he said, "You said you talked to Itachi. What did she say about the script?"

You had to give it to him—though he sometimes seemed unfocused, he missed nothing. But I'd written my line, and I delivered it:

"By the end of the conversation, she seemed pretty receptive. She's pretending to think it over, but I think I sold her on it."

He left without mentioning or even alluding to the whiskey. Confused, I pushed the middle drawer shut to find that the *Lucky Wander Boy* script that I had thrown into the bottom drawer had landed squarely on top of the Jim Beam flask, hiding it from Krickstein's view along with my Shitheap file—fittingly, since Krickstein had relegated the script to his personal Shitheap, me. The Lucky Wander Boy name had transformed a putrid piece of work into a protective talisman.

nobody does it better

• • • • • • • • • • • • • • • • • • • •

INT. SHELF #1—TIME UNCERTAIN

C.U. of the back of a BLOND, BUZZ-CUT HEAD, gazing down a long hallway. He looks to his left, and sees a wall. He looks to his right—

It is a very wide hallway. Infinitely wide, in fact.

SLOW DOLLY AROUND the blond head, to a C.U. of LUCKY WANDER BOY. For a minute (at least), he stares without expression into the camera, at us, just as he does in the coin-op cabinet art.

PAN TO LUCKY'S POV. At the far end of the hall, a SE-BIRO APPEARS. He is played by the same actor as Lucky, but with Gregory Peck hair. He wears a gray flannel suit.

PAN BACK TO LUCKY, already running away.

I got two books on screenwriting and read them through in two days. The well-made screenplay was expected to have three acts, as well as an array of plot points, midpoints, dramatic contexts; premise ideas, counter ideas, controlling ideas; archplots, miniplots, antiplots; setups, payoffs, callbacks. I had neither the time nor the expertise to argue with any of these strictures. It was easier to give in to them.

Writing my own version of the *Lucky Wander Boy* script made very little sense, I was well aware of that. There was no hope of Krickstein ever buying it or supporting it, no matter what I said or did. With very little effort, I could summon an image of Kurt in a pink tutu doing pirouettes and grand jetés through the Plant to the applause of three hundred venture capitalists, but when I tried to run the mental movie of him holding my *Lucky Wander Boy* screenplay in one hand and patting me warmly on the back with the other, it would slip its sprockets and disintegrate before my mind's eyes. I'd never written anything in the screenplay format before; indeed, the only script I'd ever read was Cheops Feinberg's abomination. Thus, my work on a *Lucky Wander Boy* script was unusually susceptible to interference from Anya—the "Why you don't take me anywheres?" of my life, the high-volume alliterative soundbites about suave celebrity soirées that streamed under my shut door and shattered the concentration I needed to make good on such a project.

Yet I made up my mind to see it through. The *Lucky Wander Boy* movie might be the game's last chance for survival and reintroduction to the cultural habitat, and production of the version commissioned by Krickstein would mean certain extinction. Moreover, the *Lucky Wander Boy* script project was an important evolution of my own grand Project, which I felt to be moving in the service of some greater Purpose. From videogame ROMs to the *Catalogue* to Lucky Wander Boy, my new enthusiasms were subsuming my old enthusiasms, swallowing them whole and incorporating them into a more complex endeavor the way the biggest, baddest organism in the world incorporated a tiny power-puff mitochondria a few billion years ago, starting the long march toward lizards and mammals and men and civilization and video games. Where my Moment of Decision would ultimately shepherd this many-splendored beast was as unknown to me as human beings were to dinosaurs, as the end of a journey is to the beginning. The centrality of Lucky Wander Boy was growing more and more evident, however; though I had fallen behind schedule with my *Catalogue* entries (I hadn't even begun Galaga or Space Invaders yet), I felt that I could not deal with these until I had put the Lucky Wander Boy entry to bed.

To do this, and to complete my screenplay adaptation of same, certain information was needed. I remembered Araki Itachi's note about Feinberg's script:

Remember 3 acts, and middle being the longest, and middle also being the WANDER stage. Also, looking at Mr. Finebug's ending, I think, "????" Playing game is mostly essential for scriptwriter. Perhaps find one who is a knower and lover of LUCKY WANDER BOY.

The screenwriting books proved her to be correct. In the scheme implied by the note, Act I would correspond to Stage I of Lucky Wander Boy, Act II to Stage II. . . .

And Act III to Stage III. The true knower and lover of the game would have broken through to this undiscovered country, or at the very least have gazed into its Promised Land through the testimony of another. Detective work was called for—but I was shouldering the script, the *Catalogue* and my job while maintaining an uneasy détente with Anya and seeing to my basic human needs. I needed some help on the Lucky Wander Boy front.

I hoped to go directly to the source, and left several messages for Itachi with the mumbling man I could only assume was her male secretary, but none of them were returned. Shortly thereafter, she began calling Portal herself, on a semiregular basis. She did not ask for me; she asked for Krickstein. Whenever Krickstein's assistant, Alicia, would call over the top of her tiny office to tell her boss that Ms. Itachi was on the phone from Kyoto, he'd yell back that he was not in the office, and to transfer the call to me. The first time I was standing in the waiting area when this happened, Kurt was escorting a beautiful Korean girl—with breasts that did not come from the Korean gene pool but may have come from a Korean factory—into his office, where (he said) they would talk about what her career options were, how she was going to play them to the hilt, how she was going to become the Korean Amber Anthony, all that good stuff. When Alicia told him Araki Itachi was on the phone from Japan, he told her to transfer it to me without acknowledging my presence, calling into question whether my name and my face were actually connected in his mind. I eagerly ran back to the midday midnight of the Plant to take the call, but Itachi never said a single word to me. As soon as she heard my voice—a click and a dead line.

Needless to say, this bothered me. But I did not get angry or fester with resentment; on the contrary, each hang-up only deepened my resolve to talk to her. Like the record hunter's desire for a legendary rarity that grows each time he enters a record store that does not have it, my longing to ask her questions about Lucky Wander Boy in general and Stage III specifically deepened, even as it grew progressively more unlikely that she would give me the answers I sought.

Twenty or thirty times she called and hung up. Then she'd ring back later—an hour, two hours, two days, a week—and ask for Krickstein as if it were the first time, daring anyone at Portal to call her bluff, which no one ever did. Her obstinacy did win her one small battle: Krickstein stopped having her transferred to me, and issued a standing order to Alicia to draw up a list of ten Very Important Places for him to be, and to put him in a different one each time Itachi called.

I would have to look elsewhere.

After Clio read the five sample entries of the *Catalogue of Obsolete Entertainments* that I'd given her, she came to my desk and dropped the pages across my computer. A protracted silence followed. I had no idea how I'd done. Like a quarter balanced on edge, it could have gone either way.

"You know what that's like?" Clio said. "It's like archaeology—no, no, I mean city planning, or—what do you call being a specialist not on cities themselves, but on the pipes and sewers and phone and electricity cables? That's what it is. Subterranean. Like you're navigating this underground river—it was aboveground not too long ago, but it's gone underground, so nobody cares where it's going anymore except you, but once you publish the map, and they see that the river is like an express subway to—

"Okay, erase that, replay, replay. Did you ever see that picture by the optical-illusion guy, what was his name—no, don't say it, I remember, *Escher*, an etching by Escher, the one where he's holding the mirrored metal ball in one hand and drawing it with the other? Think about what you can see in that picture. He's in the middle of it, right, taking up most of the ball with this fish-eye take on his face, but you can make out nearly the whole room in one version or another, only not quite, because you can't see the back of the ball. What it's more like, really, is what Escher's etching of the metal ball *would have* been like if he'd done it on another metal ball, all the way around. And not in a cramped room, but outside in the wide-open air—in the wide-open air on a *flat earth*, with the smallest brush possible, a brush that was like an atom thick. If he'd done *that* on the flat earth and you looked at it close enough with a killer microscope, you could've seen everything there was, it would've all been in there somehow, twisted and bent out of shape maybe, but *there*, with him in the middle. That's what it's like."

"That's . . . effusive," I said.

Though I'd never thought of the *Catalogue* in those terms, Clio's enthusiasm was clear. I hadn't told her about my Lucky Wander Boy script, not yet; her approval had not been guaranteed, and it would have been foolish to expose myself to more ridicule than necessary. Even after her flattering comparison, I saw no reason to widen the scope of the conversation beyond the *Catalogue*.

"Now," I said, "about the Lucky Wander Boy entry—"

"That was the only one I had trouble with," she said. "It seems too long, and it's inconsistent. In the beginning it's got this scholarly tone like all the other ones—which I like—but toward the end of it, you start saying 'I' did this and 'I' thought that. And it's incomplete. It just sort of ends."

"You see," I said, "the problem with Lucky Wander Boy from a research angle goes back to their use of the Z80X microprocessor—"

"Yeah, yeah, I know all that, you can't emulate it, and it's almost impossible to find a machine—" Her face lit up, she snapped and smacked my chest. "You want me to help you find Lucky Wander Boy! Or help you find out about it, so you can finish the entry. Am I right? I am. I'm right."

Though there were only two of us, I felt extraneous to the conversation. Not that I was complaining; I was glad to see her reciprocate for all the times I'd kept one of our talks on life support long after she'd given up the ghost. I still don't know whether the demands of Lucky Wander Boy truly forced me to enlist her aid, or just gave me the excuse to lure her into a private conspiracy, to bring her within range so I might act on Shay's inside information about her desire for me.

Reading the telegraphed beginnings of my attempted roguishness in the upturning corners of my mouth, she moved on before I could complete my lopsided smile, shifting abruptly into an exaggerated suspicion at once stylized and completely natural, with a silent-comedy purity that made me question my own more reserved, mainstream mannerisms.

"Will I get credit?"

"Like, school credit?"

She smacked my chest again. It would have been flirtatious, but it was a bit too hard.

"Like due acknowledgment for services rendered, that kind of thing. I'm not talking coauthorship. It's your baby, you'll be doing the heavy lifting, so it's your name on the cover. But I think that, if I can help you find a Lucky Wander Boy machine, I should get something."

"Something like money?"

"I'm not a whore, I'm a swinger. Something symbolic—wait, money's symbolic—something more symbolic. Something less practical, less tainted."

It was similar to the arguments that often occur over hypothetical bands formed amongst friends who cannot play instruments. I opted against bargaining.

"If you can help me find out what happens in the *third stage* of

Lucky Wander Boy, after the second-stage endless desert part, I'll *give* you coauthorship. 'By Adam Pennyman and Clio Michael Camp.'"

"Since when did I tell you my middle name?"

"You didn't. Sammy Benjamin did."

"He tried to stick his tongue in my mouth once."

"Will you help me?"

She grabbed my hand and shook it hard, but said nothing until I did.

"Deal?" I asked.

"Deal," she said.

"Did you let him?" I asked.

"No," she said.

Later that day, when I returned to my desk after soundly trouncing Linda at Eviscerator, there was something waiting for me, propped up against my monitor. It was a picture of a woman, surreptitiously printed on the photo-quality color printer and glossy paper stock reserved for Portal press releases. The woman was Japanese, and her age was a uniform haze between twenty-five and fifty. She had a certain indeterminate quality—her face had set up camp at that place where the borders of bemusement, concentration, obstinate resolve and expressionlessness met. She stared directly into the camera, right through the picture plane as if she were waiting for me, but it was a challenging kind of waiting, and I knew who she was before I read the note resting on my keyboard:

Here it is—the only good picture of Araki Itachi ever circulated, long presumed lost. It was out there. I found it. Don't ask where. Nobody does it better. Clio.

ignocracy

• •

Snow lay in a tattered blanket on the ground. Squinting, you could see the grain on the aged wood crossbeams that held up the roof of the monastery, seasoned dark brown by hundreds of winters and springs that had given birth to thousands of haikus and bamboo brush paintings. The mist almost looked unreal, which is to say tangible, as though you could reach out and spin it into a gossamer thread. Visually, the mist served a unifying function, lashing the sixty-foot virgin cryptomeria trees it floated around to the gliding birds that floated through it, provoking an insight into the fundamental impermanence of all physical things great and small, ephemeral and enduring, as my Spectral Samurai cut a mighty Bonzai Sweep with his sword in the foreground, neatly exposing the brain pan of Shay's vicious Viking berserker Njal Njalson to the open air. Njal fell, and his blood seeped into the snow with lovingly simulated capillary action.

"Your kung fu grows stronger, Pen-Yi-Mon," Shay said. He was right. This game was tied at one even, and he could sense my skills gaining on his. "Soon you're gonna leave me in the dust and go gunning for Ibn Alhrazed, the Big Boss."

The compliment was a tactic. By engaging my pride and filling my head with dreams of Final Victory, he hoped to pull me off balance and land an Evisceration, thereby winning the game. I was onto his ruse, and when his reincarnated Viking appeared, I gave him no quarter, unhesitatingly subjecting his face to a battery of tooth-loosening punches. The ease with which I manipulated the ral Samurai's legs, sword and taloned fists was threatening to strip my facility with my real limbs in the real world, and this evelopment troubled me at first. The Spectral Samurai was a girder in the foundation of the house that Kurt Krickstein built— did I want him to gird my own identity as well, or was Eviscerator just an infernal temptation, distracting me from Lucky Wander Boy? As I gave the matter more thought, however, I decided that being able to literally beat Krickstein at his own game might turn out to be advantageous, and remembered Itachi's invocation of the samurai tradition in my one conversation with her, as she described the steadfast sense of duty exhibited by Pac-Man creator Toru Iwatani. The Spectral Samurai was a point of connection with Itachi, and with her city. I had looked into it; back before the Tokugawa Shogunate moved the Japanese capital to Tokyo in 1600, Kyoto had been a big samurai town.

My concentration was such that I did not hear Lyme until he and the VC VP from Palo Alto were standing directly behind us. I could see them both weakly reflected in the game's monitor, and once I saw them, no effort of will could push my focus back beneath the surface of the screen.

". . . uh, hot babes, cool cars—you know, explosions, and—hey, check this out. Technically, I shouldn't be telling you this, it's not quite a done deal yet, very hush hush, but since we're going to be working with you guys—you see that?"

In Lyme's pronunciation of the words "technically" and "telling," I thought I heard a trace, conscious or otherwise, of Krickstein's lazy L. Lyme pointed at the screen, and his reflection pointed right at me. I could make out his grin. He had small, even teeth.

"For the movie?" Lyme said. "We're going to blow it up."

The D,S&A VC VP's eyebrows inched closer together like tiny grubworms.

"The videogame machine?" he said.

"No, no, not the machine, that monastery on the screen, in the background behind the fighting guys. It's a perfect reproduction of the famous Mount Hiei monastery complex in Japan, and we're in negotiations right now to blow up one of its derelict buildings for the finale of *Eviscerator III*, in exchange for rehabing the main wing where the monks live."

"Make sure you tell Chad about that, when he comes down. He's a big special-effects fan."

As they carried on, Shay let out a long *psssshhhhh*. It sounded like the release valve on a steam engine, or it sounded the way I imagined that would sound, never having heard or seen a steam engine outside a movie theater.

"*The videogame machine*. That's who's in charge now, man. Guys like that. Ignocrats. Well . . . welcome to the occupation, I guess."

I asked Shay if it wouldn't be better PR, not to mention more cost-effective, to blow up a simulated Buddhist monastery instead of a real one. He told me that, surprisingly, the answer was no. According to what he'd heard from the guys in the digital-effects unit, they'd found a team of four North Korean demolition experts Pyongyang had agreed to let them use, guys who'd gotten their start blowing up American-made bridges in the Korean War. Even taking into account the cost of rehabilitating the living quarters in the Enryaku-ji complex on Mount Hiei, the demolitions men were a lot less expensive than a high-end digital rendering and explosion, even if they used a cheap Australian CGI team—although after they shot the explosions with a camera, they were going to shoot them over to Australia via FTP for some postproduction touch-up work. D,S&A met this plan with great enthusiasm. It was redolent of globalization. And as far as Kurt was concerned, PR was PR.

Shay waited until the very end of this explanation to make his move. He played it perfectly. I was distracted, and forgot the Left-Left-Up-High Punch-High Punch defense combination for the quarter second it took Njal Njalson to cleave my Samurai from nuts to neck with his battle-axe. *"Evisceration!!!"* the machine bellowed through its stereo speakers. As with poker, so much of the battle was psychological, and took place outside the game itself.

When I returned to my desk still smarting from Shay's devious and narrowly stolen victory, Clio was waiting for me, tapping a pen against my cubicle's only decoration: the color photo of Araki Itachi that I'd taped to the cubicle divider as an anchor and reminder.

"I've got something else for you," she said.

Wisps of porno propositions.

"What?"

"What's it worth to you?"

"Depends what it is," I said.

She gave up on holding out, and told me that Araki Itachi would be arriving at Portal in person, in a week, for a meeting.

"Says who?"

"Says a bunch of people up front," she said. "It's been going around."

"Are people excited?" I asked.

"Only two of them. You ought to get prepared."

[from beginning of page 34 of entry] ... and while we are considering this ending-that-is-not-an-ending with the aid of religious metaphors, we would do well to ask: What can we do, if anything, to reach it? Is there any course of action we can take to ensure our advancement to Stage III? At the very least, are there preparations we can make to tip the scales of possibility in our favor, or are we predestined to either arrive there one day, or to wander the Stage II desert forever dowsing for it?

To my knowledge, no effective strategy to progress beyond Stage II has been found—but that does not mean none exists. The only points of reference—the trees—run around like philanderers each time you turn your back, and this shifting landscape precludes simple mapmaking. But perhaps there are patterns hidden in the trees' movement; perhaps the true Stage II strategy lies in descrying these patterns and reacting to them in the proper way. And the objects: the hand mirror, the red dress, the baseball cap and the rest. They have no apparent function or relationship to one another—but perhaps there are *secret* relationships. Individually useless, perhaps they are pieces of some larger mechanism waiting for a motive force to act upon them, to lift them from the mundane and sweep them into their proper places, their ordained roles.

Perhaps, then, to prepare for—or even precipitate—the great Moment of Decision in Lucky Wander Boy is to root out the concealed flux of relationships between the different elements of the game. To grow more sensitive to connections.

the smiling man

● ●

On my living room floor (there was not enough room in the cluttered office), I spread out my script notes and relevant *Catalogue* materials and began to organize them, to get a visual sense of where the holes in my Lucky Wander Boy knowledge were. Anya watched me from the couch, poised between confusion and disgust, silently demanding acknowledgment. Finally I asked her:

"What are you looking at?"

"Really I have no idea."

It was not a bad line, and she delivered it well. She had been watching a good many sitcoms lately.

"If you must know," I said, "I'm preparing for a meeting at work. A big meeting."

She waited until I left in the morning to move my notes roughly to the side with no regard for the work that had gone into arranging them. When I returned home I fixed the damage she'd done, completing the first cycle of what would prove to be a silent but bitter war of attrition spanning the next several days. There were still moments when I felt tenderness toward her. I'd see her come home at 11:00 or 11:30 with her head wrapped in the best facsimile of a Polish peasant head scarf Urban Outfitters had to offer, an accessory her boss had suggested she start wearing, and when she flushed red with shame for having forgotten to remove it and tore it off in disgust, her unhappiness cut deep into me. Many times I was right on the verge of pulling her in, squeezing her tight and apologizing for the whole awful package—her job, the six thousand miles between where we were and where she belonged, the dead space that had congealed and grown solid between us. All of it was my fault. I wanted to let her know that I knew it and took responsibility for it, and would try to do better from now on . . . but then, inevitably, just before I took the first reconciliatory step, she would kick one of my note piles aside, sometimes sending a sheet or two airborne, and ruin everything.

I came up with a list of questions to present to Itachi as soon as I received the order to take her off Kurt's hands, which I thought was likely to happen after he put in his minimal face time. Most concerned game specifics and mechanics:

—By what mechanism can a Lucky Wander Boy player reliably proceed from Stage II to Stage III?
—Is there an intermission between Stages II and III?
—Please describe in detail the first image a player sees upon reaching Stage III.

Some questions were biographical, attempting to establish connections between the creator and her creation:

—Where were you born?
—What led you to a career in videogame design? How did you get your first job at Nintendo? What decisions led you to leave and start your own company, Uzumaki?
—What kinds of pressures did you feel as a woman in a man's field, in a society that had yet to acknowledge the validity of the woman-as-artist, let alone as entrepreneur?

And:

—What kinds of games is your current company S.L.S. developing at the moment? Are you continuing in the experimental tradition of Lucky Wander Boy, or moving more toward the mainstream?

—Have you ever read the novella *Leng Tch'e* by Dafei Ji? If so, how has it influenced you?

Connections.

When the S.L.S contingency arrived at Portal, I was at my desk practicing, casually trying out my questions on the picture of Itachi hanging in my cubicle, reacting to her imagined answers. "Really . . . yes, I can imagine it would have been very difficult for you . . . oh yes, I agree, it's a wonderful book, I've written on it extensively myself." By the time I found out S.L.S. was in-house and ran to the front, the meeting was already under way in Krickstein's office. In spite of my best efforts to eavesdrop, I couldn't make out much: Lyme's voice mostly, then Alicia's, then what sounded like a man speaking Japanese. I didn't hear Itachi or Krickstein. Clio joined me, and together we waited for them to exit. It occurred to me that I might take her hand, but neither of us were the types who thrived on the kind of attention one got at the center of the employee gossip web, so I took a half step closer to her and figured that would be good enough. I felt pangs of anticipation I had not felt since I waited backstage for Miles Davis at Woodhill Grove's prestigious outdoor music venue, disguised in the food service shirt I still had from the job I'd been fired from the year before for stealing a case of cheap beer. I never got to meet Miles, because I blew my cover and got kicked out when I shook hands with his bass player, Darryl Jones, who played bass for Sting as well, which held some cachet back then, years before Sting stooped to sharing the stage with karaoke thug Puffy Combs.

I heard a strained laugh from Lyme and could tell something was wrong. When the door opened, the only people to exit were Lyme, Alicia and a slender, expressionless Japanese man in a gray suit and white gloves, carrying a gunmetal attaché. Neither Krickstein nor Itachi was present.

I had put too much hope in Itachi, and given Krickstein too much credit in assuming he'd at least show up, but there was no way to express my anger to either of them. I crumpled my list of questions into an angry ball.

"Next time you get a hot tip about Araki Itachi, remind me not to stop what I'm doing," I said to Clio, and followed Lyme, Alicia and the S.L.S. representative back into the Plant. Clio did not follow me. She did not appreciate being snapped at.

"Kurt should be back any minute," Lyme told the Japanese man, though he knew it to be untrue. Lyme did not blush from the shame of it, but I blushed for him.

The S.L.S. rep smiled. His neutral expression of a moment ago was strained, as if maintained only with great effort, but the smile was effortless, native to his face. He spoke, and though I could not understand what he was saying, I recognized his voice. He was the man I'd spoken to on the phone whenever I called Itachi. The man whose Japanese didn't sound the way I thought Japanese should.

Not knowing how to react to the communication gap, Lyme ignored it. I kept a few paces behind them as he led the rep to the corner I shared with Linda and Shay. About to step outside to join Shay for a smoke, Linda found herself cornered. At Lyme's insistence, she provided a demonstration of web design for S.L.S. Incorporated's Senior VP Mr. Marufuku, calling up a half-finished draft of the Coming Soon! splash page for *Lucky Wander Boy: The Movie* on her screen.

Two months ago, I had talked to Shay about finishing the recently half-finished Lucky Wander Boy splash page and the rest of the promotional site. I tried to explain to him how groundbreaking *Lucky Wander Boy: The Movie* could be, and told him I'd stay after hours to work on it with him.

"When you talk about Lucky Wander Boy, your eyes go glassy," he said. "Like a Scientologist."

He went on to tell me that he worked after hours for no man. The *Lucky Wander Boy: The Movie* splash page would never get done. Not knowing this, of course, Marufuku gave three polite claps with his right hand against the side of his metal attaché when the Lucky Wander Boy cabinet art appeared. On Lyme's further prodding, Linda clicked her mouse a few times and dramatically exposed the page's HTML guts for Marufuku's benefit. Being a graphic designer she knew nothing at all about programming, but managed to deliver a minute of extemporaneous bullshit on the intricacies of the code she knew nothing about to attentive nods all around. Then Lyme saw me.

"Mr. Marufuku, I'd like you to meet Adam Pennyman, our resident Lucky Wander Boy specialist. He'll be intimately involved in the development process, and I assure you he is *eminently* qualified, wouldn't you say, Linda?"

"I'm not really qualified to say. I'm missing my smoke break."

Linda walked away and left Lyme hanging there in that limp fish way that made me feel sorry for him in spite of myself, but something he'd said—probably "Lucky Wander Boy"—stirred Marufuku into action. His default smile flared as he slapped the attaché down on Linda's desk and snapped it open with an unnaturally sharp economy of movement, as if he'd done nothing but rehearse the action on the entire flight from Kyoto. Reaching into a mesh pouch in the top of the case, he removed a single sheet of paper with the same deftness, handed it to me and bowed deeply. I tentatively bowed back, and his smile seemed to harden, beginning a transformation from a mere ephemeral expression into a frozen, permanent, perfect *thing*—but Alicia interjected before the transformation was complete:

"God, I can't believe I forgot to ask, Kurt would kill me—would you like something to drink? Water, Coke, coffee—"

At the mention of coffee, Marufuku's eyes lit up.

"Sugar and cream, please!" he said.

Before leaving, he shook my hand, and I felt the reason for his gloves: the pinky space of his right glove was filled with some unyielding material, not to be mistaken for a human pinky.

He was missing a finger.

After they'd all gone, the meeting reenergized by this undeniable act of communication, I took a close look at the paper Marufuku had given me. A close look was required, since the print was excruciatingly small, so small that it took me a long time, far longer than you'd imagine, to ascertain that with the exception of the numerals, the printing was entirely Japanese. I folded it neatly and put it in my pocket.

Outside, I discussed Krickstein's planned absence with Linda and Shay as they tore through their cigarettes.

"It's not right," I said. "It's wrong, it's fucked up, and it's bad business besides."

Linda shrugged. She was a fatalist. "I guess that's what you get when you go into business with Kurt. You take his money, you've got to expect his treatment."

"I don't care if she took his money," I said. "*We* take his money. If you don't want to give people basic consideration, don't work with them. It's dishonorable. This kind of thing would never happen in the society Itachi and Marufuku come from. Honor is very big over there. We could learn a lot from them."

There was no arguing with that.

Something had to be done.

When I got back to my desk and checked my e-mail, I found that Kurt had sent me a message from wherever he was waiting out the afternoon. It mentioned an Internet copywriters' dinner meeting three days hence, location to be determined. I wondered about the placement of the apostrophe. A quick check around the Plant revealed no one with the title of Internet Copywriter besides me.

In the beginning, Nolan Bushnell created Pong, the second coin-operated video game (after creating Computer Space, the first coin-operated video game), and placed it in Andy Capp's Tavern in Sunnyvale, California. It grew gravid with quarters in less than a week, and Nolan Bushnell saw that it was good. Not long thereafter, as more video games came into being, the imperative toward economies of scale led to the creation of the first video arcade in Colonie, New York. Others followed.

Each of the games in the video arcades ran different assembly language code that, in conjunction with the brain and sensory apparatus of the gamer, created a different world with different goals, rules and (after a fashion) physical laws. In the arcade, the games were in close physical proximity, but separate from each other, and limited to one world per screen. With a few steps, the gamer could enter a different world through the persona of a different avatar and strive fruitlessly toward a different goal—but actual movement was unavoidable. Stumbling, foraging steps across unforgiving distances that allowed no Warp Skip!s or hyperspace jumps. Quadraceps were involved, hamstrings. There was a thicket of other human beings to navigate. The jarring first step away from the screen when the Game was Over and another person's quarter was waiting in the on-deck line atop the game's control panel... it was like being dragged from a wonderful dream.

Concurrently with the above, a second stream: In 1976, Fairchild Camera and Instrument released the Channel F home system, the first home videogame machine to play games that were not stored on ROM chips inside the system, but on ROM chips encased in plastic in *interchangeable cartridges*. In 1977, Atari released the VCS (Video Computer System), also a cartridge-based system, and the VCS began to sell, and sell, and sell. Mattel released the competing Intellivision in 1980.

Both Intellivision's wedge-tipped plastic cartridges and Atari's chunky rectangular cartridges eliminated the need for locomotion that fragmented the world-swapping experience of the video arcade. Sitting in a meditational position, the bodily movements necessary to toggle between Ice Trek's Viking Hero and Dracula's eponymous anti-hero and Microsurgeon's disease-fighting pod were limited to the arms and hands. Turn the machine off, yank one cartridge free, replace it with another, turn the machine on. Off, out, in, on. Off, out, in, on. O, O, I, O, O, O, I, O, cycling as through a mandala, merging the mind with different code configurations, permuting the consciousness of the gamer, who paused only to eat pillowy Coconut Snowballs and other such nourishments.

Nearly fifteen years later, the MAME emulator furthered the Cartridgeration process well beyond where cartridges themselves could take it. With MAME, the switching no longer required gross arm movements. Now the mere fluttering of fingers across a keyboard were enough to change from one game to another. With this ease, the pace of the switching increased accordingly. On Intellivision, the gamer might play a game only once before switching to another one. With MAME, he often quit in the middle. He could sync himself to one fragment after another in a state of near-complete stasis, watching the world change before his eyes.

Cartridgeration has its consequences. Prolonged exposure to this fragmentary method of relating to the world inculcates in the gamer the belief that he can have it all, serially, within a very short time span, regardless of whether any two pieces of It are mutually exclusionary. He can be chasing 'em down…and on the run. Safe…and under fire. Cute and harmless…and imposing and dangerous. As he toggles from cartridge to cartridge, game to game, goal to goal, identity to identity, his mother's long-standing promise that he can "be whatever he wants to be in this world" seems fulfilled, given a broad enough interpretation of "in this world."

This is not entirely a bad thing. The ability to simultaneously entertain contradictories can be useful…but it comes at a price. The Cartridgeration process leads one to a mode of thinking that stresses the inadvisability of choices. Any definite choice and subsequent course of action puts the gamer on one path at a tremendous possibility cost to all conceivable others. Through definitive actions, he pares the ür-configuration containing all his possible worlds to a stunted fraction of its former self. How many brilliant futures are ruled out with each step, with each decisive word? Billions, in a very real sense. The further he gets himself into any situation, the more severe the pruning of his possibility tree. Thus his inability to focus on any enthusiasm for too long, a metaphysical fickleness that functions as a defense mechanism against the death of possibility.

Being fundamentally sane, the gamer knows, of course, that his life will go on, and in the end it will finally trace out one path through the world to the exclusion of all others—but he prefers the joys of hopeful stasis, sitting in a world where all possibilities live side by side, waiting for the Moment of Decision to overtake him, for some overwhelming Reason to present itself and overwhelm him with the necessity of one monumental choice, making all other decisions moot. Why settle for less?

This intentional idling, this conscientious objection to activity has far more effect on the Cartridgerated's developing sense of self than any actual actions he might take. With so much of his experience coming in snippets, samples, recombinant swatches of game after game, config after config, and the whole thing going faster and faster from arcade to basement and basement to computer like 35mm frames being brought to speed through a projector, the flux becomes a thing in itself, and one day the gamer looks at the thing and sees that it is *he*. He is—(gerund, verb-as-noun, **He-is**—) skating across the surface of a chain of games, words, hopes, associations that has no endpoint. He has no existence save as this chain, this progression. He can choose to become two, three, four or more...but he cannot choose to stop choosing, because **he *is*** the choosing, the changing, the becoming. Like an open-water shark, he must keep moving, or *he* as he has come to know himself will cease to be.

All the fragmentation and Cartridgeration and whatnot, it probably goes a long way toward explaining how I could feel no guilt about Anya—poor Anya Budna in her do-rag, speaking Polish to no one in a restaurant on Fifth Street—while I was fucking Clio in the Portal attic storeroom during lunch the day after Marufuku's visit. It isn't that I put Anya out of my mind entirely. On the contrary, when I reached beneath Clio to hold her pixie ass in my hands so I could push deeper inside her, I noted its similarity to Anya's ass, and when I ran my hands under her shirt over hillock breasts so small you'd miss them if you went too fast, I thought about how different they were from Anya's. As physical types went, I had no preference, big-breasted and flat-chested were all the same to me (although their similarity in ass sizes led me to believe *that* might be a vector of attraction). The reason I enjoyed myself more with Clio, aside from the fact that she was actually having sex with me, was the same as the reason I could feel no guilt about Anya: whatever guilt I felt back when I first met Clio and fantasized about her, by the time we came around to the deed itself, I saw her as part of a completely different config than Anya, the bouncing bonus treasure in a quest game far more exciting and worthwhile than the dull, poorly programmed obstacle course I got whenever I plugged in the Home Life cartridge. I was not lying to Anya or cheating on her, because she was in a whole different universe, as different as Stage I of Lucky Wander Boy is from Stage II. Clio was where I was then, at that moment.

As to how I came to be fucking Clio in Portal's attic storeroom after I'd apparently burned my bridges by snapping at her cruelly and unjustly the day before, out of misplaced anger over the absence of both Krickstein and Itachi from a Krickstein/Itachi meeting:

Once Marufuku left the building and I remembered what I'd done, I threw myself into mending things with Clio. For the rest of that day and all the next morning, I displayed the kind of sincere regret that would have made my parents proud for raising me right, had they witnessed it. When she put both her hands on my shoulders at 12:45, squeezed and said, "Almost lunchtime," I happily realized that in my eagerness to right the wrong I'd done her, I had overshot my mark. As with cable channels or French fries, a small marginal expenditure would get me a far more comprehensive package. So I paid it.

Though I believe the language of passion has been too worn out by overuse and abuse to deploy effectively, one prurient detail about Clio bears mentioning: although physically very involved, greedy even, she was silent during the sex act. Screaming and grunting were out of the question, of course—we were at work and someone would have heard—but when I say silent, I mean *nothing*, no low moans or whispers in my ear, no purring, not even the sound of her breath, though I could feel her chest rise and fall deeply beneath me. Complete silence, like we'd been relegated to the secret stag reel that came after the end credits of a silent romantic comedy. Only after we wound up the reassuring, after-the-fact kissing and put all our clothes back on did she find her tongue again.

"That was nice," she said. "We should do it again."

I nodded agreement.

"Did you have that paper the Japanese guy gave you translated yet?"

"No, not yet," I said. "I will soon." It was at home, hidden from Anya. So far, after logging in about four hours on the kanji database of "Taro's Japanese ←→ English Server" site, I'd managed to identify characters for "happiness," "fat/chunky" and "discipline/punishment," located at various points throughout the S.L.S. document. The futility of attempting my own translation was fast becoming evident.

"How is the C.O.E. coming along?" Already she was referring to the *Catalogue* with insider's shorthand. She was on board, comfortably ensconced in her first mate's cabin. Explaining to her why the ship's captain had commandeered it for the pursuit of his personal White Whale would be needlessly complicated, given his difficulty in explaining just what the White Whale was to him, and why he was pursuing it.

"Fine, just fine. I'm—working. Working on it."

"Have you written any new entries—besides Lucky Wander Boy, I mean?"

"Yeah," I said, "I've done a few—supplementary essays. For the past day or so, though, I've been occupied with something else."

"Something besides me?"

I didn't know the right answer to that question, so I jumped right to a description of the invitation to the "Internet copywriters' dinner meeting" with Krickstein, to take place in two days at an as-yet-undisclosed location. I asked her if she knew any other copywriters at Portal, and she told me she did not.

I then revealed my plan to use the occasion of the dinner meeting to lambast Krickstein for his neglect of Lucky Wander Boy and Araki Itachi, to rise up and force him to confront the inanity of Cheops Feinberg's script, and indeed the whole Portal enterprise. To speak truth to power. To act.

"Why would you do that at a copywriters' dinner meeting?" she asked.

"If he threatens me or tries to hurt me, I want there to be witnesses," I said. "I bought a Halliburton attaché case to carry the script in. It set me back $225, but it's made of aircraft-strength aluminum alloy. I'm hoping it will command respect." Marufuku's attaché had an effect on me. I found myself thinking about its muted luster during idle moments, and the way he wielded it with a swordsman's grace.

"You know, you could always find another job," Clio said. "I know this one pays pretty well, but I don't know if it's healthy for you."

"This game—it means something to us, it represents—the last hope for some kind of redemption in a world increasingly devoid of—okay, that's stupid, but that we don't know what it means, that we can't encapsulate it in a 'log line' only makes it mean more. And it's almost extinct. If it disappears now, it disappears forever. This movie—it'll never live up to the game, being forced through the motions of a *story*, it'll never come close, but it may be Lucky's last chance for resurrection. We owe it to ourselves, to everyone who has ever played Lucky Wander Boy, and more importantly, to everyone who's *never* played it, and most of all, we owe it to Araki Itachi, who created the game for us, we owe it to all of them to breathe life into this thing. It's like, 'Help me, Adam Pennyman. You're my only hope. I am waiting for you!' Y'know?"

She kissed me on the mouth, hard. Our front teeth clanked painfully together, but she did not back away. Then she removed some quarter-folded papers from her back pocket, unfolded them, laid them on a file crate and stepped away, like a cat offering a dead mouse as a present. I picked it up. It was the Option Agreement between Krickstein and Itachi for the Lucky Wander Boy rights. I flipped it open at random:

—said Option being renewable at The Producer's discretion, for a further period of twelve (12) months for an additional payment of $10,000USD; and for a further period of eighteen (18) months for an additional payment of $10,000USD, also at the Producer's discretion; and for a further period of twenty-four (24) months for an additional payment of $10,000USD, also at—

Krickstein had Lucky Wander Boy for as long as he wanted it—it was his, and he didn't get to where he was today by giving away things that were his. The situation would not right itself. The need for action pressed more heavily upon me.

"How did you get this?" I asked.

"Don't ask, don't tell. Nobody does it better."

my dinner with kurt

● ●

THE CHARACTERS

KRICKSTEIN—Man in his early forties. The Boss. Power.

PENNYMAN—Man in his late twenties. A Copywriter. Truth.

BALD THICK-NECKED COPYWRITER, SKINNY SKITTISH COPYWRITER 1, SKINNY SKITTISH COPYWRITER 2, SKINNY SKITTISH COPYWRITER 3, FEMALE COPYWRITER—Unimportant, as they will not have a chance to speak.

THE SCENE

A restaurant with dingy carpeting. KRICKSTEIN, PENNYMAN, BALD THICK-NECKED COPYWRITER, SKINNY SKITTISH COPYWRITER 1, SKINNY SKITTISH COPYWRITER 2, SKINNY SKITTISH COPYWRITER 3, and FEMALE COPYWRITER are seated at a round table with a worn tablecloth.

KRICKSTEIN. All right, why are we here. The reason we're here is—a few reasons. First of all, we've got a lot of Internet projects going on—we've got websites you're writing copy for, fan sites, web shows, web games. You're all working on these projects together, only you don't know it, because you don't know each other, and a lot of the time you're working at cross-purposes. I decided this would be the best way to get everybody on the same page, with no room for misinterpretations, or any interpretations—what I tell you here tonight is the Gospel, okay, with regards to any and all portal-entertainment.com projects. I also thought, you know, it'd be nice for us to get together, have some good food and a few drinks, get to know each other so you guys can get to be friends, maybe brainstorm together in your free time. So why don't we start by going around the table and introducing—

PENNYMAN. (*Stands up, cutting him off.*) Hello, everyone, my name is Adam Pennyman, and I think the first order of business here tonight is this— (*Removes* Lucky Wander Boy *script from attaché, holds it up, drops it on the table.*) Lucky Wander Boy is definitely the most important project we have going at Portal, from a cultural standpoint, and this screen adaptation of it—let's just cut to the punch line, people. This is a piece of shit, entirely without merit.

KRICKSTEIN. (*Stands up, leans on the table, stares at PENNY-MAN.*) Excuse—are you kidding me? Are you absolutely fucking kidding me?

PENNYMAN. (*Stares back.*) Never more serious.

KRICKSTEIN. That script is what people want to see. That script is a blueprint for a movie that will cost maybe 35 if we do the effects in-house, and make twice that much at the box office, not to mention cable and video and merchandising. Money in, more money out. That's why I optioned it. That's why people option video games to make movies out of them, you little retard!

PENNYMAN. Obviously this comes as a surprise to you, but for some of us, Lucky Wander Boy is not ultimately reducible to a commodity that you buy and process and resell. Lucky Wander Boy epitomizes our struggles, our confusion, our persistence in the face of opponents we cannot even see, much less understand. It *means* something. Think about that—it has *meaning*.

KRICKSTEIN. And this wonderful, meaningful fucking thing, did fucking God give it to you? Did fucking Allah tell Moses to pass it on to Jesus and say, "Behold, give this video game to Adam Whatsisname"? No! A corporation made it. A bunch of people who didn't like it over at Nintendo, who did what disgruntled employees with *balls* do: they *quit*, they moved down the street and they started their own *corporation*, which tried to make *money* by selling *commodities*, and they did a shitty job of it, and before they knew it they were out of business. Am I out of business? No, because I know what I'm doing. I know how to sell—

PENNYMAN. You sell bullshit company tours and presentations to venture capitalists! What do you do besides stroke those guys off and speak to them in a language that only people like you and them understand? When Nolan Bushnell started Atari, they made Pong. You make speeches to VCs!

KRICKSTEIN. (*Begins to pace clockwise, then counterclockwise around the table.*) Okay, so Atari, Atari had *meaning* to you, "from a cultural standpoint"? Back in the fucking good old days, you found personal *meaning* in a Home Pong machine or an Atari 2600? You know what Atari needed to make the first batch of Home Pong machines? They needed 10 million dollars of *capital*. A guy named Don Valentine *ventured* to get them this *capital*, and that's why they could stuff your meaning in a corrugated box and ship it to a store near you!

PENNYMAN. (*Sits back down.*) I don't see why the way it was packed has anything to do with—

KRICKSTEIN. Later on, big evil corporations like Sears, Time and Warner Brothers ponied up the *capital* for your Atari 2600, which was probably just a game to you back then, and has slowly come to symbolize your lost childhood or personal empowerment or who gives a shit what else as you've gotten older and become a bigger and bigger fucking loser!

PENNYMAN. I had an Intellivision—

KRICKSTEIN. And Nolan Bushnell, your hero, the guy who came up with your Atari 2600—he was going to flush the 2600 down the toilet! It didn't sell right away, he got bored with it, he wanted to move on and make something bigger and better that could provide shits like you with even more *meaning*. That's what "meaning" people do, they diddle around with something, then they skip along to something else without seeing the first thing through. It was Ray Kassar, the new president of Atari installed by Warner Brothers to replace Bongwater Bushnell, Ray Kassar, that stuffed shirt who rode in limos who nobody liked, it took Ray Kassar, my first boss and one of my fucking heroes to keep all the dope-smoking, deep-thinking morons at Atari in line for long enough to get the 2600 on the shelves and make them the fastest growing company in the history of the United States!

PENNYMAN. (*Jumps back to his feet. Points an accusing finger.*) I don't care! It's bullshit! You sell bullshit, façades, window dressing for empty stores! I've heard what you tell these VCs, what you promise them—it's like all those Coming Soon! announcements you've got on portal-entertainment.com for web shows and movies that will never go beyond a splash page. What percentage of your promises ever come to anything? What are the chances you'll ever make a *Lucky Wander Boy* movie, as opposed to just making sure no one else does?

KRICKSTEIN. (*Demonstrates the following using items from the table:*) Okay—when the mommy sea turtle (*a dinner roll*) sends all those cute little baby sea turtles (*tears crumbs from another roll*) down the beach to the sea (*marches the crumbs toward a pitcher of water*), she does it knowing that only three or four will ever get there alive. The rest are gonna get picked off by seagulls (*smashes some crumbs with a salt shaker*), or rabbits (*stabs some crumbs with a fork*), or whatever, okay, and sure, the mommy sea turtle cries about it, but there's nothing she can do. She didn't make the world that way, but that's how it is, and it's probably just as well, otherwise I'd be sitting here at this table up to my ass in fucking sea turtles. If everybody like me saw every promise through, there wouldn't be any room to breathe, there'd be so much crap building up every-where, turtles and rabbits and movies and every fucking thing—but you *need* the promises to keep the machine moving, to keep people working so they have the money they need to spend on the prom-ises that make it to the sea! (*Throws a handful of roll crumbs into the pitcher of water*) Thank God for my bullshit!

PENNYMAN. (*muttering to himself*) How can this be?

KRICKSTEIN: Who do you think makes your world possible? (*Chucks a dinner roll at Pennyman. Misses.*) Who do you think is behind everything, *everything* that you love, all your goddamned personal meaning? A bullshitter like me, you little shit! (*Chucks a dinner roll at Pennyman. Hits his shoulder.*) People who get things done so people like you can sit around getting nothing done and feeling fucking profound about all your nothing! (*Chucks a dinner roll at Pennyman. Pegs him in the eye.*)

PENNYMAN. Ow! (*muttering to himself*) This can't be happening, it can't be playing out this way. . . .

KRICKSTEIN. Now shut up and eat your pierogis! With sour cream!

PENNYMAN. But I hate sour cream. . . .

my dinner with kurt (real)

● ●

For the Internet copywriters' meeting, Krickstein picked a restaurant a few blocks from Portal Entertainment, one of his favorite spots, a quaint place with exposed wooden beams, creaky wood floors, threadbare linens and shabby carpeting that served great Polish food—a place called Warsaw Gardens. When I first made eye contact with Anya, I wanted to flay my own skin from my body and leave it draped over the back of the chair while I ran home. Never before would I rather have been playing Pengo more—but when my eyes met her beautiful, nuclear-green eyes, I saw she'd been practicing the L.A. smile in the mirror, and I relaxed a bit. She was good. She had a knack for cultural mimicry. It was as if I'd never seen her before. I tried to talk to her, to explain why I was here humiliating her like this, but she would only reply in Polish, gesturing to her boss with a shake of her do-rag, washing her hands of me with a shrug.

Sitting directly across from me at the round table, Kurt addressed us. "All right, why are we here. The reason we're here is—a few reasons. First of all, we've got a lot of Internet projects going on—we've got websites you're writing copy for, fan sites, web shows, web games. . . ."

We were the only diners in the restaurant. Whether this was by Kurt's design or coincidence I did not know. To my left, a thick man in his late thirties with a denim shirt and a waxed head squinted at Krickstein intently, looking away only to take notes in a small leather-bound notebook. To his left was a skinny, skittish guy around my age with long, unkempt hair; to my right was another guy around my age, similarly skinny and skittish, only with neatly combed hair and tortoiseshell glasses. The guy sitting to his right was skittish to the point of being unable to sit still for more than ten seconds without shifting his position. To his right and next to Krickstein sat a plain, slightly horsey woman. Looking at her newly pressed skirted suit filled me with an inexplicable sadness, so I stopped, instead reaching beneath my chair to feel the reassuring presence of my aircraft-strength attaché with the *Lucky Wander Boy* script inside, ready for use as a prop when I made my case. By all rights, I should have been the most skittish of them all, but I was not. I kept one detached ear on Krickstein, and waited calmly for an opening to present itself.

"So why don't we start by going around the table and introducing ourselves. Ah—Adam. You start."

I rose. "Hello, everyone, my name is Adam Pennyman, and—"

Anya emerged from the kitchen and stood at Kurt's side with her ordering pad. He turned away from me to scrutinize her breasts, and gave her the "wait one minute" sign with both hands. While trying to remember where I'd seen him use that gesture before, I lost my train of thought.

"—and it's nice to finally meet you all."

After addressing us as "my fellow scribes," the guy on my right introduced himself as Eric something-or-other, and made a joke that I've done him the favor of forgetting. Then the others introduced themselves, ending with the bald guy to my left, who sounded depressingly like a day player reading his single line as a stock mob hitman. After he told everyone to call him "A.C., like air-conditioning," he strayed from protocol and ventured a suggestion. "Y'know, Kurt, I was thinkin', maybe we could go back around the table the other way and have everybody here give their opinions on what kinda direction the next Eviscerator movie should take—like brainstorming, just like you said, Kurt, 'cause I know we're all fans—Am I right? Fellas, miss? *I* got an idea. I think it oughta be a comedy."

"A comedy," Kurt said.

"Yeah, you know, with like, funny karate numbers, and a lot of great one-liners, and maybe even a song. I think that could be real funny."

There was a blank intensity to Kurt's disbelieving stare, as if he were trying to make Air Conditioning disappear by force of will.

"That is completely retarded," Kurt said. "Completely. You're Internet copywriters, you're not here to talk about Portal movies, okay. Don't even think about Portal movies until you see them on the screen."

Dead air, until Anya motioned to her ordering pad and told Kurt in Polish that she was ready to take his order: "Tak słucham." Directly translated, it meant "I am listening." I had heard this phrase many times in her lengthy after-work invectives, but never as I was hearing it now, free of singsong contempt. She really *was* listening to Kurt, and he clearly found her Polish charming enough to merit his full attention. Turning away from us to face her, he began to order for everybody, which was a slow process with Anya's simulated incomprehension. Kurt acted like their inability to communicate was the funniest thing in the world, a move I recognized from my Kasha-poaching days in Warsaw.

I took the time to glower briefly at Air Conditioning; he had offered an opinion on a Portal project without being asked, and shit my nest by doing so. Perhaps it was for the best. I could talk to Kurt privately after the meal. He might be more receptive to a less confrontational approach. When I returned my attention to my boss and my girlfriend, the latter appeared to be whispering something to the former. Breaking the house rules?

"Pssst." It was Eric, the copywriter to my right. "Adam, hey. . . ."

"Yes?"

"How long you been doing work for Portal?"

"Uh—I don't know, six or seven months—" I wanted to ascertain whether Anya had deemed Kurt worthy of a lapse into English, but Eric persisted as Kurt ordered for the table.

"So hey, man, tell me something. What do they give you per page?"

Per page. "What do they give you?"

"Asked you first."

"You started it."

He was forced to concede the point. "Okay. I get thirty."

"Dollars."

"Yeah, per page of work."

"For each draft?" I asked.

"No, final draft, however many it takes. Come on, your turn."

Luckily, in his hunger to find out where we stood relative to each other, Eric read in my niggling questions only common mistrust, rather than total incredulity at his day laborer's wages.

"Me too. Thirty."

He relaxed a bit. We were lodge brothers. "Sucks, don't it? Still, keep it under your hat." In an over-enunciated whisper: "I think they only get twenty-five."

As Kurt was winding up his order, I heard the front door of the restaurant open behind me, and saw Kurt leap from his chair abruptly enough to startle Anya. She scurried back to the kitchen.

"Hector! My man!"

It would be hyperbolic to call him "wide as he was tall," but the race between Hector's height and circumference was close. In his sweatsuit bottoms and "USA Wrestling Nationals" T-shirt he lumber-jogged over to Kurt, who threw a few play karate punches at him, which chuckling Hector swatted aside as if Kurt were seven.

"Everybody, this is Hector Yusgiantoro, the *real* reason I wanted to get you all together here tonight."

"You're tricky!" Hector said. Kurt winked at him and continued.

"Hector was an Olympic wrestler, bronze medal in '68, and after he finished his wrestling career, he went on to become a trainer. Wrestling. Judo. Jujitsu. Ultimate fighting. He has probably trained more champions than anyone else you will ever meet, okay. Now he's a professional Motivationalist—I've been working with him steadily for almost a year, and he has totally, completely changed my life. So now you're all going to listen to him, and he's going to totally, completely change your lives. I absolutely promise you, one hundred percent. It's all you, Hector. Set 'em straight, I gotta go take a leak."

Kurt left for the bathroom, and Hector fell gratefully into his chair. His skin was very smooth, as if his Maker had hybridized a giant baby with a toad. After a few deep breaths, he pointed directly at me.

"You," he said.

Then to Air Conditioning:

"And you."

Four more "you"s.

"I want you all to get out there and be champions. This is no time for losers. *You* are the champions . . . of the world. Each and every one of you. . . ."

Now that I'd been taken into Eric's confidences, I knew where the other Portal copywriters had been hiding: at home. None of them were salaried. They were all freelancers. All except me.

I divided them into the thick and the dead. In the latter category, the three skinny guys and the woman in the saddening suit—together they exuded a defeat so palpable it tinted them all gray, colored them with sallow surrender as they made pitiful attempts to muster signs of enthusiasm, cocking their heads at random intervals during Hector's spiel to counterfeit attentiveness, afraid to roll their eyes at each other or me even in Kurt's absence. In all fairness, I did not roll my eyes either. Then there was Air Conditioning, whose enthusiasm was entirely genuine as he took down as many of Hector's words as he could capture in his designer notebook.

"—and you can't let that fear get in your way. Because you know what fear is? Do you? Anybody? I'll tell you what fear is: False Evidence Appearing Real. That's all F.E.A.R. is—False Evidence Appearing Real. I want to tell you a story. When I was a young man growing up in Guam, my old man was real strict. I didn't do what I was told the first time, I got the belt. I didn't do what I was told the second time . . . I got the buckle."

Their situations were worse than mine, much worse. Doing some mental calculations, approximating where necessary, I figured out what I would earn at the rate of thirty dollars per page, given my current workload. It came to about one-sixth the salary of a typical Polish Urban Professional. I could not pay my rent on that. I could not live on that.

"So this one time, some friends and me lit off some firecrackers in the soccer field . . . and we got caught by the principal. He called my mother up, made her come and get me. And the whole ride back home, all she said to me was, 'You're gonna get it when your father hears about this.' I begged her, 'Please don't tell him, Momma,' but she wasn't hearin' it. 'You're gonna get it. Boy are you gonna get it.' That was all she'd say."

What set me apart from them was obvious: before he moved on to bigger and better things, Sexy sneaked me in the back door and got me salaried. My sinecure was modest enough to fly below Kurt's radar, as long as I didn't wave any flags and cause him to think about me for longer than ten seconds. As soon as that happened, things could get much worse.

"I waited in my room. I thought about all the beatings I'd gotten in my life, and I waited for the worst one of them all. And then I heard the front door open. My old man was home. I heard my mother's voice—she was telling him what I'd done. He climbed up the stairs. *Thunk. Thunk. Thunk. Thunk. Thunk. Thunk. Thunk. Thunk.*"

What if Krickstein *had* found me out? What if this whole dinner was just a ploy to let me know how much worse things could get for me, a pierogi- and kielbasa-cloaked threat? I wanted to lock gazes with him and search for some sign to affirm or rule out this possibility, but I could not. He was still in the bathroom. My only portal to Lucky Wander Boy was Portal Entertainment. If I got fired, my rescue plans would fall apart, and Lucky Wander Boy and Araki Itachi would be without a champion. I began to feel the F.E.A.R.

"As my old man stood there in the doorway, I almost . . ." He looked to the horsey woman, held out his hands in apology for the indelicacy, ". . . I almost peed my pants. And he looked right at me and said, 'Your Momma told me what you done.' I couldn't say a thing, I could only look at him like some kind of rabbit.

" 'I bet you think I'm gonna give you a beating,' he said. 'I bet you're afraid. Right about now, you must be pretty afraid.' 'Yeah,' I said. 'I'm afraid. I been sitting here afraid for two hours.' 'Well let me tell you something,' he said. 'Today you ain't gonna get a beating. Those two hours of fear . . . *that's* your beating.' "

Kurt returned, pulled up a chair and sat down. Hector was too wrapped up in the climax of his story to notice.

"So I sure got off easy, huh? The hell I did! My old man was right. Those two hours of fear—of F.E.A.R., the *false evidence* of my beating, that was the worst beating I ever got. Having my jaw busted would've been better than those two hours of F.E.A.R. So I want you all, every one of you, I want you to drop that F.E.A.R., just drop it! 'Cause you know what? You're all champions, each and every one of you!" He rose to his feet and rose his hands into Touchdown position.

During the instant of silence that followed the Motivationalist's final exclamation, I checked Air Conditioning and found him transfixed, face frozen in Eureka! rapture. Then Krickstein shattered the silence with his applause, which everyone at the table quickly took up.

Yes, I clapped too, but just barely. I suddenly felt very tired and drained of will, like the victim of a psychic beating, far too weak to hold aloft the Lucky Wander Boy standard in the prevailing winds. Over the course of Hector's motivational speech, I had lost all motivation. A dull throbbing pain began to pulse behind my eyes, and I wanted very much to go home.

The rest of the dinner was a haze, a bluish fog. The smell of the sautéed butter and sight of the drizzled sour cream on the pierogis nauseated me, and the fine gristled texture of the kielbasa nearly made me gag. I ate as little as I could get away with. At the first available opportunity I left without talking to Kurt or saying good-bye to Anya and walked home, greedily drawing in the clean air that blew off the ocean less than a mile away. My headache had begun to clear by the time I turned onto the street that ran between Portal and my apartment.

It was well after dark, but Vato Hat, the day laborer who'd

nearly incurred Krickstein's wrath weeks before, was still standing on the corner. I nodded to him, and he nodded back. My facile sense of superiority to Vato Hat and his *vatos* that used to make me feel better about my lot in life when I passed them on my walk to work had disappeared. Both Vato Hat and I ate or starved according to the whims of others, we were both largely ignored except as productivity devices—but he had no F.E.A.R. That much was clear. He was all confidence and self-possession. Which was more devoutly to be wished: a living wage, or freedom from F.E.A.R.?

"¿Cómo está el puto?" he asked of Krickstein.

"Él es el jefe, como siempre."

He was the boss, like always.

CATALOGUE OF OBSOLETE ENTERTAINMENTS
GAME: FROGGER
Format: Coin-Op Arcade Machine
Manufacturer: Konami
Year: 1981
CPU: Z80 3.072 MHz
Sound: 1 × AY-8910 1.789 MHz
Screen resolution: 256 × 224 pixels

In Frogger, you must try to get your frog safely across a road, median strip and river while dodging various dangers, into a frog haven on the top of the screen. When you fill up all five frog havens, they empty out, you start over, and the game gets markedly more difficult, with more dangers introduced. That is all.

Everyone loves Frogger. Boys and girls, women and men, rich and poor, high and low. Who doesn't love Frogger? It draws its power from our shared memories of powerlessness. Wherever we are now, at one time or another we have all felt the poor frog's anxiety in the face of the world's intransigence, its blind and callous disregard for our happiness or well-being. We are not killing anything in Frogger, except the occasional fly. It is all we can do to stay alive, avoid the fast cars, snakes, gators and weasels long enough to get a ladyfrog and make it to the top of the screen for our moment of rest. More than anything else, we'd love to stay in that Frog Haven forever, existing in a state of amphibian bliss—but we are forcibly dislodged, and have to repeat the whole ordeal. Most of our antagonists do not even know we exist. They are not "after" us. We are not a target. We are just in the way.

poor guy

● ●

My car jerked to a crawl in front of Portal, which would not have been worthy of note, except that I wasn't in it at the time. Shay, Linda, Ted, Clio and I were sitting on the grass, leaning against the building and eating lunch. I rarely drove the '89 Honda; I walked to work and the grocery store, and given the certainty of the car's eventual breakdown, the bus always seemed a better bet on those rare occasions when I had to venture more than a mile afield. The last time I'd been behind the wheel was when I gave Anya a driving lesson several weeks before—a failed bid for rapprochement. We hadn't been seeing much of each other lately. She said she was putting in a lot of overtime at work and "chilling with friends," whom I had yet to meet, though the recent overcrowding of her shoe rack did suggest she was making more money.

Now here she was, lurching down the street in erratic, Brownian fits and starts, riding up on the curb, bringing my bumper within inches of the fire hydrant in front of Portal, fitting perfectly the profile of the average local driver. She glanced at Portal's front door, then at me, then at the front door again. Then she gave me a smile, and a limp wave, and a goofy thumbs-up, completely incongruous behavior, as if she were pulling her gestures from a grab bag. I braced myself for her emergence from the car, my heart began to kick as I struggled in vain for a smooth way to introduce her to Clio and vice versa. But fate was kind—a BMW SUV honked loudly behind her, and she zigzagged into the street like a spooked chipmunk and drove away.

"Who was that?" Clio asked.

"Just someone I used to work with. When I worked on that *Viking!* movie."

She squinted in an expression of exaggerated suspicion, so obviously ironic that it seemed to mask something genuine.

The SUV dropped off a day laborer in a green vinyl windbreaker and drove away. The laborer, flush with a twenty-dollar bill in his hand, waved at Vato Hat across the street and yelled in Spanish that he would buy them both lunch. When he moved to cross over to the Tacos Burritos Mariscos truck, however, the traffic patterns militated against him, sending a steady stream of fast-moving vehicles that kept him on our side of the street for a long while. When he finally made it to the double yellow line, a lumber-bearing semi pulled out from the lumber yard, barring his path for long enough to allow a convoy of other freight trucks to catch up to it. The draft from one of the trucks tugged on his windbreaker as if trying to tear it off, sending the laborer back toward our side of the street. He narrowly avoided being clipped by another SUV, which honked at him six or seven times, and ended up back where he had started on the grass.

"Remind you of anything?" Ted said.

"Poor guy," Clio said.

"Never send to know for whom the horn honks," I said. "It honks for thee."

"You've been like this all day," Clio said. "That must've been some copywriters' dinner meeting."

I still felt the queasy BYYEWwww of defeat rumbling in my gut from last night, but I didn't want to go into it. I told them briefly about the Motivationalist who had found inspiration where others would see only child abuse, and mentioned a slight downgrade in my sense of job security. It was all Shay needed.

"Krickstein's a fucking crocodile," he said loudly. We all turned reflexively, expecting to find Kurt standing right behind us the way movie monsters always were, but Shay maintained a haughty forward glance, even stretched his arms in a yawn to flaunt his utter lack of concern. "You're riding on his back and he doesn't notice you, but as soon as you register in that dinosaur brain of his, he flips you into the air and bites you in half with those stalactite teeth. We're all one-hundred-fucking-percent disposable."

As we watched Windbreaker have another go at the traffic and pondered the truth in Shay's words, Tamar burst out the front door. She was always bursting into places and bursting out of them; it now caused me only minor discomfort. She told Shay curtly (and in a subtle but undeniable way, Kurtly) about our urgent need for a new *Eviscerator III* Coming Soon splash page, because the VCs were coming soon, tomorrow in fact, and we needed the page finished by the time they arrived.

"Impossible," Shay said. "Anyway, it's the first I've heard of it."

"Well I just heard of it from Lyme, and now you've just heard of it from me. Come on." She snapped her fingers.

"Ja wohl!" he said, and Seig Heiled, knowing that Nazi jokes made Tamar especially angry.

"Wow," Ted said, grabbing Shay's abandoned, half-eaten cheeseburger. "He really doesn't give a shit. I kinda wish I didn't give a shit."

Linda shrugged, tacitly agreeing that it was a shame Ted couldn't not give a shit like Shay. I felt the need to speak up; Ted was a beautiful guy, but he wasn't someone you wanted to emulate, exactly, if you had plans to accomplish anything as such.

"I'll tell you, the only reason I give a shit is because of Lucky Wander B—"

Clio chopped the last syllable from my sentence with a sharp look of naked betrayal, one that laid bare the nearness of our secret devotion to her heart, and the maternal jealousy with which she held it there. In her eyes, I was teetering on the cliff of a great infidelity. It was right there, I think, swallowing my words and shrugging with sheepish reassurance, that it suddenly occurred to me that Clio was in love with me—which meant it was only a matter of time before I began to feel like I was in love with her too. It had come at a bad time. I felt unsure of my footing, carrying as I was the enormous burden of a great many Things To Do without the comfort of the knowledge of what those Things were as of yet. This was one more angle to consider, and I had never been very good at multitasking—but it was impossible to predict or control what sprang up between two people. We would just have to deal with it as best we could.

Leaving them with only the cryptic beginning of a revelation, I turned away from Linda and Ted in time to see Windbreaker make it across the street, triumphant, amid the backpatting and laughter of Vato Hat and his friends.

winner

• •

"You wait and see," Shay said. "I'm just the beginning, man, my 'insubordination' was just an excuse. This was bound to happen, because it's all a fucking pyramid scheme, and pyramid schemes are unstable by nature. Portal Entertainment is just a prop in Krickstein's Crisco MBA schtick, a carrot on a stick he uses to trick other Crisco MBAs into giving him money. Mother FUCKER—"

I tore Shay's head off and sheathed my sword in his exposed windpipe.

"I don't know," I said. "You like playing this game, right?"

"Live for it—*die*, bitch!"

Shay ran the two horns of his Viking helmet through my eyeballs, and I turned my head from side to side, trying to understand why I couldn't see anything through these new binoculars for a few slapstick seconds before giving up the ghost.

"So, to develop and produce this game, somebody had to *venture* some *capital*. Someone who understands that end of things," I said—but *why* would I say this? Devil's Advocate was a rhetorical stance, not a call to defend a true Adversary.

"But Pennyman, the scheme, it's not even a pyramid, it doesn't have the three dimensions it'd need to be called a pyramid, it's just the façade of a pyramid, of course it's going to fall down eventually. What the hell do we *do* here, what service do we provide, what product do we *fuck me!*"

I completely flattened his rib cage with a flying side kick, forcing geysers of blood through his ears, eyes, nose, mouth.

"If all the baby sea turtles made it to the sea in one piece," I said with impacted masochism, "we'd be up to our asses in sea turtles." I was ashamed of myself. This defeatism, this self-doubt—I was not worthy of the Spectral Samurai. Shay's analysis gave off the light of truth, but I was stuck in the shadows, obscured by clouds of fear—fear that if what Shay was saying was true and all our Portal days were numbered, that Lucky Wander Boy, the *Catalogue* and the vague-but-significant Project to which I'd devoted myself would fall apart before coming to fruition, even before I got to look upon this fruition from afar and see what it might entail. The fear that all my sacrifices would come to nothing but a hazy ghost of what might have been.

"You've got the wrong reptile," Shay said. "It's not about turtles for him, it's about crocodiles, remember? A pyramid-building crocodile—he'd have been worshipped as a God in Ancient Egypt, you lucky, lucky, goddamn little *BITCH* what are you *DOING*—"

It took him a second to realize what was happening. I don't think Shay was aware of the Spectral Samurai's ability to administer the Death of a Hundred Cuts. Why should he be? He never played the Samurai, the series of joystick pulls and button hits required was protracted and convoluted (not to mention unpublicized by the company), and to the best of my knowledge, the Death of a Hundred Cuts was a Chinese, not a Japanese, innovation. But the Eviscerator designers either did not know this or chose to ignore it. The butchery began with Njal's eyebrows, then moved on to the hackles of his shoulders, his nipples, his fingers, his toes and so on, with each cut taking half as long as the one before it, until my Samurai's blade was a steel cloud surrounding a rapidly diminishing Njal Njalson, soon reducing him to his constituent parts, still-quivering fragments of Shay's glory. Do not think the connection to *Leng Tch'e* was lost on me; I believe the sequence of cuts was precisely the same as in the novella. And so it was, with this fabled act of dismemberment, that I stole Shay's title from him in his last game as a Portal employee, and ascended to the plateau of Eviscer-ator Winner through the avatar of the Spectral Samurai.

Shay finished the last long drag of his cigarette. He ashed on the Plant floor, stubbed his cigarette out on Eviscerator's front panel and tossed the dead butt into the middle of the common area. He shook my hand.

"Well done, well done. It's you against the machine now, Pen-Yi-Mon. You against Ibn Alhrazed, the Big Boss. I'm out."

I said I would do my best to deserve the honor, and promised to beat the machine eventually. Shay picked up the file box filled with the items he'd torn from his cubicle walls the night before. At 9:30 P.M., an exhausted Shay had gotten up to go home—but Lyme was still at Portal, having stayed behind to prevent this very eventu-ality, and he told Shay he could not leave until the coding for the complicated *Eviscerator III* Coming Soon! splash page was finished in time for the VCs' arrival tomorrow morning. Shay told him that if they'd known the VCs were coming and needed to have the splash page finished by the following A.M., someone should have told him about it before that afternoon, and that he wasn't staying unless he got overtime for every hour after 5 P.M. Lyme said he was paid by the week, not by the hour, Shay said that didn't make him an indentured servant, Lyme called Krickstein at home on his cell phone and told him what Shay was demanding, Krickstein demanded to speak to Shay, and when Shay reiterated what he'd told Lyme, he was sum-marily fired. Now he was leaving, and passing the Eviscerator mantle to me as Clio and Linda bore witness. I could tell that Clio was proud.

Shay fired his parting shots. "Good-bye, Grover's Corners! Good-bye, everyone! Good-bye, Tamar—torture a Palestinian for me! Good-bye, Clio—keep banging Pennyman, a spent copywriter is a docile copywriter! [I told her with a shrug that I hadn't told him.] Good-bye, Ted—stay real, stay fat!"

He put down his box of personal effects to pull Linda into a bear hug, slapped her on the back and picked up his box again. As he crossed the threshold out the back door into the daylight, he took one last backward glance, saw me watching him, and called out:

"Farewell, Pen-Yi-Mon. Keep your eye on the Pharaoh."

Shay left. Linda watched him go, sucking on a Blow Pop with the despair of a freshly orphaned child. I patted her on the shoulder—somewhat awkwardly, I'm sure, but the thought was there—and Clio stepped up beside me and squeezed my hand. Together, we wallowed for a moment in the Melancholy of the Left-Behind. Clio and Linda went back to work, but I wallowed for a bit longer, staring out the back door at the parking space where Shay's car used to be. Tamar saw me musing, blinking after the remnant rectangles of outside light that flash-floated across my field of vision. Still angry about Shay's Israeli-baiting, she told me to get to work.

correspondence

● ●

On the Monday following the Thursday of Shay's departure, I eaves-
dropped on an executive meeting taking place in Krickstein's office
while gnawing on a hard bagel left over from the previous Friday.

"We've got to talk to these people!" Kurt's voice rolled over the
communication gap. "Alicia, where are my plane tickets—exactly!
They're not here, they're nowhere. This Mount Hiei monastery explosion thing has to be a done deal before we can put together a final
budget on this fucking film, and we need a final budget on this film
before D, S&A will fucking release the final *funding* for the film, and
D, S&A likes explosions! I want those tickets on my desk. Chad from
D, S&A is coming down here himself on the fifth and I want to be on
a plane to Kyoto by the seventh. Get me a good interpreter, I know
how to talk to goddamn Buddhists."

"Kurt," Lyme chimed in, "while we're talking about Kyoto, I
was going through your e-mail, and Araki Itachi sent you a new, uh,
memo, concerning the *Lucky Wander Boy* project—"

"Yeah, I know how I want you to deal with that, Tom. I want
you to get a shovel, a big fucking shovel, I want you to drive out to
the Mojave Desert and bury that memo, bury all copies of the
Lucky Wander Boy script, and bury a fucking Lucky Wander Boy
machine if you can find one! What reason could you possibly have
to be talking to me about this now?"

"I just thought, since the contract does give her Meaningful
Consultation Rights—"

"A *shovel*! It's dead!"

"So," Lyme said, "we're giving it back to—"

"Lyme! It's mine, I don't give things that are mine to women I've never met, it's going to sit here and rot in the fucking *meaningful* dungeon, next item!"

It was easy enough to get Lyme to forward me Itachi's memo; all it took was a few innocent questions about the progress of the Lucky Wander Boy project. The whole thing was a buck he desperately wanted to pass, and sending me the memo fostered the feeling that someone was dealing with it. Itachi's Krickstein strategy had evolved in a masterly way, reaching new levels of dissimulation:

For Kurt Krockstain, Mr.:

Progressings on LUCKY WANDER BOY moviescript with great anticipation is awaited, but unseen? Hoping writer Finebug is fired, new writer hired, writer who has mainly played game knowingly and in excellent condition. PLEASE, emphasize the Objects of Centrality beyond screwdriver (of course!), but also shovel, red dress, mirror, briefcase, axe, baseball cap. As per interim, re: discussion before.

I am waiting for you!

Sincerely,
Araki Itachi, CEO
S.L.S. Inc.
Kiyamachi-dori 32
Kyoto, JAPAN 604
(011) 81-75-433-6252

The last line before the closing was likely meant for my eyes. Itachi surely knew the memo would be swept onto my desk by the wave of non sequiturs that preceded it. She was a woman to be admired, and not merely in the way men usually admired women. Indeed, I had studied the proportions of her face many times in the past few weeks, staring at her picture on my cubicle wall, but it was not until that very moment that I made it through the thicket of faintly insinuated qualities and saw her beauty. Like her cleverness, she kept it well hidden, to ward off the sort of dabbler who slavered over the cheesecake shots that littered www.portal-entertainment.com.

Really, I was the only one equipped to champion her. It was my duty not to let her down. That night, I attacked my *Lucky Wander Boy* script with fresh enthusiasm, whistling the game's opening fanfare as I worked.

It was coming along rather well. I seemed to have a knack for this screenwriting thing. The first act was exceptionally taut, not so much defining Lucky's character as establishing his archetype, while setting up the necessary "jeopardy" and "narrative tension" to pull the viewer into the second act, which would be the most demanding and rewarding two hours of cinema they'd ever experienced. That night, in a keyboard frenzy, I wrote the entire "plot point two" scene "bridging" Act II and Act III—a scene in which a sun-scorched and weakened Lucky, at the end of his tether and divested of all his possessions, finds a large *shovel* (this *Lucky Wander Boy* screenwriter knew enough to be "emphasizing Objects of Centrality"). With it, he tries to dig through the desert, which (it is implied) is merely an illusion, a sort of ironic mirage hiding the Haven Zone beneath—which is to say the third act, the point in the script beyond which my current knowledge would not serve to take me. We were both digging, Lucky and I.

And Anya as well. A half hour of Martha Stewart on flower arranging almost derailed me early in the evening, but she turned off the TV unexpectedly, and went out to the dilapidated porch we shared with the nice, chain-smoking couple across the hall whose names I did not know. The sound of her digging came through the slat windows and mingled with the clacking of my keyboard, as she scooped the dirt and cigarette butts from the barren flower planter with a rusty spade that had been out there since we moved in, and dumped it over the side of the porch. She scooped until the dirt was all gone and kept on scooping, out there in the dark, the spade scraping across the wood of the planter like a cat clawing at a closed door.

nothing! nonsense, crazy!

● ●

Through the several kinds of shock that hit after I read her note and realized what she'd done, I managed to feel a sharp, parting tinge of admiration for Anya. Not once had I seen her so much as peeking over my shoulder while I was at the computer, not once had I ever seen her use or even power-up a computer, but she had nonetheless figured out how to erase my MAME emulator and every one of the 1,423 games I'd diligently collected over a period of several months. She had not just thrown them into the Trash and selected Empty Trash from the Special pull-down menu. By itself that would have been impressive, but intuitive, feasible. No, she threw them all away, emptied the trash, and used the Wipe Info function in the Norton Utilities program to make them irretrievable, to pave over the space where they'd been rooted with the endless repeating sequence: 010101010101010101. When I mention her "native intelligence," I do so without condescension. Every MAME game was *gone*, and the printed-out note left no question as to who was responsible.

Although the end came swiftly, there had been warning signs above and beyond the usual hostilities. She'd been gone a lot lately, for one. It had occurred to me that she might have found someone else. More than just occurred to me—I strongly suspected it was coming, as I've said before. But since I could hardly blame her if that was the case, I took a don't ask, don't tell approach, which was why, if It had indeed come, I still had absolutely no idea where It had come from.

Shortly after she dug up the porch flower planter, she gave up on détente and started taking the offensive, stepping into conflict instead of merely opening her arms to it when it came. Two days before, for instance, I tried to engage her in conversation. She saw me looking through the Yellow Pages for affordable Japanese-to-English translation services with Marufuku's kanji-covered sheet beside me, and asked me what I was doing. I tried to explain Lucky Wander Boy to her—nothing too involved, just a brief summary of the game and how it differed from all the other video games she'd seen—but I did not even make it to the Mega-Sebiro of Stage I and the varying effects of the Warp Skip! button before she exploded.

"You talk nothing! Nonsense, crazy!" She fluttered her lower lip with her fingers to make gibberish sounds, and stomped out of the apartment.

It wasn't the stomping out that got to me—she had done that before. In combination with the lip thing, however, her choice of phrasing tunneled back into my memory far enough to hit a well-spring. It all rushed in at once—how often I'd spoken to her—*at* her—at length about things for which she cared nothing, things that were no more a part of her experience than bread lines, privation and drunk fathers drinking unlabeled vodka were a part of mine—and in a language she only half understood to begin with. Anya and I lived in near-parallel worlds, only intersecting in a very small space. Now the last, vestigial remnant of my Stage I was gone for good, as her note made clear:

Adam—
You are not good for me, Adam, and I not good for you. We are not good. It never is very much fun anymore, you know? Once, yes, but not now, not for the longest time. I see all the 12 Warning Signs—we are Dysfunctional! Mostly you. Always inside of doors, never outside. You have issues. I am trying to help you when I erase from

your computer things that are not good for you, but I think there is no help, mostly.

I am OK. I go to explore what are my career options, and how I will be playing them to the hilt, and maybe to be a successful actress or other good stuff. Do not go finding me, prosze. I will be far away over oceans from you. I worry about me, you worry about you. Be more healthful, go outside. You are losing your <u>hair</u>.

Love, Anya

I paused this round of Dumped! for long enough to grab a picture in a silvered frame of Anya and me on the banks of the Vistula River, and check my hairline against it in a powder-blue ceramic hand mirror she'd bought on one of our weekend trips to Krakow. I dropped the hand mirror on the coffee table nearly hard enough to crack it.

She was right. A recession was under way.

She had taken almost all of her clothes with her in my oversized duffel bag, but left a lot of her knickknacks behind. A miniature vase filled with dried flowers. A heart-shaped hatbox. A ceramic beer-cat we stole from a Japanese restaurant after splitting a whole bottle of sake. A handcrafted incense burner I bought her for no particular reason. A palm-sized red bean-bag dog she'd named Pikpak (how could she leave poor Pikpak?). These things were invisible to me before, but I noticed them all now. For the first time, I saw the sheen of her own reality that Anya had spread over mine, just as it began to fade. A single dress remained, a red spaghetti-strap thing I'd bought her, the only piece of clothing I ever bought her—it. It was draped over the couch like a limp and lifeless shadow, as if she'd been on the verge of taking it when she remembered where it had come from.

It didn't strike me as the sort of thing I would do, but I spent at least a half hour thinking about all the last times: the last time we made love (5 months ago), the last time we screwed (1.5 months), the last time I saw her naked (1 month), the last time I touched her hand with tenderness (1 month), the last time I saw the steep nape of her neck as she lifted her hair (1 week), the last time I heard her laugh, truly laugh the way she had at the beginning (4 months), the last time we went out for dinner (2 weeks), the last time she passed the salt (2 weeks). They all became milestones, retroactively. I sat on the couch where she'd sat so many mornings and watched me with rancor as I ate breakfast, and thought about what it would feel like to live a life in which the abovementioned things would never be possible again, not with Anya—

But I could not imagine what it would feel like. Not because it was all too much for me to take and I was too sensitive to handle it. No, when I peeled myself from my own thoughts and examined them in their nakedness, I had to confess I could only feel what it felt like to be *thinking about* what it would feel like to live a life without these pieces of Anya in it. Some blockage prevented me from getting to the feeling beneath . . . or was the blockage a protection, a buffer against the truth that there was really nothing there, no feeling at all, no ghosts of love and loss hiding in the mental machinery? Andy Warhol once said that once you saw emotions from a certain angle, you could never think of them as real again, and thinking about Andy Warhol kept bringing me back to thinking about my hair and looking at it in the blue hand mirror, and given that my live-in girlfriend had just walked out on me, this inordinate concern with my receding hairline tended to support Warhol's position. Eventually, to take my mind off my situation, I called Clio and told her to come over, which she did. Although I lived within walking distance of Portal, she had never been to my place (for obvious reasons), and I'd only been to her place in North Hollywood once (it was a trek, and I preferred to stay off the highways). All sex had occurred on Portal premises. I hid the remaining traces of Anya in the closet, although I almost forgot the red dress, only seeing it as I stepped into the living room to open the door for Clio. I quickly covered it with a throw blanket patterned with guitars, drums and musical notes—a housewarming gift from my parents, a subtle suggestion that rekindling my interest in music might be a healthy, productive thing for me to do in my spare time.

redemption of physical reality

● ● ● ● ● ● ● ● ● ● ● ● ● ● ● ● ● ● ●

Now that the MAME games were gone, I desperately wanted to play them. Though Pengo, Zaxxon, Kaos, Qix had largely fallen by the wayside along with the *Catalogue*, displaced by Lucky Wander Boy–related matters, I thought about them for the first time in weeks. When I returned home from work the next day, however, and began downloading the MAME emulator again to start from scratch, I saw the Sisyphean task of reacquiring the games stretching up over my head, 1,423 steep and foreboding steps. I knew I would not be able to enjoy playing any one game until I had all of them, so I went down to the video store to get a movie instead, to take my mind off my loss.

I went with the intention of renting *Buckaroo Banzai: Across the 8th Dimension*. I did not go to Blockbuster, because no one should ever go to Blockbuster for any reason, even if they do have multiple copies of *Buckaroo Banzai*. I went to Videonaut, a video store owned by real people who had a stake in the store doing well, people who stayed after hours painting funny pictures on the store windows in liquid tempera, people who could provide useful information about the movies on the shelves, people who knew my name, and were always glad I came, and knew which new releases I might like.

"Adam! You like Japan?" asked Anthony, the Videonaut-on-duty. His hair was getting very long. He was in bad need of a shave. He had made a point of seeing every movie in the store.

I told him that, indeed, I did like Japan very much.

"Well, you've got to check this out," Anthony said. "We just got it today, it's a movie by Kitano Miyake, the hottest young director in Japan, he's made eight movies this year alone. He shot this one on sixteen millimeter in two weeks. I saw it this afternoon. It's out there, way out there, but—let's just say I've already reserved a place for it on my top-ten list for the year, and it's only March."

"Great," I said. "Let's have it."

He handed me the box from behind the counter. On the homemade cover, an ancient photograph of a reed-thin Chinese woman, lashed to two wooden poles with strips of animal hide. Together, they might have formed the skeleton for a teepee. A crowd was gathered around the woman, and a man with a shaved forehead and a long braided queue snaking from the back of his high, even-brimmed hat was pinching her eyebrow with one hand, and holding a long knife in another.

The title of the film was *Leng Tch'e*.

I flipped the box over. The actual descriptive text was too small to be legible, but a critical blurb was printed in a larger font:

"A gruesomely touching story of love, loss, and the redemption of physical reality."

—Film Threat Magazine

I nodded to let him know I'd take it. I was nearly struck dumb, but not quite; when Anthony returned with the film adaptation of *Leng Tch'e* in its orange Videonaut box, I asked him if I could take the original box with me. He handed over the homemade box without a second thought; I got the sense he was no stranger to strange requests, on either the asking or receiving end. He even refused to let me pay for it, though I would have gladly paid double, because the moment I saw it, I knew it was portentous. It was a sign, an omen, it shouted to me in thin, white, sans-serif letters, not just a phrase, but an explanation and a goal:

THE REDEMPTION OF PHYSICAL REALITY

The words lured my eyes to the box as it sat in my lap on the drive home, and I puzzled over their relevance, a relevance that had yet to show me its face. At the first red light I encountered, my eyes barely made it from the box to the windshield in time, and I came within two inches of ramming into the rear bumper of the old Beetle in front of me, on which a bumper sticker read:

Not all who wander are lost.

—J. R. R. Tolkien

Connections were making themselves known. I did not know whether I was watching them come into being for the first time, or whether they had been there all along and only become visible to me in the calm that followed Anya's departure. Whichever the case, I felt that, bit by bit, I was reading the thought of Lucky Wander Boy in the mind of the world.

The brutal realism of the film's actual "Leng Tch'e" scenes got to be a bit much, even in black and white, or possibly *because* of the black and white; all the simulated violence to which I'd been exposed through Eviscerator et al. had been lovingly rendered in the colors of the real world, but it was all too easy to imagine this shaky dismemberment footage as an authentic artifact. I did not know much about the history of Chinese-Japanese relations, but the term "Rape of Nanking" stuck out in my mind like a naked flagpole, so I figured that, in a Japanese movie about violence toward a Chinese woman, there was likely some subtext I was missing. Eventually I treated the film as a piece of inverse pornography, fast-forwarding through the graphic scenes to watch the exposition, which expanded poetically on the resonant bits of the narrator's life, often in voice-over dialogue. The subtitles were taken directly from the text of the Ana translation of the novella:

So I listen as my husband plunges himself into the young *hsiao* flute player, her feeble moans reminding me of the scant sighs of pity I will soon hear amidst the jeers and incriminations at my own execution. When my husband finishes, I wait, I watch her dainty feet bound with strips of binding cloth as they carry her out the door and over the rise.

I also watched all the beautiful, extreme close-ups of the dropperful of opium being dripped into the narrator's mouth, stranding her on the border between this world and the next.

When I'd finished my scan of *Leng Tch'e*, I did not see what *The Redemption of Physical Reality* had to do with either the movie or its source material, which if anything seemed to be a tale of Redemption through Fragmentation—but *Leng Tch'e* had important connections to Lucky Wander Boy, so I took it on faith that the phrase did too, in some way that I would soon descry.

Late that night, after the last beater car had come or gone with a raucous sputter and the birds had fallen silent, leaving only the horror-movie shrieks of the local cats as my downstairs neighbor's red tabby asserted his dominion, in the corner of my computer screen after it fell into a dark, power-saving sleep I saw a reflection of the slat window behind me. When I moved in closer to the dark screen and squinted my eyes, in the horizontal bands of that reflected slat window I glimpsed my Moment of Decision looking back at me, impassive, unreadable. He was Japanese, bearing a slight resemblance to actor Toshiro Mifune, which was only fitting—yet he was also not-Japanese at the same time. He had a Spectral Samurai topknot, yet he did not. The particular and the general coexisted in his face; he was at once an image you could draw if you had that facility, and undifferentiated, faceless, the great protean Primary. Since he only existed in my mind at the time, he was allowed these contradictions, this shift and sway.

He did not want to stay in my mind, however. The Moment of Decision means nothing until he is born into the world. And what does he do, once he leaves the womb of possibility? Well, I cannot speak for everyone's Moment of Decision, that would be presumptuous—but my Moment, what were his plans?

The Redemption of Physical Reality

Along with my Moment's face, the meaning of this phrase in relation to my own situation was coming into the open. I postulated the following:

In my attachment to MAME, my thrall to its glamour and fascination, I had overlooked the crucial element the emulated arcade games lacked. Back in Warsaw, I'd been too quick to agree with Jeffrey that the essence of a game was in the running of its code, I'd sided too easily with the config against the Thing Itself. The MAME games were facsimiles that came so close to covering all salient points of the originals that I had not noticed what was missing: their *aura*. Their uniqueness, their spark, that something (or nothing) that resides in the Game Itself—not just in the circuit board but in the beaten-up plywood cabinet, in its side decals, in the ten-watt bulbs behind its translucent plastic marquee, in the synergy of all these things together—and is not passed on in a digital copy, however perfect.

Perhaps the MAME emulator was only the first stage in the establishment of the true relationship to the games that I—or my Moment—was striving for. Because once you allowed for the existence of the aura, the Games Themselves became powerful things. With their auras intact, the Games Themselves could be brought to the service of a world that was all wrong, a world that needed *redeeming*. They could unite opposing sides of the screen—my experience with Microsurgeon had shown that much—and fix what was broken beneath the glass and above it, restoring Classical order and proportion and simplicity. In great acts of healing, of sympathetic magic, of *tikkun*, they could kill every wrong thing.

Now, thanks to Anya, the impotent MAME replicas were gone, spurring me to search for the real things. They were still out there, I had seen them in low-profit retreats, half deserted, lying fallow in their obsolescence as Next Big Things sprouted up all around them, taking a sabbatical to reinvigorate themselves. And if it still existed anywhere on American soil, Lucky Wander Boy would be among them.

It was a hypothesis. My knee hit the desk, sending a vibration through the wood that triggered my mouse, waking up the sleeping computer. My Moment of Decision disappeared from the screen, replaced by a search engine page, into which I immediately entered the word "samurai." Coincidence surfing, I rapidly and randomly selected a matching result, and was taken to "Seicho's Samurai Quote Of The Day Page," on which the following appeared:

> Lord Naoshige said, "The Way of the Samurai is in desper-
> ateness. Ten men or more cannot kill such a man. Com-
> mon sense will not accomplish great things. Simply
> become insane and desperate."
> —Yamamoto Tsunetomo,
> *Hagakure: The Book of the Samurai*

My Moment of Decision had manifested himself in order to point me toward a course of action, and to take away the F.E.A.R. that prevented me from acting. I was falling into line with a new way of thinking, a brand-new config. For days, I carried the over-due *Leng Tch'e* video box like a devotional object everywhere I went—Portal Entertainment, the various rooms of my apartment—meditating on its meaning and message during every spare moment.

An hour of research turned up Re-Play in Costa Mesa, forty-five minutes south on the 405 expressway. "Dozens of Classic Games . . . at Classic Prices." They had Pac-Man, Ms. Pac-Man, Tempest, Robotron 2084, Frogger, "many other games." It seemed made to order—

—but as it turned out, Re-Play was all wrong. The arcade was very brightly lit, with an atmosphere better suited to a supermarket. To get to the Classic gaming area, you had to walk through Re-Play's real moneymakers: the modern shooting games with real simulated auto-matic pistol recoil, the jet ski and motocross simulators with tilt-sensitive controls, the live-action dancing games in which children jerked around like clumsy marionettes on weight-sensitive pads, drum-ming games, lots of two-player beat-'em-ups. The cacophony seemed familiar at first, but it was composed of the wrong kind of noise, lots of overorchestrated cheese-funk MIDI soundtracks, massive explosions and voices, real voices, not synthesized but digitized from real actors. Rather than working in harmony to create an aural ambience, each sound fought tooth and claw for supremacy over the others, and the final result was far too rich, a distraction, like a pound of saffron in the rice.

When I got to the Classic gaming area, there was no Lucky Wander Boy. I hadn't really expected them to have it, but still I felt deflated, the tiny slump in the soul that came with each losing Lotto ticket. Determined to make the best of it, I stepped to the Tempest machine and started to play, but the kids milling around the arcade behind me were an impossible distraction. They were all wrong. Baggy clothes on the girls . . . the guys could have baggy clothes, but the *girls*? Any girl in an arcade should be wearing tight black jeans. It was not open to discussion. Her body type was irrelevant. And everyone primly obeyed the No Smoking signs, not understanding that they were there to be ignored.

The past was not what it used to be. For my act of redemption, I would need a more controlled environment. To get back to basics, I would have to go back down to the basement. Metaphorically, of course.

fetish

● ●

Acquiring the original home consoles was easy; were it not for my initial preoccupation with MAME, I would have done it sooner. Vintage videogaming technology was readily available on eBay to the highest bidder, which I was every time. In two weeks, I owned an Intellivision, an Atari 2600, an extra Atari joystick to replace the broken one that came with the 2600, and a total of about fifty cartridges for each system. Sum total expenditure: $155.00.

Living alone, I began to comprehend the reason I'd persisted in spending time with other people from grade school to the present day, beyond the satisfaction of basic animal urges. Some minimal degree of personal coherence and consistency was probably necessary to operate successfully in the world of men, which is the world we must live in, for better or worse. It was only through association with other people that I maintained this coherence and consistency. Mirroring their gestures, using them as libraries of phrases and norms, I kept relatively close to the local baseline, and was allowed to carry on in the world largely unnoticed.

Impressing Anya into servitude as my mirror and library, as a trampoline to keep me in social shape, was tremendously selfish and I regretted having done it. As unpleasant as it had been for her, however, she was no longer here. This was a good thing. With the arrival of the Atari and Intellivision, I left the world of men and entered into a different space—one of experiment, of ritual, of various forms of antisocial behavior necessary to tease the aura from these old games, through the consoles and phono plug cables and out the TV screen, sparks from a forgotten time that would come to heal whatever had been broken and deliver me into action of some kind. Anya would not have appreciated these ad hoc rituals. Not at all. Her absence was probably for the best.

After purchasing and assembling a tangled mass of equipment from Radio Shack that allowed for easy switching between the Atari and Intellivision, I laid all the functioning Atari and Intellivision cartridges out in an intricate three-leveled mandala. Its widest circle was exactly 8 feet in diameter, and consisted of 34 cartridges. Its middle circle was exactly 5 feet in diameter, and consisted of 21 cartridges. The inner circle of the mandala was exactly 3 feet in diameter, and consisted of 13 cartridges. I sat in the center of the mandala, with the Atari exactly 2 feet to my left and the Intellivision exactly 1 foot to my right. 1 (me), 1, 2, 3, 5, 8, 13, 21, 34, 55—the first nine numbers of the Fibonacci sequence were present. This sequence pops up in everything from the Great Pyramids to sunflowers to rabbit breeding to the stock market to electronics. The symbol of the Fibonacci Association, dedicated to further interest in the Fibonacci sequence and related matters, was a pentagram in a circle, much like that used in ritual invocations.

Starting at 12 o'clock in the outer layer and working inward, I moved through the layers of the mandala clockwise-counterclockwise-clockwise, playing one game of each. I would list the games in order, but this would be tedious. I began with Raiders of the Lost Ark (Atari), Ice Trek (Intellivision), Kaboom! (Atari); I ended with Dracula (Intellivision), Yar's Revenge (Atari), Microsurgeon (Intellivision). Before playing each, I pricked my finger, using a safety pin sterilized with a lighter and rubbing alcohol, raised a drop of blood, and wiped it on the edge of the cartridge; by the time I was done all my fingertips were extremely tender, but rituals that do not include bloodletting are not the real deal. This ritual took five and a half hours, during which I listened to Rush's *2112* on repeat seven and one-third times.

So I receive my life a second time, back and forth, piece by piece. . . .

—Leng Tch'e

Pieces of my life I'd written off as gone forever were here now, in actuality, like resuscitated memories. I was working through them again, living them again, but now they were under control. My control. My life had been confused and without center, but by returning to this starting place and going over it all slowly and with volition, I could find it. What had been buried for me and me alone, what had been lost. The solid can disintegrate, but the intangible can also receive form.

With an X-Acto blade, I cut a square from the carpeting in front of the TV, and wiped the dusty, chipped hardwood floor beneath with a damp rag. I then Krazy Glued an Atari joystick to the floor in front of the TV, and taped the color photo of Araki Itachi that Clio had given me to the entertainment center so it hung directly above the TV. Removing my pants and underwear, but not my shirt or socks, I sat before the joystick in lotus position and plugged in the Adventure cartridge (one of the closest things to Lucky Wander Boy I had at hand, with its acquirable objects, and Holy Grail surrogate, and potentially interminable wanderings through castle rooms and hallways). I shuttled my gaze between Itachi and the game in smooth and steady one-second intervals—when my eyes were on her, I tried to bore through the picture plane to get to the woman beneath—and played the game with my right hand while masturbating with my left. This was not easy, as there is nothing overtly sexual about Adventure. Though the dragon is snaky and phallic on the box cover, in the game it resembles a duck more than anything. Perhaps that was for the best—as it stood, I climaxed in perfect synchrony with the acquisition of the magic chalice and successful completion of the game, after which I anointed Itachi's picture with a ritual dab on her forehead. Semen is often used in true magickal ceremonies, or so I have read.

Ever since I had unveiled the beauty that lay beneath the layers of Itachi's inscrutability, I'd begun to feel the first stirrings of desire that always lurk beneath the blanket of aesthetic appreciation. Instead of blindly giving in to it or roughly suppressing it, I wanted to elevate this desire, to harness it and impress it into the service of something greater. It was not a sidetrack, or a hindrance. My desire was a motive force. I thought of her as a metaphysical carrot on a stick, pulling me in the right direction, toward a sacred space where the dead pieces of the world around me would begin to shimmer with sparks of herself.

The weekend after the semination ritual, I began to grow impatient with the lack of results. What to expect from an improvised ritual was anyone's guess, they were wildcards, but I had expected *something*—some sign, some tangible effect on the world, an indication of potency. When none of these appeared, I began to rethink the idea of the aura. Perhaps when things have been in our presence often enough and long enough to collect the familiarity that breeds simple nostalgia for machines like Atari and Intellivision in the minds of millions of people, perhaps by this time these things have been stripped of their aura for good. Perhaps it simply washes away like the topsoil of a denuded forest, leaving behind a desert that will never see an aura bloom again. Try as I might to bring them into a strange and sacred space, I was not getting at the essences of these games. They were the Things Themselves, yet somehow they were not—they were my remembrances of the things taped to their corpses like Araki Itachi's picture taped above my TV. I flipped to a passage in *Leng Tch'e* that obliquely made an important point:

> I hold no grudge against the men who scatter my parts to the five directions, because each piece of my body is a hindrance to my immortality; as I shuffle off each part, I become further invested in timelessness. . . .

The real reason these games had reappeared in my life was to be shuffled off again. Nothing would be changed or redeemed by them—they were merely another stage on the path as MAME had been, bringing me closer to my ultimate goal by the deceitful means of promising more than they could deliver, coaxing me in the direction of the difficult, the unavailable, the experience that cannot be replicated, forged or reproduced.

Lucky Wander Boy, I knew, still had its aura, wherever it was. It still had the mythic sparks given off by the rubbing together of rarity and time, and the charge grew stronger in direct proportion to the game's distance from my current situation.

As if to herald the arrival of this Friday insight, a great flash hit on Saturday morning, while I played Raiders of the Lost Ark on the Atari—my final attempted ritual. Though it could not be called a successful game, Raiders had been a valiant effort on the part of programmer Howard Scott Warshaw, probably the predecessor that came closest to Lucky Wander Boy territory before the thing itself arrived. Having gone to Santa Monica Beach and filled a pillowcase with sand using the spade that Anya had left in the empty porch planter, I sprinkled a ritual semicircle of sand around my television, to create a resonance between the outside of the screen and the inside, which would soon become Howard Warshaw's approximation of Tunis. Then, sitting a foot from the TV with a blanket draped over my head and the screen, I took in the steam of its images, listening to the sound through headphones to better concentrate on their simple purity. In my jury-rigged video isolation tank, the picture of Araki Itachi my only company, I willingly entombed myself to get closer to the game's changeless beige desert and the keys to the past that might be buried there, imagining that I might dig some kind of tunnel through game-space and end up in the second-stage desert of Lucky Wander Boy. Moving through the Temple Treasure Room and the Room of the Shining Light, the Marketplace and the Mesa Field, I got inside the secret mesa and began to dig with my shovel, digging toward the final goal: the Ark, which presumably contained the hi-res tablets that the game-Jehovah gave to the game-Moses in the lost millennia of game-history, and as I got closer I was flooded by a brilliant, blinding white light—

Clio yanked the blanket off my head, sweeping up the picture of Itachi with it. She had come over unannounced, and although I sat five feet from the door, I had not heard her come in.

"Get up," she said. "Leave a message on Lyme's voice mail, call yourself in sick for tomorrow. If we leave now, we'll get there by tonight."

"Get where?" I asked, rubbing my eyes.

"We're taking a field trip. Bring the paper that Makurufuku guy gave you. I think we might be able to kill two birds with one stone. Come on, hurry up—places to meet, people to go."

CATALOGUE OF OBSOLETE ENTERTAINMENTS
SUPPLEMENTARY ESSAY: "ON GEEKS"

"Geek" calls to mind certain endeavors and pursuits today, as it called to mind oral chicken decapitation a century ago: computers, comic books, science fiction, mathematics and hard science, certain kinds of obscurantist films and music, video games, and at the farther reaches, *Star Trek*, role-playing games, and the geek *non plus ultra*, *Star Trek* role-playing games. Then there are the personal-appearance signifiers used to identify a geek on sight, the social-profiling scheme whereby snap decisions to harass or exclude can be made. Unusually skinny, or fat, wearing sweatpants, with the wrong kind of glasses, acne, and the telltale T-shirt (Green Lantern, Rush, Atari, *Star Wars*, *Star Trek*—anything with the word "Star" in it probably tags you[1]). Circa 1995–2003, sculpted facial hair might show up as well, a belated bid at being let inside a club he will forever be shut out of—though the hall-of-mirrors relationship between the geek and the alpha male grows increasingly complex, as women's magazines and men's magazines declare various forms of Outside to be In.

All of these associations and identifications obfuscate the heart of the matter, the essence of what defines the geek and sets him apart from his fellow man, and far, far apart from his fellow woman.[2] The core definition of geekhood encompasses the above preconceptions, and a great deal more besides:

A geek is a person, male or female, with an abiding, obsessive, self-effacing, even self-destroying love for something besides status.

The "status geek" exists, of course, but there is little point in discussing him, because he belongs to an all-inclusive category. We are all hard-wired to be status geeks, approbation geeks, doing whatever we can to impress and impress upon.[3] It is an imperative that can only be

---

[1] Yes, "Porn Star," that means you.

[2] Which is not to ignore the female geek, in many ways a doubly unfortunate creature.

[3] "... the individual or the family do not ask themselves ... what would suit my character and disposition? Or, what would allow the best and highest in me to have fair play, and enable it to grow and thrive? They ask themselves, what is suitable to my position? What is usually done by persons of my station and pecuniary circumstances? Or (worse still) what is usually done by persons of a station and circumstances superior to mine?" John Stuart Mill, *On Liberty*.

blocked by personal deficiency—only when some missing rung prevents a person from climbing their social ladder will they find themselves on a fallow patch of ground where other, more fragile interests can take root. I think of all the geeks that I have known or known of, and I am certain that, in the formative period during which their personal obsessions were beginning to develop, almost every one of them would have left their geek love behind in a second if status truly seemed within reach (or sex, or money, they are all linked in a big transitive circle, impossible to disentangle). The heroic pointlessness of the specialist is an evolutionary door prize. It beats the lot of the stag sea lion bull who, unable to whip the eight-hundred pound ass of the king of the beach, crawls off to the other side of the island to live and fish and die alone, but it is still primarily a consolation for the also-rans.

In line with the above reasoning, those happy few, that band of surfeited brothers who dumb genetic accident has granted both the brains necessary for geekhood and the savoir faire to work the People-Who-Know-People circuit will hardly ever choose the former. They may seem to at first glance, while they discourse to a circle of martini connoisseurs on their deep spiritual appreciation of John Coltrane, but they are dabblers. After making their money, they move on to professional dilettantism, a bit of this and a bit of that, learning enough to write a passable in-flight magazine article. It does the trick, they make an impression, like a nineteenth-century Belgian colonialist hacking apart a few dozen Congolese to take their diamonds and present them to his Belgian sweetheart upon returning home, while declaring his love in an accent I'm told the Parisian French find buffoonish. The cultivation of "geek chic" is a deeply cynical, pernicious, even nihilistic attempt to plunder lives that are more often than not emotionally destitute already, to steal their sole prized possession and trade it on the open market for a minute of juice with a sexual target, a fleeting hit of superiority in a friendly discussion, the shimmering mirage of depth for an in-flight magazine profile.

In the unlikely event of an afterlife with presiding deity, the geek chic set will get theirs.

In truth, the typical geek pursuits cited earlier represent only the most visible tip of a vast iceberg. People find many, many havens from their species' unpleasant and often brutal prime directive, and manage to live entire closeted geek lives without having to endure the indignity of the label.

Sports is one of the most clever ones. Or gambling. Or gambling on sports. Or cars. Or clothes: there are millions of clothes geeks out there, Moses figures all, gazing out lovingly over the cut and drape of the magazine landscape, and all the while being too fat or stocky or awkwardly put-together to ever fit into their size-two Promised Land. A geek loves *something* more than the fear and respect and desire of his fellow men and women. Comics, clothes, heroin. Anything.

A great irony too familiar to inspire any awe is that most great achievements, the ones that outlive their achievers, are born in this place that people only go by default—the geek place they enter with hung heads and shuffling, defeated feet. The corollary irony, less powerfully obvious, is that in this place effects are unimportant. Means are unimportant, ends are unimportant. Geeks heed Heidegger's call to set aside the *Herausfordern* or "challenging" relationship to things that makes "the unreasonable demand that [things] supply energy which can be extracted and stored as such."[4] In its place, geeks stick to "keeping watch over the unconcealment . . . of all coming to presence on this earth," or their own small corner of it. They encounter their comics or cars or computer games as pure *Quidditas*, whatness, thereness for its own sake, the *Gelassenheit* or "releasement" that Joshua Glenn parses as "the gentle coaxing from things of their own best potentiality"[5] without trying to control them or beat them into conformity with the useful.

Indeed, the vast bulk of geeks, like the vast bulk of their status-seeking brothers, will achieve nothing of note—but this does not stop them. It would only stop them if they considered the end result, and if they considered the end result, they would not be geeks. Victims of

---

[4]From Martin Heidegger, *Basic Writings*, trans. David Farrell Krell (Harper & Row: New York, 1977), p. 296. Harmless incongruity of the coexistence of John Stuart Mill, Martin Heidegger and sports betting in the same essay: duly noted. Not-so-harmless omission of mention of Heidegger's unsavory Nazi activities circa 1932–1945 (Nazi party membership card # 312589): duly noted.

[5]In "Anorexia/Technology: An Introduction" from *Hermenaut* #14.

the Mosaic curse, they look down into Canaan from their own private Pisgahs without any hope of ever being allowed in, and like Moses they acquiesce in this state of affairs, though unlike him they have done nothing to deserve their exclusion from the land of milk and honey. For they may be oppressed by the figures of beauty, and they may be ugly—but they have the music. While the hedonistic treadmill carries the others through cycles of momentary appeasement and slow, scraping dissatisfaction, the geeks will penetrate deeper and deeper into the music the others cannot hear, its notes independent of the demands of the world that pull people through jobs and parties and bars toward their end. They will hear its forgotten strains and study its evolution in all its branching intricacy, and in the unlikely event of an afterlife they will have their music to carry them, they will never grow tired of it, they will still be going and going and going long after the others have overdosed on the maximum conceivable pleasure and chosen self-extinguishing over the ultimate boredom hangover that follows. Their passion is like a red dwarf star—it may not burn as hot, but it burns longer. It burns near forever.

convention

● ●

Clio insisted on driving the whole way. She always insisted on driving. She went to an all-girls college, which may have had something to do with it. As soon as we hit I-10, she set her Jetta's cruise control on eighty-five and kept it there. We stopped twice for gas and bathroom breaks, and once for a McDonalds drive-thru. All food was eaten in the car. By late afternoon, we were moving through the Painted Desert, its clay-red striations reminding me of a monochromatic version of Dig Dug's layered screen (which was more varied than the real desert, it must be said, covering as it did the whole hot end of the color spectrum). By sundown we were driving past distant New Mexican mesas. At around 11:30, on Route 70, we skirted the White Sands National Monument.

I looked at the free road atlas she'd gotten with her car insurance. "Looks like we're about forty miles south of White Sands Missile Range. That's where they've got the Trinity Site." No response. "You know, where they detonated the first atomic bomb."

Clio gave a bemused *hmmmm,* saving her thoughts for the road, and our destination.

"You still won't tell me the special secret reason we *had* to come to this thing?"

"If I did," she said, "it wouldn't be secret, and once 'secret' goes, 'special' goes too, and then all you'd be left with is a reason. A plain old three-for-a-dollar reason. Trust me, it's better this way."

I agreed with her on the virtues of secret reasons, and did not push the matter any further. I trusted her.

We pulled into a Best Western in Alamogordo just after midnight. Although an impromptu road trip like this was supposed to kindle passion, we were both too tired to screw, and fell asleep as soon as we slid between the dubious sheets.

Nothing about the exterior of Alamogordo High School distinguished it from the generic high school template. I should have feigned greater excitement, but memories of my own high school years made this impossible.

"Come on," Clio said, flicking my earlobe hard enough to hurt. "This is it! You're a modern primitive, man, and this is your tribe!"

"I don't think I'm very tribally inclined," I said. "Maybe a tribe of two."

By the way she flicked my ear again, more tenderly this time, I could tell she thought I was referring to her and me. If she'd been a Jewish girl, she would have made me say it outright, but she evidently came from people who knew when a simple request for clarification could knock down the whole house of cards, so she took it on faith. I had spoken without full forethought, however. The tribe of two might have been Clio and me—or it might have been me and a Lucky Wander Boy machine, in the kind of cyborg synergy that arose between an artificial intelligence and Bombay bombshell Persis Khambatta in the underrated *Star Trek: The Motion Picture*. Or—dare I say it? Me and Araki Itachi? I think I meant all of these simultaneously. In my mind at that point, our future together was like Schrödinger's Cat, in an uncertain superposition of life and death.

Like the school itself, the Alamogordo High School gymnasium was what you would expect, with a high ceiling and a handsome, olive-green Alamogordo Tigers banner stretched across its rafters, flanked by a couple of state championship pennants. The white, hand-painted banner announcing the EIGHTH ANNUAL ALTERNA-CLASSICGAMING-CON suffered by comparison, as did the twenty-five-odd participants in this final day of the conference, dwarfed as they were by the rising bleachers. Most of the participants were also exhibitors, responsible for one of the fifteen or twenty picnic table booths. Some of these were purely educational displays about one or another aspect of Classic videogame history, but more of them featured vintage merchandise, and the salesmen could be distinguished from the spectators or curators by the proprietary ticks with which their heads kept jerking back toward their own booths to make sure nothing was missing.

There were a few tables of straight licensing paraphernalia: "Pac-Man Fever" 45s, mint condition boxes of Donkey Kong cereal, Space Invaders lunchboxes, the Q*Bert board game, various T-shirts, even the very same Pac-Man clock I had on my office wall, on sale for three times the price I paid. One table was covered in vintage fan magazines from the years 1981 to 1984—*Electronic Games, Video Games, Videogaming Illustrated.* The *Electronic Games* from 1982 went for $35 a pop, the ones from 1981 for $50, and the first issue for $100. Another table specialized in rare home systems—an original Magnavox Odyssey, an Atari Home Pong, a Fairchild Channel F, two Bally Arcades, a Coleco Telstar arcade (I particularly liked the look of this one, a triangle with different kinds of controllers crammed in on all sides, a pistol, a steering wheel, a paddle knob), and the centerpiece, an ultra-rare GCE Vectrex home vector system in its unopened 1982 box, exhibited with show-and-tell pride, its $450.25 price tag printed in seventy-two-point type on a dot matrix printer. At center court, someone had set up a lone Asteroids machine with tensor barriers surrounding it on three sides, like a single mangy panther at a roadside zoo.

"Now," I said, "the big secret?"

"Still for me to know," she said, scanning the crowd. "Why don't you socialize?"

We each paid our five dollars entrance fee, and I did my best. The first guy I approached was manning one of the three or four paraphernalia tables. He wore a flannel shirt in the face of the mounting heat, and a beard not unlike my own, though bushier. After introducing myself, I asked where he was from and learned that he lived in Minnetonka, Minnesota, and I made some dull comment along the lines of "It must be nice coming down to such warm and dry weather this time of year."

"I'm here for three reasons," he said. Humorless, almost confrontational, he counted off on his fingers: "Classic. Video. Games."

"He wasn't very nice," Clio said as we walked away.

"Don't mind Zach," said a guy in a Green Lantern T-shirt who'd overheard her. He looked like a newsprint image of a regular guy stretched lengthwise on Silly Putty. "He's been P.O.'ed for the past few years, ever since eBay forced his store out of business. I'm Tom." He shook Clio's hand first, then mine.

"Yeah," said another guy as he approached us with his cheese-fries belly peeking out from the bottom of his Green Lantern T-shirt, "a lot of CGers don't see much reason in coming out anymore, except to that mainstream expo in Vegas that was cool when it was World of Atari, but is *so* weak now. All the newfangled stuff's starting to seep in, and there's media coverage, and you know what that means—"

"Van Burnham, J. C. Herz, Zoe Heller—it's all about the big-name chicks now," Green Lantern #1 chimed in. "No offense."

"What about the Tokyo Game Show?" Clio asked.

"The Tokyo Game Show?" Green Lantern #1 said. "You know how much a ticket to Japan costs? Tell me where I can steal one and I'll go."

"The only ones left here are us *hard-core* guys," said Green Lantern #2. "Oh, my name's Jack. I'm this guy's brother." He also shook Clio's hand first.

"And I am Charlie, aka GameDemon," said Green Lantern #3, shaking Clio's hand. "Now you've had the honor of meeting us all." In a drug dealer's scheming whisper, speaking mainly to Clio but gesturing indifferently to include me, he said, "If you guys are interested, my frères and myself are offering a full line of vintage *adult* games for sale at very competitive prices, over at booth número seven. Custer's Revenge, Bachelor Party, and Beat 'Em & Eat 'Em cartridges, all in their original packaging. We've even got an original five-and-a-quarter-inch floppy of the text adventure Soft Porn for the Apple IIe—*if* you're interested in that kind of thing, that 'cup o' tea.'"

After the sixth guy had come over to shake Clio's hand first, I surveyed the floor. There were two other females in the gym. One of them was tremendously overweight and stood slackly behind a homemade exhibit on the Atari/Intellivision advertising wars, waiting to hit Rewind on her TV/VCR whenever George Plimpton took his final tweedy potshot at the Atari 2600, signaling the end of the tape. The other was less overweight and far less resigned, hiking up the front of her overalls, lifting both her arms to run both her hands through her straw hair in a blatant animal bid to hold on to her dwindling court of admirers, and when two more of her available males turned to see what had pulled their fellow suitors away and, catching sight of rail-thin Crayola-haired Clio, paused pregnantly before turning back, the woman's eyes took on the sharpness of steak knives.

My compassion for these women's predicament was all but buried under the avalanche of irritation I felt at having driven 850 miles for this. I put my arm around Clio's shoulder and herded her aside, speaking quietly into her ear.

"This is retarded," I said.

"Snobby snobby. Maybe *you're* retarded. I think they're fun."

"Your prerogative." A sudden spike of anger toward her surged through me, and I walked away before I said anything I'd regret later. On the other end of the court, far from the conventioneers, stood a rack of basketballs, probably left over from a Saturday Tigers practice. I took one, dribbled a few times and started taking shots, pretending not to notice the stares. Walking into the gymnasium holding Clio's hand made me the alpha male by default. I had never been an alpha before, not in my own country, and thus had no idea how I was supposed to act in order to fulfill people's expectations. Ignoring one's female in favor of an athletic display seemed like a suitable thing to do, but I couldn't be sure. Although I should not have cared one way or another, the fear of falling from my newfound position made me uncomfortable. There was also the suspicion that GameDemon had been right, that everyone here *was* hard core, inside, the real deal. I wanted to believe that I was too—I'd have to be to write something like the *Catalogue of Obsolete Entertainments* with any authority—but they were forcing me to confront the possibility that I still had a long way to go, and this irritated me.

The basketball hit the rim at a funny angle and ricocheted over my head. I jumped to catch it, but not high enough. When I turned, I saw the ball heading for the Rare Home Systems table, and sprinted after it.

The proprietor of the Rare Home Systems table watched with terror and loathing and heroically threw himself over the Vectrex box. I was running after the ball, but I was not gaining on it. On the contrary, it was pulling away from me. With a pure and concentrated dread, I understood that to have any chance of heading off a disaster, I would have to dive for it. I had not dived after anything for years. I hadn't dived into a swimming pool for years. I tried to run a quick analysis to determine which held the greatest potential for disaster—diving, or not diving.

The straw-haired overalls girl jumped across my path to grab the basketball, and came to a stop with a rubber-soled squeal.

"Thanks," I said, huffing.

"You shoot like a girl," she said, and sunk a jumper from the three-point line.

"You want to get us kicked out of here before we get around to our special secret reason?" Clio asked after smacking me in the chest.

I took a deep breath. "I think it's time for you to reveal this special secret reason."

Clio scanned the crowd.

"I don't think—no, there! There he is. That's him."

Sitting alone in the top row of the home-team bleachers, someone in a long black coat and a red baseball cap watched us expectantly. Though we made eye contact, he made no move in our direction. Only when we reached the top of the bleachers did he stand to shake our hands. When he raised the brim of his cap, I saw he was Japanese. It is not fashionable of me to say so, but I found this propitious, though his fleshy face remained as flat and impassive as the face of my Moment of Decision when I saw him out of the corner of my mind's eye.

"Adam Pennyman, Tetsu Bush."

"Any relation to—?" Just an attempt at levity. I thought it would help.

"My original name was Bushi, which means 'warrior' or 'samurai' in Japanese. My parents had it forcibly shortened for them upon arrival in this country. One thinks that this sort of thing no longer happens—but one is so often wrong, isn't one?"

Keeping my face as indifferent as his, I gleefully noted the samurai connection.

Tetsu turned to Clio. "You have brought the discussed item?"

"Yes. Adam's got it."

"Good."

He stood. We were alone in the bleachers, but after a quick G-man once-over, Tetsu decided we were not alone enough.

"Come on," he said, "I do not trust these gatherings, even one as pitiable as this. They perpetuate the commodification of uniqueness. Let's go somewhere we can talk."

This was the perfect thing to say, but I did not want to let him know I thought so just yet.

"Like where?" I said.

He put on dark sunglasses. "Your car's in the lot? Good. Follow me. And be sure to keep up. I drive fast."

In the car, as Clio's Jetta struggled to keep up with Tetsu's black Nissan 300ZX, I listened to the song "Subterranean Homesick Alien" by Radiohead on the stereo, in which I recognized my own childhood aspirations, transfigured and returned to me with a certain alienated majesty:

I wish that they'd swoop down in a country lane
Late at night when I'm driving

Take me onboard their beautiful ship
Show me the world as I'd love to see it

I had dreamed that same abduction dream many times, mostly during quiet nights in a summer camp in northern Wisconsin, provoked by a surfeit of visible stars. Absently gazing at Clio's white-knuckled grip on the wheel, I wagered with no one in particular that the "beautiful ship" in the song had been inspired, as my own imagined rescue ship had been, by the beautiful Mother Ship at the end of the original 1977 version of *Close Encounters of the Third Kind*, before Spielberg himself took it out of the film three years later. A certain kind of arcade can resemble that Mother Ship if you are high enough, or if you are extremely myopic and not wearing your glasses. Shards of colorful light, a crystal cathedral in the air, listening for that famous five-note theme, or some permutation thereof.

Tetsu pulled into the parking lot of a stark square building, darkly mirrored like the sunglasses of some great, abstract beast, with two silolike rectangles abutting it. The reflected sands made the building a dun shade of gold, and near the front door I could make out a marble slab that read INTERNATIONAL SPACE HALL OF FAME. We got out of the car.

"Are we going in? Is there something we have to see here?" I asked.

"Not inside," Tetsu said. "Around this way."

Walking past a huge conical rocket ship engine and the original Sonic Wind rocket sled ("reached a ground speed of 632 MPH on December 12, 1954"), and past a simulated launchpad, we came to a cactus garden. Beneath two flagpoles, overlooked by what strongly resembled a Beethoven bust but must have been someone else, a bronze memorial plaque read:

WORLD'S FIRST ASTROCHIMP HAM
BORN 1956 EQUATORIAL AFRICA
DIED 16 JAN 1983 NORTH CAROLINA ZOOLOGICAL PARK, N.C.
HAM PROVED THAT MANKIND COULD LIVE AND WORK IN
SPACE

"Wow," I said.

"And look down there, between here and the campus. What do you see?"

Following his finger, I looked into a shallow valley, beneath a desert sky with a cloud layer so flat it reminded me of the trompe l'oeil ceilings of the Paris casino in Las Vegas. In the distance, a college campus was just discernible. About five hundred yards closer to us, a poorly situated parking lot floated like a concrete island on the sand, moored to nothing.

"A parking lot," I said.

"Do you know what is buried beneath it?" Tetsu said.

The moment he asked, I did.

"The Atari cartridges," I said.

Tetsu nodded with a stoic frown.

"Wow," I said.

"You understand why I chose this spot for our meeting."

I nodded back. I understood. It was a place of resonance. Of intersections.

CATALOGUE OF OBSOLETE ENTERTAINMENTS
GAME: CHINA SYNDROME
Format: Atari 2600 VCS home videogame system
Manufacturer: Spectravision
Year: 1982
CPU: 6507 4-bit processor 1.19MHz
Screen Resolution: 320 × 200 pixels
Sound channels: 3

This game is a dull attempt to license, license, license the popular 1979 movie of the same name, starring Michael Douglas, Jane Fonda and Jack Lemmon. The goal is to keep a nuclear reactor from melting down by catching the loose atoms in the crosshairs of your atom catcher. Visually uninteresting and prematurely released to the public without proper testing, it rapidly goes from tiresomely simple to impossible; a chain reaction does not provide a good model on which to ramp the difficulty level of a game.

A few weeks after *The China Syndrome* film came out in 1979, the devastating explosion at the Three Mile Island nuclear facility occurred, raising the specter of bona fide meltdown. A few months after The China Syndrome game was released for the 2600, an explosion of cheap marketing schemes and knockoff games like it led to a glut in the home videogame market, an inverted pyramid of supply and demand that soon began to totter. Consumers had no way to distinguish the wheat from the chaff, so they bought the less-expensive games, which is to say the knockoffs. The quality companies like Activision and Imagic could not compete with these me-too jackals, and once-quality Atari compounded their own problem by licensing, licensing, licensing popular properties like E.T. and the arcade Pac-Man only to turn them into home games not much better than China Syndrome. Everyone was forced to dump inventories at fire-sale prices to recoup as much of their losses as they could. Consumers soon stopped buying, resentful at having been duped by fancy packaging into buying substandard product, and soon no one could survive, thanks to the retreat of capital, leading to the Great Videogame Crash of 1983. A thirty-fold contraction of the industry took place, and many great programmers and designers lost their jobs, not to mention the regular people who answered the phones, poured the coffee and wrote the press release copy. The bubble had burst. The Classical period of videogame history had effectively ended.

In 1983, rather than follow the standard practice of unloading extra inventory at bargain prices to cut losses before closing up shop, Atari's El Paso manufacturing plant loaded its surplus cartridges into fourteen trucks and drove them out to Alamogordo, New Mexico, where they were buried in a landfill. When the rumor hit that someone had found the landfill and was digging up the cartridges for free, Atari steamrolled the landfill to crush them all—tens of thousands of ETs and Ms. Pac-Mans and Raiders of the Lost Arks—and had the whole thing paved over with asphalt.

Removed, yet connected: the same year, in the same town, Ham, the first U.S. chimpanzee sent into space in 1961, was also buried after dying at the age of twenty-seven—the death of the monkey who (along with the Russian dog) had been the birth of humanity's first true hope of escape from the fallen world. At last count, Ham had 111 descendants, some of whom served the air force like their progenitor, and more than half of whom were buried far less ceremoniously than he after serving as test subjects for AIDS research in an Alamogordo chimp research lab.

Alamogordo-adjacent: the Trinity Site, where the Manhattan Project detonated the world's first atomic bomb in 1945, vaporizing completely the iron tower that held it—the birth of humanity's first justified fears of apocalypse, sketching the outlines of the China Syndrome and other nightmare scenarios. Coming attractions for a thousand possible manifestations of the Demiurge's wrath.

Also nearby: Roswell, New Mexico, where some residents claim another kind of explosion and covert burial took place in 1949, when *something* fell screaming from the sky. The army says it was a weather balloon. Some experts believe it was a prototype fighter jet flown by Japanese test pilots. The popular imagination has lit upon an altogether more exotic craft and occupants—coming to take someone away, perhaps, when a bug in their system lead to a Great Crash that dashed the unarticulated hopes of some desert dreamer without his even knowing it. In an elegant parallel, Robert H. Goddard's pioneering rocket lab was also in Roswell. There, a process was set in motion that might someday allow us to provide entities in a galaxy far, far away with a Roswell crash of their own. Maybe someday we will do the saving. Become a place to escape to instead of from.

In a one-hundred-mile strip of New Mexican desert, the smashed and scorched hidden heart of the modern era lies interred beneath the sands, sands through which the ghost of Oppenheimer's Destroyer of Worlds will still speak its indecipherable click language, given a strong enough Geiger tongue. Like all history, this heart is comprised of corpses: corpses of game cartridges, thousands of microworlds destroyed, their plastic exoskeletons crushed beneath one more parking lot; corpses of pilots, perhaps, of one alien extraction or another; corpses of rockets, corpses of bombs; and the corpse of Ham, the faithful son of Uncle Sam, named after Ham the son of Noah, that antediluvian geek, that original Curious George who had to look and had to know the naked truth about his father, no matter what cataclysms it would bring upon him.

It is tempting to call it a shadow history—but that would be a misnomer. Though burned out and buried, these things are no mere shades. They are the shapes that cast the shadows, and we are the shadows they cast. They are the ghosts more real than the haunted, and they are waiting for us, inviting us to dig the tunnels that will connect them, to create the network that binds them all together with secret knots, so that every action and every event ripples, echoes and reflects upon every other. Apocalypse and redemption, above and below, the Great Crash and the Great Escape, all waiting for us on the other side of the sands.

grave exchange

● ● ● ● ● ● ● ● ● ● ● ● ● ● ● ● ● ● ● ●

"Tetsu knows about Lucky Wander Boy," Clio said. "He's been to Stage Three."

Tetsu gazed out across the desert, where so much was hidden, and did not respond to her assertion.

"You have," I said.

Deliberately, he nodded. My pulse rose, but I made sure to maintain a critical distance.

"When, and how?"

It took me a moment to adjust to the odd formality of his speech. It was as though he was reciting a prewritten statement from memory:

"I was born in Japan, and grew up in Kyoto until my family moved to Santa Clara, California, for my father's work in 1984, when I was sixteen. As a boy in Kyoto, I lived on the outskirts of the Gion district, near the banks of the Kamo-gawa River. I say 'river' only for your edification—in Japanese, 'gawa' means 'river,' making the phrase 'Kamo-gawa River' redundant. Gion was home to Kyoto's geisha houses and many beautiful old buildings, but after the war, more modern architecture and entertainments were woven into the area. The Kujaku Densha *geemusentaa* or video arcade was one of these, only three blocks from our apartment, across the river on the Kiyamachi-dori amidst the bars and vomiting youths. I spent much of my boyhood there, starting from the age of eight. At that time, most of its games were electromechanical in nature, but the true video games were not long in coming. I was one of the first ten people to play one of the first ten Space Invaders machines. It took the fourth Donkey Kong machine only ten minutes to reach Kujaku Densha from the Nintendo Corporation, located across from the Heian-jingu shrine a mile and a half away. It probably took Araki Itachi about twice that long to walk from her old office at Nintendo to her new office at Uzumaki, around the corner from Kujaku Densha, after she quit, or was fired. At different times, she told different stories."

"You knew her?" I asked.

"Yes. She hired me herself as a playtester for Lucky Wander Boy when I was only twelve. She walked into Kujaku Densha, saw me playing Yosaku To Donbee, my intensity and focus impressed her and she offered me a job on the spot. She told me there were three of us playtesters, but I only met one other. During the eight months that I worked for her, I probably played Lucky Wander Boy more than anyone before or since. When school got in the way of my pretesting schedule, I did not go to school, and only certain family connections saved me from being expelled. It was during this time at Uzumaki that I reached the third stage of Lucky Wander Boy, while sitting on a red, white and blue bar stool Itachi had stolen from an American-themed bar down the street."

Although I tried not to show it, I believed him. The precision of his enunciation and diction could well have been a result of prolonged contact with Araki Itachi, whose speech patterns were similar. She might also have conferred upon him this compelling, hermetic intensity, the way a saint might grant a person grace. My hunger for any and all Itachi information and apocrypha was so strong, it sent out waves of need even Clio picked up on.

"What was she like?" she asked.

"She was a handsome woman," he said, "but she would not always talk to you. She had a system, I believe, some complex and personal form of divination not unlike the traditional *onmyoudou* system, which determined whom she would talk to on any given day. More than once I caught a glimpse of my name on some inscrutable chart or other, next to the names of the other testers. At other times she would speak only through cryptic messages folded into tiny origami sculptures, or scrawled in dust, or transmitted in some other, similarly arcane manner. The only name that did not appear on any of her talk charts was that of Vice President Marufuku—"

"I met him! We met him!" My enthusiasm was becoming difficult to contain.

"She would talk to Marufuku on all days. My theory is that his disorder exempted him from her system."

"Disorder."

"He suffered from a strange form of aphasia. Although he could read and understand speech perfectly well, he could not actually speak himself. His own utterances were complete nonsense."

"What do you mean?"

"I mean nothing, nonsense, crazy collections of random Japanese phonemes. Often bits of words would emerge, or two or three words would be jumbled together, but there was no syntax, or none anyone could puzzle out, and nothing could be made of his statements as a whole. He was rumored to be former Yakuza. I was relatively bold for a twelve-year-old, but I never asked him. There would have been little point."

Another connection fused in my mind between Marufuku's missing finger, and a half-remembered piece of Yakuza lore concerning their standard punishment for deeds left undone. But my eagerness to hear what Tetsu had to tell me—the real reason we had come all this way—made it difficult to dwell on this for long.

"And so you made it to the third stage," I said.

Tetsu nodded.

"What was there? What did you see?"

Tetsu smiled for the first time since we'd met him, but just barely. "My experience on Stage Three was hard won, and much of its value lies in its uniqueness. By telling you about it, I run the risk that you will claim my experience for your own, thereby chipping away at this uniqueness and diminishing the value of my experience. You may promise not to do this, but this promise means very little to me, as I do not know you from—pardon me— Adam. For one who values the uniqueness of his own experience as I do, this risk would be considerable, wouldn't you say? You would not expect me to take it for nothing."

Thinking I got the point, I reached into my pocket and took out my wallet, but he touched my hand, stopping me.

"I am not a whore. Ms. Camp has led me to believe that you have something else for me, something more in keeping with an even exchange of ideas. In another pocket, perhaps?"

From my back pocket, where Clio had put it before we left L.A., I removed the sheet of Japanese writing that Marufuku had handed me at Portal.

"This for the truth about Stage Three?"

Tetsu nodded.

"The *truth*?"

"Mr. Pennyman . . . though I live here now, I was socialized in a place where codes of honor are taken quite seriously."

I unfolded the paper and handed it to him. Poker-faced, he read it in about twenty seconds, the whole thing, his index finger flipping down and up the page in a blur.

Then he told me about his ascension to Stage III.

Through the daze that followed, I had the acuity to ask him about Marufuku's sheet.

"It is information pertaining to S.L.S., Ms. Itachi's new business venture."

"What's the nature of this venture? What kind of games are they working on? Is it—are they taking it even farther? Is it possible?"

Tetsu held out his hands and smiled again. His eyebrows lifted into matching forty-five-degree angles; I impertinently noticed their bushiness. "As one who values the uniqueness of experience, Mr. Pennyman, I can hardly be expected to leave this transaction with fewer secrets than I came in with. It has been a pleasure."

He bowed indifferently to both of us and walked off toward his car.

"You made a copy of it, right?" Clio asked as Tetsu got into his Nissan.

I could think of no answer to her question I wanted to hear myself say.

We watched the black car turn into a flyspeck against the beige, and out of the corner of my eye I surreptitiously watched Clio watching the car. Everything I had just heard, everything I had just been given, I had received through her efforts, through her dedication to me. My new knowledge of Stage III and the color picture of Araki Itachi served as two tent posts to which I could lash myself and stand tall against whatever lay in store for me, and I owed them both to Clio. As predicted, the ties between us had begun to tangle into something I might call love—but these things she had given me, they were planted in the ground between us, and I knew they would grow, perhaps into something so big and solid that neither of us could reach around it to touch the other. Her gifts could well tear us apart. Pulling her to me, I squeezed her tightly, feeling her thin ribs pushing against mine, and her smile bled so much happiness I had to staunch the flow with a kiss, and I felt that our future together was more uncertain than ever.

[Compiled in accordance with the testimony of Tetsu Bush (né Bushi), whose claims of having been a Lucky Wander Boy playtester at the Uzumaki Corporation appear to be well founded.]

Of all the items one can acquire in Stage II of Lucky Wander Boy, the mirror is the most crucial. In itself, the mirror does nothing. There are configurations of acquisition, however—patterns of object retrieval—that will activate the mirror, and allow it to realize its true function. Or such is one conjecture, as the precise nature of this object configuration is not known. It must exist, however; of all things, the transition from Stage II to Stage III cannot be granted by the grace of random number generators, whatever other aspects of the game they determine. We cannot be expected to be delivered from the Stage II desert by faith alone. Our choices must play a part in our crossing over.

When the player achieves the proper configuration (or one of the proper configurations) by accident or design, the mirror's potential is unlocked. Floating from Lucky's pocket of its own accord, it hangs in the space before him as if dangling from an invisible stick by an invisible thread. As Lucky runs forward to grab it again, the mirror maintains its distance.

But then the desert rises up on either side of him in towering waves of sand, like the Red Sea around Moses. When Lucky stops, they stop; if he turns around, they begin to recede; but as long as he continues moving forward, the waves grow. Curving inward, they eventually meet over his head, forming a tunnel of sand that should cave in just as the walls of water in the Red Sea should have fallen, but it does not.

The mirror outpaces Lucky, firing down the tunnel like a bullet, leaving a shimmering trail. If Lucky keeps running for about twenty seconds—and at this point, which Lucky would not?—a blue-green glow appears at the end of the tunnel like a reflection of light off the waters of an oasis, and the glow grows larger as Lucky gets closer.

There is no oasis. There is only Lucky's pocket mirror, grown to fill the mouth of the passageway. When Lucky nears this mirror, he sees a reflection of the tunnel behind him, but unlike the rest of the game, the reflection is rendered in crisp vector graphics,[1] like an intricate laser light show version of the tunnel and himself.

For the whole of Stage II, you have been looking at the back of Lucky's head, or at best the hint of his cheekbone as he turns his head. It has been maddening at times, but over the course of hours and days you have gotten used to it, and the itch to see his face has faded, flaring up only now and then. When Lucky steps right up to the mirror, however, you get to see him. You get to look upon his face.

It is your face.

Whoever you are, in the material world, playing the game. Your face is in Lucky's mirror, broken down into innumerable vector-sketched polygons.

Then you step through the mirror, into Stage III. The vector world, with its complex filigrees of sharp colored lines, open and airy, like the inside of a Gothic cathedral or a giant Mother Ship. You see the sound of thousands of singing equations. Unlike in Stage II, you cannot see the back of your head any longer, just as you cannot see it right now. You are out of the picture because *you are in the picture*. Total immersion.

What is inside the mirror?

Tetsu Bush found the beach at Okinawa in summertime, where his mother and father used to take him once a year until he was seven, the ocean ebbing and flowing in waves of blue and green topographical-map lines. Six hundred and fifty miles from Okinawa, yet only ten steps away, was the Maruyama-koen Park in Kyoto in springtime, where the cherry

---

[1] Adapted from *The Free On-Line Dictionary of Computing*:
Vector Graphics: The representation of separate shapes such as lines and polygons, and groups of such objects, as opposed to images composed of arrays of pixels arranged in rows and columns ("raster graphics"). The advantage of vector graphics ("drawing") programs over bitmap ("paint") editors is that multiple overlapping elements can be manipulated independently without using different layers for each one. It is also easier to render an object at different sizes and to transform it in other ways.

blossoms bloomed in pink and white lines as delicate as a *sumi-e* ink painting. His mother, father and grandfather were there, in both places simultaneously, the only people whose faces he could see. In the park, his mother had a pink rice cake for him, wrapped in leaves from a cherry tree.

According to Mr. Bush, the other Lucky Wander Boy playtester who reached Stage III saw something completely different. He would not tell me what. He did not feel he had the right.

Moreover: Once you reach Stage III and it gives you those things, places, people you want the most, you are free to stay for as long as you need to. Not in the same way you are free to walk around Stage II—until it gets dark, until the arcade owner kicks you out, until you've had enough of bland beige nothingness and throw yourself into a bottomless chasm. In Stage III, you are not only given things, but time—or rather, you are taken out of time, to the place the Egyptians thought their mummies' *kas* went, a place that is only place and nothing else, unchanging. When asked whether he felt Lucky Wander Boy truly had this effect on the world at large, or merely affected some psychotropic manipulation of his own consciousness,[2] Mr. Bush declined to speculate, outside of commenting that he might be able to make a more definite pronouncement had he been wearing a wristwatch at the time. He estimated his total (subjective) time spent on Stage III at 30 minutes. When asked why he would walk away from the machine after so short a time, he said that he as-

---

[2]There is some evidence to suggest the latter. Vector graphics present apparently solid shapes that are really a ceaseless frenzy of motion, lines drawn and redrawn over and over again many times a second, like laser light shows. In addition to providing a degree of fascination to the laser light show experience over and above what might be expected given the smoking of massive amounts of weed, this stroboscopic motion has been known to trigger epileptic fits. Perhaps—no allegations, but perhaps—this strobe effect also played a part in the unfortunate death of eighteen-year-old David Migdal in Friar Tuck's Game Room in Calumet City, Illinois, on April 3, 1982. After putting his initials on the vector game Tempest's high score list two times in a row, Mr. Migdal suffered a massive seizure as he put a third quarter in the slot, and had expired from a brain aneurysm by the time paramedics arrived (Richard Bradley, "Video-Game-Related Death In Suburbs" in *Chicago Tribune*, April 4, 1982, p. 4.). If this were the case, it would prove that vector graphics have the power to exert a direct influence on the back brain, a power that could be put to hypnotic use by someone with the proper skills. Interestingly, Calumet City is only forty-five short miles from the Bennigans Restaurant where my own videogame dreams died like Mr. Migdal.

sumed he'd hit upon the correct sequence of object acquisition, loss and reacquisition, and could therefore reach Stage III whenever he wished. In later attempts, he found to his dismay that he'd either misremembered that sequence or misunderstood the whole mechanism. Whichever the case, he never reached Stage III again, and by the time his family moved to Santa Clara, there was not a Lucky Wander Boy machine to be found in any public place in the entire United States.

weasels

● ●

The chickens of rumor were coming home to roost. Back at Portal after only a Monday's absence, I found that the landscape had changed considerably. Linda had been fired, for one; I arrived to find her packing up her stuff. She had voiced her opinion that the deadline on a certain assignment was "bullshit" within earshot of Krickstein, and lost her job immediately. We were all in a limbo line, and the bar was being lowered. When Linda turned to give us the good-bye look, cigarette in her mouth and a box of belongings cradled in her arms, her smile suggested she had been "let go"— not as in "kicked out," but as in "released from involuntary confinement."

She was not the only one. Over the weekend, Tamar had been fired and replaced.

Tamar, tireless partisan for the management class, hard-ass taskmaster who made my experience in steerage far more labor-intensive than it would have been otherwise: gone. When Clio told me, she squeezed my shoulder in an expression of silent exultation, since more than once I'd expressed the fear that the Israeli would be the catalyst of my own dismissal, but I could not feel joy at Tamar's misfortune—it was irrefutable evidence that these firings were not free-floating instances of conflicting personalities as they might seem in Shay's and Linda's cases, but instead the protruding tip of some larger-scale new order. This could not bode well for me, and I was the linchpin in the fate of Lucky Wander Boy, the only thing that held it together and held it aloft in the fierce storm of reptile regression that blew into Portal each morning with Krickstein's arrival.

Tamar's replacement fed the "new order" theory. At twenty-five years of age, Alan Freint had already acquired a flutter-lipped sigh as an unthinking mannerism, betraying the broken resignation of a draft horse. Looking like he might suffer from a mild form of progeria, Alan could be construed as a consolidation attempt on Krickstein's part, for he was an Alan-of-all-trades—in addition to human resource management and producing web content, he also had a background in HTML and Java-script programming. And he did "a bit of writing on the side."

"So, I guess one thing I'll probably have you guys do is fill out daily shift reports," Alan told us after introducing himself. "Nothing fancy, just a daily breakdown of the projects you worked on over the course of the day, and how many hours you spent on each. Kurt and Tom are going to be reassessing the direction of the site in the next week or so. You know, stressing accountability, determining the viability of our web shows, that kind of thing."

Soon thereafter, Alan left to help Kurt prepare for the big D,S&A meeting about *Eviscerator III*. Although she had less to worry about than anyone, Clio exaggerated her disappointment with this new shift-report regulation out of solidarity for my predicament. She was a good person, a caring person. I would have liked very much for our weekend in the desert to mean the same to me as it did to her, to believe (as I knew she did) that it was the beginning of something rather than its likely end. At that time, rather than wrestling with these issues, or the concept of the daily shift report and its implications for someone who averaged just over an hour of work a day, I applied myself to Eviscerator for the better part of two hours. An hour and three-quarters into my game, Clio came to check up on me, to see if I was all right.

"Ted, get over here!" she said. "Pennyman's about to reach the Big Boss!"

Ted the artist lumbered over in time to see my Spectral Samurai put the finishing touches on Chedaki, Ibn Alhrazed's alien capo.

Using an involved button-and-joystick combination that had been no more than an Internet rumor, I sheathed my sword, thrust out with both taloned hands, and pulled out both of Chedaki's three-chambered hearts.

The Eviscerator earth began to shake. Twin replicas of the Great Pyramid of Khufu rose from the ground, and numerous UFOs came to circle around them. Although I had studied the game's mechanics and strategies for many, many hours, I had remained oddly detached from its backstory, and this was the first time I'd recognized Eviscerator's ill-conceived allusions to Ancient Astronaut theories. Was I meant to suspect that Chedaki's insectoid alien race had played a part in the construction of the pyramids, or even the very inception of life on Earth, as suggested by fringe-of-the-fringe Alien Origins enthusiasts and the movie *Quatermass and the Pit*? This led me directly to the thoughts of alien salvation and apocalypse I'd had in the New Mexican desert, which strongly resembled the Eviscerator desert, which strongly resembled the Lucky Wander Boy desert, which my Close Encounter with Tetsu Bush in the New Mexican desert had taught me how to escape. All connected, related, waiting to be unified into a greater whole. This line of inquiry was cut short as the Big Boss arrived, spit up by the sands.

Ibn Alhrazed wore an Arab kaffiyeh and a pharaonic false beard, shimmering robes and wraparound sunglasses, and wasted no time in launching an initial fusillade of deadly fireballs at me, for which my research had prepared me. Clio gasped with excitement. Ted said, "Fuckin' A."

Then Krickstein's voice began to reverberate throughout the Plant.

"We've got a motto here that encapsulates the philosophy of Portal. 'Don't ask why—fun is fun!'"

Pharaohs lurked on either side of the screen. Clio, my gaming muse, ran for cover, and Ted disappeared as well, but I did not leave the game. To do so would have been to call attention to my loafing and admit guilt, and besides, why was it there if we weren't supposed to play it? An employee playing the Eviscerator machine was a part of the calculated casualness and premeditated unpredictability central to the Portal ethos. My concentration had been shattered, however. When Ibn Alhrazed delivered his fabled Finger Snap, I was unprepared to counter, and I blew up very suddenly and anticlimactically, splattering the Big Boss with blood, innards and strips of skin. He washed his hands of me in a simulated Nile. My game was over—an evil omen? No. Wars were neither won nor lost in their first major battle. I was confident that with diligence and work, Ibn Alhrazed would go down.

Returning to my desk, I pulled up a month-old business-related e-mail and pretended to contemplate its contents as I watched Krickstein lead the D,S&A venture capital team around the Plant with the Eviscerator battle-axe slung nonchalantly over his shoulder. I recognized the VC VP who'd been to Portal before, and studied him as he sneaked occasional glances at Krickstein's real fake weapon, clearly wanting to hold it himself, and ashamed of this desire. I had never seen any of the other three men, but the one with the pressed khaki pants who walked in step with Kurt while the others trailed behind had to be Chad, the D,S&A CEO the VC VP had mentioned in conversation with Lyme. He was easily ten years Kurt's junior. He looked to be a few years older than I was. His neatly trimmed beard was identical to mine.

"We're about all the stuff we all loved as kids, and we still love here: guns, chicks, cars, explosions—"

"Right on!" said Chad. "You know, I consider myself an explosion connoisseur of sorts. Nothing like you guys, I'm sure. But I'm a fan."

"Then let me tell you something—you have bet on the right horse. The day after tomorrow, I am flying to Japan—"

"Yeah," Chad said, "I was going to ask about the monastery thing. Are we gonna blow that baby? It's a done deal?"

"All but," Kurt said, twirling the battle-axe.

"'Cause I am *so* gung-ho on the monastery thing. It is *the* payoff to the third act. Totally necessary, dramatically."

I watched the shiny top of Krickstein's head as he walked the men along the far aisle between the tweed cubicle dividers. His voice grew indistinct down by *Eviscerator III*'s digital effects section, where the behavior of a virtual bullet as it penetrated a virtual chest was simulated for Chad's benefit. Ted had shown me this simulation before—with the push of a button, all blood could be erased from the scene, for MPAA approval. Kurt set the battle-axe down by the back door and shook out his arms as he might after a set on a Cybex machine. When he herded the men back in my direction, I picked up the sales pitch again.

"We're edgy, we're very good at what we do, and we're devoted to maximum exposure and penetration. Have a look at this—"

Lagging behind, Chad interrupted Kurt with a call to the rest of his party to check out the Alien Bimbo Range online gamelet, in which the participant had one second to identify and shoot the bikini-clad girl whose extra eye, extra finger or other anomaly exposed her as a malevolent alien. In anticipation of the D,S&A meeting, Kurt had Clio hastily retrofit the Bimbo Range into an Eviscerator ad last week, turning the "malevolent aliens" into "malevolent alien cohorts of Ibn Alhrazed" and making minor graphic changes to promote the illusion that no expense was being spared in the promotion of *Eviscerator III*, giving the film the flavor of a fait accompli. The D,S&A team gathered around Chad to appreciate the game while Chad stroked his beard and chuckled. Before I could stop myself, I stroked my own beard in sympathy. Kurt was pleased to see them responding to it, but Chad had disoriented him with his blithe interruption, a thing Kurt did not brook in Portal's day-to-day operation. He came over to my desk with the stagger of a man who'd just been woken up from a nap.

"Outta the way," Kurt said. *Snap snap snap.* "I need this computer."

I stepped away from the desk, away from *my* desk, as Kurt called up the *Eviscerator III* splash page Shay had lost his job over, and soon had the D,S&A team hovering around the desk looking at it. Chad sat in my chair.

"We are very Do It Yourself here, because we want It done

right, because we are *not* Hollywood. Whatever you know or think you know about Hollywood, flush it all down the toilet. It doesn't apply here. Anytime you're dealing with Hollywood, there's some middleman, some *weasel* who doesn't add value and takes as much credit as he can grab and sends your costs soaring through the fucking roof, pardon the French. If we find a weasel in this company, we make him into a fur coat, okay?"

He wasn't kidding. The weasel herd was being culled. I retreated to the kitchen and waited there. I thought of myself as a refugee from my own desk, which got me to thinking about Vato Hat and the other laborers outside. I pictured them wandering through the Chihuahuan desert, and crossing the Rio Grande to a place where things could be better, where they could earn a living. Then, in my mind, Vato Hat and his *vatos* were no longer in the Mexican desert, but wandering through Lucky Wander Boy's Stage II desert. With the right knowledge—the knowledge only I could give them—they could cross over to the place of their dreams, a place without difficult choices. They would not have to leave their families behind, if they had them. If they did not have them but wanted them, the right family would be waiting for them there. I had acquired this knowledge at the cost of potentially greater knowledge: the contents of the S.L.S. information sheet were lost to me. What if it contained a revelation that supplanted even Tetsu Bush's Lucky Wander Boy testament?

When Krickstein and the VCs moved on, I returned to my desk. While trying to translate the S.L.S. sheet myself, I had bookmarked Taro's Japanese ←→ English Dictionary Server on my browser. I called it up now, and fed it the only Lucky Wander Boy–related words I had left :

Uzumaki: whirlpool; eddy; spiral
And:
Araki: logs in bark; rough wood
And:
Itachi: weasel; skunk; mink; ermine
Weasel.

From the corridor connecting the Plant to the front offices, I watched Krickstein show the investors out.

"So you'll call us the minute you get back from Kyoto," Chad said. Krickstein said he would. Handshakes all around. D,S&A left.

Krickstein bounced back into the waiting area with a half grin that indicated no emotion, being a permanent facial feature.

"So how do you think it went?" Lyme asked.

"Great! Great. We need the monastery thing."

Kurt dropped down onto the couch and called Curly over. He began to tap the mutt on the muzzle with random lefts and rights, taunting him, "Come on . . . fight back . . . fight back . . . come on, don't be a pussy, fight back. . . ." The taps grew harder, and soon his hands closed into fists, and he kept on hitting, he kept on punching the dog in the mouth, "Fight back . . . fight back. . . ." Curly growled and raised a quivering upper lip but he would not fight back and he would not run away. He just stood there and took it.

Clio wanted to come home with me at the end of the day, but I told her I had work to do.

"What kind of work? You haven't said a word to me since you told me you weren't eating lunch today." She poked me weakly, tentatively. "Something's wrong. Tell me what, I'll fix it. Nobody does it better, remember?"

I promised her that nothing was wrong, and gave her a few of my most recent *Catalogue* entries to pacify her. As I walked out the front door, I promised to call her later, but forgot all about it when I got home.

That night, while I was looking in the bathroom mirror and stroking my beard, Chad the explosion connoisseur from D,S&A came to mind and refused to leave, so I took my beard trimmer from its charge rack, pulled the adjustable guide comb off and shaved my chin clean, finishing the job with a safety razor. Then, with the aid of the Polish hand mirror, I did the rest of my head. It took a while, shaving all that thick hair with a beard trimmer, but I had nowhere special to go. When I was finished, I sat on the couch and examined my work in the hand mirror, rubbing my hands across my skull. The

feel of the remaining peach fuzz beneath my fingertips was a pleasant sensation, and I liked the new look. It was very ascetic. No hairline remained, receding or otherwise. Bits of hair fell like snow onto
the white couch with each stroke of my hand, but I did not mind.

I made some ramen noodles for dinner, ate them, and went directly to bed, where I lay watching the dark for a good while.

The night after I had narrowly failed to prevent my grandmother's death, I had done much the same, staring at the dancing
green numbers of my LED clock. On the border of sleep and waking, just before the dream-light washed out the dark of my bedroom, I heard my grandmother's voice, heard it not in my head but
in the room with me:

It's all right, Adam, she said. You did good.

This time, however, there was no LED clock, and I was not
asleep. I heard this voice with full waking ears. It told me it was
waiting for me, but I already knew.

CATALOGUE OF OBSOLETE ENTERTAINMENTS
GAME: EVISCERATOR SPECIAL EDITION
Format: Wish Fulfillment
Manufacturer: Adam Pennyman
Year: 2001
CPU: R.E.M.

In this game, by a curious nocturnal logic, I am at once myself and my enigmatic Moment of Decision, a dual persona that becomes triune by occupying the gilded, steroid-nightmare body of the Spectral Samurai. In a similar way, Kurt Krickstein is both himself and Ibn Alhrazed, but in this case Ibn Alhrazed is at a disadvantage, for he is forced to occupy Krickstein's unimpressively regular body. A war trumpet plays Lucky Wander Boy's opening fanfare, calling us to do battle. Even more exacting in its realism than the coin-op version, this game is coated in a thousand garish reds and maroons, as the Spectral Moment of Pennyman disembowels Ibn Krickstein again and again and again before the façade of the Mount Hiei monastery. In Eviscerator Special Edition, the monastery and its surrounding trees are located not on Mount Hiei, but in the Lucky Wander Boy Stage II desert, which shifts from beige to white to beige again, beating out a periodicity of torment for Ibn Krickstein. The manner of his disembowelment seems unremarkable in a general Eviscerator context, but bears a closer examination:

After slitting open Ibn Krickstein's belly with my sword, I pull out his intestines and nail them to a sixty-foot virgin cryptomeria tree that sprouts from the sand, driving a railroad spike into the wood with my taloned fist. Then, smacking him with the flat of my blade to move him along, I impel him to circle the tree, winding his guts around it until his body cavity is empty and he falls to the ground dead. I can say with certainty that this method of Evisceration is not in the Spectral Samurai's repertoire, and despite its surface similarity to seppuku, I know it to be a uniquely Viking form of homicide. That would seem to explain how it finds its way into Eviscerator Special Edition, for the Viking berserker Njal Njalson was always Shay's avatar of choice in our many games together, and I had been thinking about Shay that same day in conjunction with Linda's and Tamar's firings—

But to the best of my knowledge, I have never seen Njal Njalson kill anyone in this manner, either. This raises the question of *how* I know of the Viking penchant for disembowelment-by-tree. The answer begins to bring us closer to the hidden meaning of Eviscerator Special Edition:

More than four years ago, I got a job working as script researcher on a straight-to-video movie entitled *Viking!* Getting the job was easy; I sent them a resume, and they hired me straightaway. Once there, I was asked to read many of the thirteenth-century Icelandic Sagas and provide encapsulations for the producer and director, along with a compendium of the Sagas' numerous Schwartzeneggerian witticisms to aid the writer in his quest for verisimilitude. I enjoyed the reading, and my enthusiasm infected both the producer and director, who loved my inspired paraphrases of Egil's pithy and poetic wrath, Kjartan's fierce love for the unquestionably hot and blonde Gudrun, and *especially* my vivid descriptions of the disembowelment-by-tree to which the Vikings so relished subjecting their defeated enemies.

When giving my lengthy lunchtime presentations, however, I did not have in mind the Austrian former Mr. Olympia second-runner-up who was attached to play the lead, nor the petite Swedish soft-porn actress he'd insisted on for his female costar, nor the black lava moonscapes in the photos the director and producer had taken during their three-day stoned location scout outside Reykjavik. My point of focus, the image from which I drew my power, was a 16-x-16-pixel videogame sprite from the Intellivision game Ice Trek: the horn-helmeted Nordic Hero, tearing across a tundra of a light blue that, though one of only sixteen colors the Intellivision could generate, was perfectly suited to the representation of ice, facing numerous challenges and hardships until he arrived at the evil king's Ice Palace and melted it, making it into the evil king's tomb.[1]

After my *Viking!* bosses found out that, contrary to my resume, I had not attended Harvard and had been the Head Researcher on neither *Orlando* nor *Erik the Viking*, they fired me immediately, but

---

[1] Tomb → pyramid → pharaoh → Krickstein.

while under the protection of the Nordic Hero, I had held a real producer and a real director under my sway. My power over them had
transported me to their level; during my briefings, there was no need
to dodge my bosses, I felt no desire to run for the safe haven of my
cubicle. I was not just swimming with the crocodiles—I was passing
for one.

The Frogger allusions are intentional, for the Frogger metaphor
brings it all into focus. In Frogger's river there are weasels[2]—but not
Kurt Krickstein's weasels, not the persistent nuisances and bottom-line
disappointments that I was by vocation and Itachi by name, those hap-
less creatures destined to be skinned and made into fur coats. In Frogger, the weasels are aggressors, right up there with the crocodiles. They
are in charge, as I was in Eviscerator, which for all my preference for
more peaceful games was the only one I'd ever been the best at. That
was the kind of weasel to be. Through the iron laws of correspon-
dence and association, the Nordic Hero's Viking violence had manifested itself in Eviscerator Special Edition to let me know that the
Spectral Moment of Pennyman had arrived on the dream threshold.
He was waiting to be made flesh, to become an avatar in the original
sense of a deity incarnate, descended to earth. The time had come to
bend the aggressor's power back upon itself and use it against him in
an act of symbolic jujitsu. To beat the BYYEWwww once and for all.

I was the weasel.

---

[2]Or otters. They're both mustelids. Close enough.

part iii

BOY

He is only a shadow, occupying a hazy space somewhere between memory and lived life, and this makes it possible to contemplate his end with a measure of detachment.

—Dafei Ji, *Leng Tch'e*

preparation

● ● ● ● ● ● ● ● ● ● ● ● ● ● ● ● ● ● ● ●

When I returned to the Plant the following morning, the Eviscerator machine was gone.

"They came for it just after you left yesterday," Ted said somberly. "Kurt's swapping it out for the new Eviscerator: Bloodgame."

Clio rubbed my clean-shaved head in consolation, and I caught her eyeing my naked scalp with worry, but there was no need. The moment I registered the empty space where the Eviscerator machine used to be, I moved beyond it. I think she thought I was in a state of denial. She was wrong. I was definitely in a state, but not that one. The Eviscerator machine had served its function, and with its duties toward me discharged, it could only become my Golden Calf, a tempting false idol in the Portal wasteland. I was glad to see it go.

She wanted to join me for lunch, but I told her I had some thinking to do, and would prefer to be alone.

"Oh," she said. "Well . . . I wanted to talk to you about these C.O.E. entries."

I told her we could do it some other time.

"I just think it's a shame to let it go in the wrong direction like this. This 'supplementary essay,' 'On Geeks'? It's cute and everything, but isn't it out of place in the C.O.E.? Didn't you tell me the C.O.E. was supposed to be about the games themselves? And the 'China Syndrome' entry . . . supposedly that one's about a specific game, only it doesn't talk very much about China Syndrome at all. I don't understand where you're going with all the stuff about nuclear testing, and Roswell, and the space chimp. It feels like wheel spinning, it makes you sound—a little—I don't know, are you sure you're all right?"

It made me sad that my partner and coconspirator who once Got It so powerfully had allowed It to slide beyond her ken, but at the pace things were moving, with connections branching out to form newer connections at an exponential rate, even the staunchest Fellow Wanderer could get left behind. I promised her we would talk about it later, and left by the back door. The Eviscerator battle-axe was still propped against the wall next to the door, where Kurt had left it.

During my lunch break, on my way to the taqueria, I bought a pair of work gloves at the Salvation Army store, and a handful of old screwdrivers. I saw Vato Hat and nodded, and he smiled at me. We were on good terms.

When I returned from lunch with the gloves in my pocket and the screwdrivers in my bag, I found Lyme waiting for me in the front waiting area.

"Heyyy, Travis Bickle. Come meet Hillary Opeth."

Hillary Opeth was the new VP of Development. When she'd come in for her interview the week before, word had spread around the Plant that she had been the blow-job queen of Fox Family Television, her last place of employment. She wore a long black sweater-jacket with black leather pants. When she bent over to put down her purse, I got a glimpse of her necklace: a leather thong dangling an ankh medallion. An *Egyptian* ankh. It was coming to pass. Signs were snowballing.

"Hillary's just come on board to whip all you creative types into shape," Lyme said. He would not be getting what he was hoping to get from Hillary Opeth, that much was obvious from the distaste with which she accepted his compliment, her smile flickering like a fake fireplace light on her unsuitably thin lips.

"I've heard a lot about you," I said with uncharacteristic boldness.

"I've been reading over your copy for the various sites," she said. "I don't think it's quite there. *We* may know all the fifty-point words, but we can't assume our audience does. We have to be sure this stuff is smart, but not too intelligent. We'll talk soon."

I ran an irony check and came up empty. Then, off an over-obvious head signal from Lyme, she took her leave, shutting the door behind her.

"Adam, buddy . . . we've got two things to talk about."

He flipped open his desk drawer with two fingers while kicking his feet up on a chair, a move he'd obviously seen in a movie somewhere. On any other day, his total failure to achieve the desired effect would have made me uncomfortable. He pulled out my Jim Beam flask and my Shitheap folder, and set them both on his desk.

"Why were you in my desk drawer?" I asked. My tranquility perturbed him. He made a No Foul gesture.

"I wasn't snooping, I was only looking for your copy of the *Lucky Wander Boy* script. Kurt wanted me to—collect them all. If you'll read your contract, you'll see that *this* is not allowed, but nobody has to know about it, this time. Nuff said on that." He tossed me the flask. "As for this stuff. . . ."

He flipped through the Shitheap. The inevitable return of the repressed.

"Can I assume this is all stuff you've finished?"

"Yes," I said, craftily literal.

"Yeah, well, before I assume that, I'm going to have Alan check on it all. If you happen to remember anything in here you may have forgotten to do, something that may have skipped your mind . . . I can give you a few days' grace period, say three or four. You've been here a while, and I like you. After that, though, I'd have to tell Kurt."

I nodded.

Later in the day, Kurt came through the Plant like a whirlwind.

"Why don't I hear typing? Why is everybody talking! Work, everybody get to work! No more weaseling around around here . . . no more weasels. . . ."

And he was gone as quickly as he'd come.

Once again, Clio wanted to come home with me. She was more insistent this time, but so was I. I told her I had work to do, work that required solitude. She asked if there was someone else. I told her it wasn't like that at all, though in a way of course it was.

"I'll talk to you tomorrow, then?"

I nodded.

She hung around for an extra half hour, waiting for me to reconsider, but I stayed put, and eventually she left without me.

As I waited for more people to leave, it occurred to me that in the battle between self-effacing love and the mindlessness that made meaningful love impossible, battle lines sometimes grew hazy. Situations arose where the champion of the former had to appropriate the techniques of the latter. This thought seemed worth saving, so I typed it up and saved it in a file labeled Samurai! In the periphery of my vision, I saw Lyme watching me type, self-satisfied, thinking I was working on the Shitheap material. I was sure to say good-bye to him when I left, and to Ted, the only one left in the Plant. Walking out the front, I cut back around and stole down the outside hallway into the kitchen, where I put on my Salvation Army gloves and waited for Ted to go to the bathroom. Then I sneaked out the back door, taking the Eviscerator axe with me. When I was through, the only evidence on the weapon would be fibers from the gloves and Krickstein's own fingerprints. They could make what they wanted of those.

When the moment—the Moment—came, I found that either the blade was duller than I'd thought, or that I needed to join a gym. Where I'd expected a clean cut, I got only a dull thud and a meek squeaking sound. It was not as pretty as I'd pictured, but I was not perturbed. I persevered. All told, it took me about ten swings to do the job.

dismantling of our hero

● ●

The sixth blow of the axe landed squarely at the point where the doorknob met the door with a metal-on-metal clank that was not nearly as resonant or exciting as the metal-on-metal clanks from the film for which the axe had been created. This loosened the doorknob considerably, but it took a few more blows to knock it off completely and allow me access to the Plant.

It was deserted, of course, at 11:30 P.M. There was no one to stop me from turning on all the lights. To my night-adjusted eyes they lit the Plant like a midnight sun, putting the sinister rows of flashing LEDs on the black IBM server monoliths in their place. All Portal's invidious Internet activity pulsed through their circuits, and their hard drives held reams of backup data like a halfwit's handprints in wet concrete—but they were vulnerable. I took in a chest-broadening lungful of the stagnant air, and punched in the code before the alarm went off. Lucky had been my on-screen avatar. Now I was his. What was my first responsibility as his earthly incarnation? I had a plan, one that found vindication in Itachi's original script note. I removed the note from my desk drawer—though I no longer thought of it as mine. I had shed that desk and the dead skin of the life that came with it.

And centralness of screwdriver, making for dismantling of Our Hero.

Many of the day laborers who frequented Portal's block spent the night in apartments or shelters, but a few actually lived on the street outside Portal. Vato Hat was one of those. I woke him gently, and his reflexive shielding of his head with his forearms in rabbit fear made me sad. As soon as he recognized me, however, the fear disappeared, replaced with relief, embarrassment and anger. My perceptions were heightened now, and even in the dark the edges of things sparkled with an exhilarating phosphorescence. In Spanish, I told him to wake up his friends and follow me. I had a great opportunity for him. He was a proud and bold man, and normally he would have told me what I could do with my midnight opportunities, but he sensed that, at that special moment, I was not merely the *peon* of a *puto*. Right there and then I was entirely self-possessed, as unwavering as an arrow shot into hell, and worth following for as long as I possessed such qualities. He woke seven other men quietly, judiciously handpicking them from their sleeping places up and down the street, and brought them all back to me.

"Vengamos," I said, motioning toward Portal with my hand. "Soy un amigo."

I led them into the Plant and gestured grandly to the wall of machinery, laughing at its helpless insect hum. I received a suspicious look from one of the men who thought that being in this building in the middle of the night with someone like me was not a good idea for someone like him, but it was all right, because Vato Hat was their alpha and he and I had an understanding. I smacked one of the IBM monoliths and said the words I'd prepared for the occasion, not trusting my high school Spanish to improvise something suitable:

"Las cosas del puto, sus computadoras . . . ¡son tuyos ahora! Si ustedes: quieren, pueden robarlos y vendarlos. Si no quieren . . . está bien. No hay ninguna problema."

It was all theirs if they wanted it. From my backpack, I removed the screwdrivers I'd bought that afternoon, to give them a better idea of what I had in mind.

There were none of the slow-blooming smiles of tacit camaraderie I'd seen when I preenacted the moment in my mind. They spoke gravely amongst themselves for about a minute, with Vato Hat doing most of the talking, and although his speech was far too rapid for me to pick out details, his body and face spoke the language of persuasion. Their discussion ended abruptly as they fell into laserlike coherence and looked to me for a final confirmation. I nodded, and they went to work.

It was the most impressive display of teamwork and productivity the Plant had ever witnessed, the workday Kurt only dreamed of seeing his workforce deliver. The man in the green vinyl windbreaker had a Swiss Army knife, and I distributed screwdrivers to Vato Hat and the rest, leaving me with one extra that I slid into my back pocket. Vato Hat also made improvised tools out of items from the surrounding cubicles: staple removers, paper clips, the thin edge of a Slinky. He began unscrewing and unplugging the server towers and laying them upside down in a neat line along the seam of the cement floor, and the others soon caught on and helped him. After all the blinking LEDs had been extinguished, the men gathered around Vato Hat as he demonstrated proper dissection techniques, unscrewing the black casing and deftly removing the motherboard, memory chips, hard drives and other fenceable parts from the first machine. His coworkers began to follow his example, and he then divided his time between breaking down machines himself, acting as a foreman doling out advice, and surveying the rest of the Plant for other exotic equipment like the Silicon Graphics workstations to mine for critical parts. He had things under control. I felt comfortable moving on to the front offices.

Gliding into the waiting area on a wave of nowness, I hurdled the couch and stomped across the huge glass coffee table. I knew it would not break, or that if it did, I would not get hurt. This was a peak experience. I had heard about them, but I could not remember the last time I'd had one without chemicals. But here it was, better late than never, better now than ever, there was no need to try and no need to think, only surf around the office and wait for an inspired action to suggest itself, and whatever that action was, it would be *right*. Beneath my foot, today's *Variety* announced the high-profile sale of Cheops Feinberg's spec script *Tag 'Em 'N' Bag*

'*Em* for $1 million–against–$2 million. I placekicked *Variety* through the communication gap into Lyme's office. Then I kicked the rest of the magazines off the table because it seemed like something I would enjoy doing, and I was right. It was. But it became clear to me I had not yet reached my destination.

Kurt's office. That was the place to be.

I entered without plans or intentions, a blank slate, open to whatever opportunities presented themselves. I might destroy everything, leaving no chair unturned, no equipment unsmashed, no paper untorn and no latex creature unmelted; I might just stick each of his pencils up my ass, one by one; or I might do nothing at all. It was thrilling, not knowing. I maintained the suspense for as long as I could stand it. Then I began a countdown, marching around the room in a rain dance cadence with increasingly louder stomps. In ten seconds, I'd know what to do. In nine seconds, I would see it through. In eight it would happen, in seven it's done, in six satisfaction, in five I'm the one, in four, in three, in two, in one—

I stopped in front of Kurt's desk and slapped my hand down on a manila envelope on which Alicia had written "KURT TRAVEL DOCS," which happened to contain a Japan Airlines ticket envelope and a passport. In the ticket envelope were two first-class, round-trip tickets to Osaka, Japan, leaving tomorrow morning at noon. One was for Kurt Krickstein.

The other was for Anya Budna.

Normally, this would have caused me distress and confusion. I would have thrown myself into a dark, depressive circle of compulsive wondering about how this could have come to pass, remembering (too late) Kurt's extended absence from the table at Warsaw Gardens while Anya was on duty, and her subsequent absences from our apartment, and her odd appearance at Portal behind the wheel of my car, and her aping of his standard pussy sales pitch in her farewell note to me. I would have most likely torn up the tickets in an impotent rage—but I did none of this. I had opened myself to options, and I felt the outer edges of my personal possibility wave tickling me like the little fingers on the lip of the "Great Wave" in the famous woodcut painting by Hokusai. Instead of obsessing, I kept moving, like a shark, like a true predator. I opened up Kurt's passport and studied his picture.

Then, in a small wall mirror with a silvered Art Nouveau frame, I studied my own face.

The revelation that, with a shaved head, I did not look entirely unlike near-bald Kurt Krickstein would normally have caused me *great* distress. I was younger than he, but as I've mentioned, his features were cartoonishly childlike. We had similar lips, the same eye color. With a few minutes of effort, I could twist my face into the same goofy smile as the one captured by Kurt's passport photographer. But I felt no distress. Oh no—

Because I could use his face. I could steal his empty soul. I, the Spectral Moment of Pennyman, could fight Ibn Krickstein using a little piece of him as my weapon.

I tore the LAX-Osaka flight coupon from the ticket packet, folded it, put it in Kurt's passport and put the passport in my pocket. I returned the rest of the ticket material to the Japan Airlines envelope, rubbed it down with my sleeve and placed it back on Kurt's desk just as I'd found it.

I was doing something! This was happening!

"I am doing something! This is happening! I AM DOING SOMETHING! THIS IS HAPPENING!"

I shouted as loud as I could as I tore through the Plant. I had not run as fast as I could for years. I'd forgotten how much I loved the sensation of running as fast as I could, even if I could not run very fast. One of the night laborers looked at me and laughed as he participated in *tikkun*, the healing of the vessels and straightening the girders of the crooked world, redeeming the old by dismantling the new. It did not matter that he was unaware of doing this, his good deeds would still be inscribed in the Book of Life, as would all of ours. We were taking away a usurper's ability to ruin, to cheapen. We were anonymous heroes—the only real kind. Still running through the maze of cubicle dividers, the circulatory system of Portal Entertainment and Development, I began to sing "hero" songs. I started with Pat Benetar's "I Need a Hero," and moved on to Tina Turner's "We Don't Need Another Hero," but that didn't seem right. We most certainly *did*. I didn't even think about thinking about that Bette Midler song, which would have ruined everything. And weren't there any "hero" songs sung by men? "Jukebox Hero" didn't fit, I didn't remember any of the words to "Pac-Man Hero," and besides, this was not a joke—

David Bowie! I'd wished I could swim like dolphins could swim, many times! And Bowie was into kabbalism before it was a thing to do. He would understand the subtle action the micro(cosm, computer) could exert over the macro. Running, jumping, singing, shouting:

> Though nothing will drive them away
> We can beat them just for one day
> We can be heroes
> Just for one day

One of the Mexican guys sang along for a bit. I knew he'd probably heard "Heroes" in a TV ad for Microsoft or FTD, I knew that, but I chose to believe he had the Bowie album instead. I ran and sang until I collapsed panting on the ground. Some of the laborers clapped.

"¡Qué bueno!"

By 1 A.M., Portal Entertainment and Development was dead, Eviscerated, the bulk of its innards neatly packaged in sound-muffling mats from the Portal green-screen set. The latex gargoyles had been unable to protect it. Its aura had been stripped away, and its constituent parts would be fenced and resold to unwitting consumers. I approached Vato Hat and patted him on the shoulder, complimenting him on his computer knowledge:

"Sabes mucho de las computadoras."

"Sí," he said, "los estudiaba en el Instituto Tecnológico Autónomo de México, a México D.F."

The men stole out the back door with the fruits of their labor. Vato Hat was the last out, and before he crossed the threshold into the night, he turned and shouted to me:

"¡Oye, muchacho!"

He threw me his "Vato" hat, and I caught it.

With great pride tempered by great humility, I put the hat on. The brim was damp, and the residue of his exertions mingled with my own.

I spent an hour returning the gutted black-box shells to their positions on the racks and putting everything else in its right place, like a harmless movie-set version of Portal. With a bottle of 409 and a rag from the cleaning supplies cabinet, I spent another hour wiping down everything the men had touched and cleaning my footprints off the coffee table. I put every magazine back, including the one I'd kicked into Lyme's office. It took me another half hour to find the fuse box and yank the fuses. Putting the gloves back on, I smashed the box with the battle-axe for good measure. Then I smashed the alarm keypad in the same fashion, making a silent apology to the alarm company representative who would catch the heat for an alarm system so easily vanquished. Until poor Alicia got someone to come and get the electricity going again, the whole deal would just look like an act of mindless vandalism.

Except they'd know someone had broken in, and if nothing was missing, they would get suspicious. So I took the only three Mac computers in the Plant and threw them in a Dumpster down the street, and did the same with the Eviscerator axe, and the pants Bruce Willis wore in *Die Hard*, which hung encased in Plexiglas on the waiting room wall. I'd never understood what they were doing there, but I thought it was the kind of thing a petty thief would take.

I went straight home, across the 10 overpass to my apartment, and allowed myself three hours of sleep until the sun came up, at which time I began to pack a carry-on.

monster of selfishness II

● ●

She did not even need to say it, it was written in the lines of hurt and reproach on her forehead as she turned to look at me one last time before leaving—but she did say it, quietly, with quivering lips:

"You're a selfish monster, you know that?"

I wanted to explain to her that I was not, I wanted to make her see. When she ran down the stairs and out the door, I ran after her.

How Clio came to be at my house at 9:30 A.M. the morning of my departure:

Given the state of things at Portal Entertainment, no one noticed my absence except Clio, who noticed it precisely because of the state of things at Portal Entertainment. I tended to gravitate toward women who were smarter than I was, and she'd figured out the connection. Someone was bound to figure it out, I guess, and I was grateful it was Clio.

Denials would serve no function, at this point. When she asked if I had anything to do with the situation over at Portal I claimed full responsibility, and could not resist intimating that they didn't know the half of it yet. I asked her if in the midst of Kurt's rants she'd heard him say anything about flight cancellations. She told me that he had indeed asked Alicia if she had taken out trip cancellation insurance, which of course she had, but that to the best of Clio's knowledge, Alicia had been given several dozen immediate tasks of higher priority than squaring things away with Japan Airlines. This was a lucky break for me—it meant I'd be spared having to make any sketchy explanations to airline personnel about why I was trying to fly on a cancelled ticket, and I've never been very good at that kind of maneuvering. I also asked Clio if Alicia had found Kurt's passport. She said that Alicia had muttered something to her about not being able to find it, but the barrage of shouted orders with which Kurt had hit her after discovering all the mindless vandalism and petty theft had shell-shocked poor Alicia to such a degree that she wasn't sure whether she'd put the passport in the manila envelope with the plane tickets in the first place, and she was therefore afraid to tell Kurt it was missing. In a rare moment of Sherlock Holmesian clarity immediately following my assault on the Portal palace, I had envisioned precisely that sequence of events.

When Clio saw the carry-on with built-in wheels lying nine-tenths packed on the floor, and my gunmetal attaché lying open on the couch and filled with papers, she assembled an even more accurate picture of what was truly going on. She presented her theory to me and I verified it, unwisely mentioning that I had only taken one of two available tickets to Japan.

How Clio tried to get me to change my mind in one way or another:

First, she employed an "It will never work" opening gambit, but I foiled this with my stern resolve. She then tried to convince me to let her come with me to Kyoto; amidst all the chaos, she could easily run back to Portal and steal the other ticket. I countered with the fact that she did not have a passport with a name that matched the name on the other ticket. She said she could buy a ticket at the airport. I told her it would cost at least two thousand dollars on such short notice, but she countered by producing a credit card with a four-thousand-dollar credit limit. I said she would still need a passport, and that she wouldn't be able to run to North Hollywood and back to the airport in time to catch the flight. Taking the offensive, she suggested I wait for her at the airport and book us both seats on the next available flight. I thought about this for a good twenty seconds, until it occurred to me that by the time the next flight rolled around, Kurt would have figured out what had really happened at Portal, cancelled the tickets and put out a call for my arrest. That was checkmate. Sadly, I told her it just wouldn't work. She tried to threaten turning me in to Kurt herself, but you're not allowed to strike out offensively after you've been checkmated, and besides, I knew she never would.

For the first time since I'd known her, she began to yell at me; I knew that from her perspective, limited though it may have been, I fully deserved it. She asked me (rhetorically) whether I was "sick-in-head" or just "thick-in-head," and expressed disbelief that I was actually going to run out on something as good as what she and I had going just to satisfy the compulsions of a "geek quarterlife crisis." I absorbed this all in penitent silence, so she went on to tell me that I was not even a real geek, and that my whole obsession with Lucky Wander Boy was nothing more than a lame evasion to distract me from my worthwhile *Catalogue of Obsolete Entertainments* project, which I'd allowed to go to seed because a *real* geek endeavor like that would involve thousands of hours of diligent geek labor, just the sort of *real* commitment that I did not have the courage to make. Using my own "On Geeks" insights against me, she accused me of the cultivation of geek chic, and said that karma would see to it that I got mine. Then she wondered aloud what had drawn her to such a lame and pointless guy, and asked how on earth she could be so in love with me. I wanted to tell her that I was not pointless at all, that for the first time in my life I was comfortable saying I had a Point—but I said nothing.

Why she finally decided my selfishness was too much, and left my apartment:

It would seem a logical follow-through to the abovementioned harangue, I know, but this was not the immediate reason for her exit. While she was catching her breath and wiping away her tears, she looked inside my open attaché and saw the stack of paper I had fatefully thrown in faceup, bound with two brass brads:

LUCKY WANDER BOY
(acts I & II)
by Araki Itachi
screen adaptation by Adam Pennyman

She asked me what it was, and I told her it was my incomplete version of the *Lucky Wander Boy* screenplay that I was going to present to Araki Itachi herself. Clio lifted the script to flip through it, bewildered that I hadn't told her about it after all this time, far more hurt than she'd have been if she found out that all through our honeymoon phase I'd had a live-in girlfriend. Upon picking up the script from my case, she saw Araki Itachi's picture laid carefully below it. She then charged me with wanting Araki Itachi in a sexual way, and using her to get closer to Itachi. I said this was not true, which was in itself not true, although it was not exactly false either; my relationship to Araki Itachi was complex, and it would have been very difficult for me to tell Clio exactly what Itachi was to me. She went on to tell me herself: Itachi (she claimed) was a woman I did not even know who could not possibly have any interest in me. Seeing the corner of Anya's red dress peeking out from beneath the throw blanket, she uncovered it, and said she supposed this was another gift for Itachi, and there was no easy way to tell her it was not. With an uncharacteristic malice that she wielded as a shield against the pain of betrayal, she warned me that Itachi probably wouldn't look so great in a slinky dress like this one, seeing as she was forty-five years old if she was a day. I told her that Asian women tended to age well, and it was then that she called me a selfish monster and left the apartment.

Why I let her go:
    I didn't at first; I went after her. There was something poignant about the ache I felt, standing there on the sidewalk as I watched her get into her car, that made her sexier to me than ever, made her resonate with me all the more. As she pulled away from the curb, she

reentered the realm of the ideal, in my mind she was baptized as the One Walking Away and reimbued with all the concomitant mystery. My desire was directly proportional to the square of her distance from me, reaching a near-infinite apogee as her car disappeared around the corner, and just before her rear fender disappeared from my sight I was overwhelmed by a blinding, white-hot need to be with her and stay with her forever, to live a normal life with her, a boring life, a regular life. A regular life with Clio was the other side of the velvet ropes for me, it was the Canaan I'd never be allowed to enter.

I consoled myself: If she turned the Jetta around and came back, my desire could well recede according to the strict dictates of the inverse square law—and the possibility cost of her return would undoubtedly be Stage III. Now that my Moment of Decision had arrived, I could hardly turn away from the course of action I had chosen. Thinking along schematic lines, I saw that like Lucky Wander Boy, my recent life could be divided into stages, delineated by my romantic involvements, and that each stage had the seeds of the stage to follow planted within it. Anya had been my Stage I, and it was Anya who pressed me to take her out the night I ran into Sexy Sammy Benjamin. This meeting was a direct pipeline to the hopeless cubicle desert of the Plant, where I met Clio—my Stage II—and became fully aware of my role in the fate of Lucky Wander Boy. Clio had both gotten me the picture of Itachi and taken me out to the real desert in Alamogordo to learn the truth about Lucky Wander Boy's Stage III, and the magical role that the mundane objects of Stage II played in its attainment.

Now, back in my living room, I looked at Itachi's picture lying on the couch next to my metal attaché (or briefcase), and the red dress hung over the back of the same couch, and the spade (which is certainly a shovel of sorts) jutting from the mouth of the sand-filled pillowcase propped against the coffee table. Reaching into my back pocket, I removed the extra screwdriver I'd put there during the dismantling of the Plant, and placed it on the table next to the hand mirror, which I then picked up and used to examine Vato

Hat's baseball cap, still on my head. In her message to Kurt, Itachi had asked him to:

PLEASE, emphasize the Objects of Centrality beyond screwdriver (of course!), but also shovel, red dress, mirror, briefcase, axe, baseball cap.

(The axe was still at Portal, but I had certainly emphasized the hell out of that.)

The flavor of destiny seasoned all. Of course, I had read about self-referential mania, about people who thought the clouds were whispering about them behind their backs and the rustling trees were spreading their secrets in a sign language of leaves, but I did not strike myself as this kind of person. On an even deeper level than I had imagined, my whole Stage II had been devoted to very subtle, subconscious preparations. Now I was ready to cross over the water, as I had done before to Poland and Anya—I savored the parallelism—to Japan and Araki Itachi. She had to have a Lucky Wander Boy machine, and it was at that game cabinet with her at my side that Lucky Wander Boy's Stage III and the Stage III of my life would come together, recursively, like a snake eating its tail. The complexity of the relationships between the world outside that game cabinet and the world beneath its glass screen occupied my thoughts for most of the cab ride to the airport.

suspense

● ● ● ● ● ● ● ● ● ● ● ● ● ● ● ● ● ● ● ●

I handed over the flight coupon and the passport.

"Hmmm . . . it says here you've got a round-trip ticket, Mr. Krickstein?" the woman said. "This is only the LAX-Osaka coupon."

"I thought I'd save you the trouble," I said.

"All right then . . . and you were supposed to be traveling with another person, a Ms.—"

"Budna. She left me this morning."

"I'm sorry to hear that, sir."

Embarrassed, the woman rushed me through check-in without looking me in the eye.

interruptus

● ●

THE CHARACTERS

PENNYMAN—Man in his late twenties. Player/knower/lover of the game Lucky Wander Boy.

MOMENT OF DECISION—Samurai whose age cannot be determined, as he has no face.

ARAKI ITACHI—Beautiful, mysterious woman between twenty-five and fifty years of age. Creator of the game Lucky Wander Boy.

MONKS—Men of various ages in the traditional monastic garb of Mount Hiei, with straw boots and canoe-shaped hats.

STEWARDESS—Woman in her early twenties, employee of Japan Airlines. Perky, but determined where her job is concerned.

THE SCENE

A secret, unused wing of the Mount Hiei monastery in Kyoto. Outside the monastery, PENNYMAN stands with his MOMENT OF DECI-SION. The Moment wields a samurai sword. Pennyman wields a gunmetal attaché containing his Lucky Wander Boy screenplay. Twin receiving lines of monks stand with heads bowed respectfully, creating a human aisle leading to the wooden front porch of the monastery.

MOMENT: We have arrived. At last, we have arrived.

PENNYMAN: Yes we have. Now that we're on speaking terms—don't take this the wrong way, but—I've got to say that I find your lack of a face somewhat disconcerting.

MOMENT: I have no face because I am merely a facet of you. Now that we have come together, you and I—you and your destiny—are one and the same. Non-different. A separate face for me would be a redundancy.

PENNYMAN: Oh. Well, that sounds okay. I didn't mean to be ungrateful or anything—but if we are one and the same, why do you need to be here?

MOMENT: Because only I knew the way.

Pennyman nods.

On the porch, ITACHI emerges in a robe of hand-painted silk. All present are stricken by her beauty.

ITACHI: (*to Pennyman*): Welcome, Adam Pennyman, and thank you. This holy place was to have been destroyed by barbarians from the East, but now it has been saved and re-consecrated by your efforts. You have earned the title of Shogun.

MOMENT: (*whispers to Pennyman*): It originally meant "barbarian-quelling General."

Pennyman nods thanks.

PENNYMAN: It was my honor, ma'am. But now I'm not sure what to do—I'm—

MOMENT: (*whispers to Pennyman*): A *ronin*. A masterless samurai.

PENNYMAN: I'm a *ronin*, a masterless samurai. I found my master evil and wrong, so I abandoned him, and now I am roaming, searching for a new one.

ITACHI: Do not worry. *I* will master you. Come—

Itachi turns. On the back of her robe, the art from the Lucky Wander Boy videogame cabinet is reproduced, in the style of the Edo period painter Hokusai. As she walks into the shadows of the monastery, she drops the robe. She is naked beneath it. From behind especially, she is sylphlike, ageless, of a different world.

ITACHI: (*calling from the inner dark*): I am waiting for you, Adam Pennyman. . . .

Tumescent, Pennyman moves to join her, when the STEWARDESS taps him on the shoulder.

STEWARDESS: Your dinner, sir.

PENNYMAN: Where did you come from? Go away. I'm busy.

STEWARDESS: Your dinner, sir.

She holds a Bento box dinner. Pennyman briefly examines its contents with confusion. He recognizes none of these foods. They all seem extremely unpalatable.

ITACHI: (*from inside*): I am waiting for you. . . .

PENNYMAN: Please, not now, I have to go. . . .

The stewardess's hand touches his shoulder, and he finds himself unable to move.

STEWARDESS: Sir? I have your dinner for you, sir.

She waves the box beneath his nose. He squints at its corner compartment, in which something that looks like uncooked duck quivers, drenched in a sauce that looks vaguely seminal.

ITACHI: I am waiting. . . .

STEWARDESS: Dinner, sir, dinner. . . .

Somehow, Pennyman is no longer standing. He is seated in a first-class airplane seat. When he looks to his side to entreat the aid of his Moment of Decision, he sees the sleeping face of a sunburnt Australian tourist beneath his Moment's samurai helmet.

ITACHI: Waiting. . . .

STEWARDESS: Dinner dinner dinner dinner dinner dinner. . . .

PENNYMAN: Ah, hell.

en route

● ●

Kansai Airport sat on an artificial island in Osaka-wan Bay. Throughout the complex, information counters had English-speaking staff who explained the hotel options available to someone in my price range, and pointed me up the elevators to the train station.

I took the Keihan Main Line from Yodoyabashi station in Osaka to Shijo station in Kyoto, and pulled my bag down Kawaramachi Street toward the street's terminus at a park that sloped gently upward to the east. The shingled roof of a shrine rose higher and higher over the edge of the park's gates as I got closer, as if aroused by my arrival, and as I reached the end of the gates, a geisha and her young apprentice left the park, *clack clack clack* in wooden sandals. I paused to appreciate the absolute perfection of this moment, then turned right down Higashioji-dori.

The Amenity Capsule Hotel was only ¥4,000 a night (about $40). My room was 3.5 feet across, 3.5 feet high, and 7 feet from end to end. When I lay down on the mattress, lifted my right leg and flexed my foot, my toes touched the screen of the small white TV in the upper right corner of the capsule. Through the curtain at my feet, I could hear a cell phone and periodic flatulence, but the hotel was mostly empty, as it was only 8:30 P.M. Putting in my earplugs anyway as a precaution against the drunks who would no doubt arrive after missing their last train, I turned off the light and closed my eyes. My hard-won sleep on the flight to Osaka had been scuttled by an overindustrious stewardess, and I would need to be at my peak tomorrow. The urge to relieve myself to Itachi's picture presented itself, but I resisted, preferring to let the energy build.

At 9 A.M. a man came by to kick me out of my capsule. I left my suitcase with the front counter attendant, but insisted through pantomime on taking my attaché upstairs with me. In the locker room, I changed into a flimsy robe and entered the communal bath, attaché in hand. Next to the door, a sign told me there were No Tattoos Allowed through a cartoon of a cute, sad, heavily tattooed Yakuza being shown the door. The bath room was full of naked Japanese businessmen. I proved to be an instant conversation stopper. Maybe it was the attaché, maybe it was my shaved head, but I had to rid myself of accumulated travel grime, so appreciated or not, I soaped up and went to soak in a hot tub. Keeping my hand on my case, I closed my eyes and took in deep breaths of steam, moistening lungs dried out from plane air. When I finally opened my eyes again, the room had cleared out.

Pulling my wheeled suitcase along with its built-in handle, I went out looking for a gift for Itachi, but I didn't have much luck. The only suitable flower arrangements I could find cost upwards of $150, and in my rush to escape from L.A., I had forgotten my credit card. A small beige teacup caught my eye in an antique shop because it was the exact same shade of beige as the Lucky Wander Boy desert at the peak of its beige phase, but when I inquired about the price, the shopkeeper told me it cost ¥879,200. This was just over $6,600, but more importantly, it was *exactly* the record high score for Donkey Kong, the highest score possible. I was on the right track.

I had not come to Kyoto on a sightseeing expedition, and had little interest in seeing this temple or that garden. I was there for three reasons: Lucky. Wander. Boy. Still, I wandered around for a few hours, because arriving toward the end of the business day would give me more time with Itachi. Sticking to Kiyamachi-dori, an endless strip of bars and restaurants, I walked up and down the street, switching hands on my suitcase and attaché for the sake of variety, sometimes stopping for a can of Roots coffee from a vending machine. Although the word "coffee" appeared nowhere on the can, I knew it was coffee from the start, because a billboard in both English and Japanese showed a can of Roots being held alluringly by Brad Pitt. Each time I passed Kiyamachi-dori 32, where a small, unassuming brass placard read S.L.S., Inc., I wrestled with the issue of desire. What to do when the carrot on the stick comes within reach? How would an adult Dante have dealt with being thrust into a room alone with Beatrice? I decided to remain in the Moment, and deal with situations as they arose; this strategy had worked well for me so far.

Six or seven tiny cans of coffee into the afternoon, I began to feel a bit edgy (in the original sense of the word, before youth marketing got ahold of it), so I decided to allow myself a beer, only one, to settle me down. The first bar I came to was called Hollywoodland. At 3:30 in the afternoon it was already a third full, mostly teenagers drinking ten-dollar bottles of Budweiser. A four-piece band played "Wish You Were Here." On my way in, I passed a young man with a perm and a leather jacket on his way out, who glanced my way before vomiting explosively on the sidewalk. His friends followed him out. I left right behind them, and watched for a while as they juggled conflicting impulses: comfort their friend, keep their expensive shoes clean.

Another bar had no name at all, English, Japanese or otherwise. The only people inside were the bartender, myself, and a three-person band. On a seven-feet-by-nine-feet stage, a thirtyish man with neatly combed hair, wearing a plush sweater with a collared shirt beneath it, milked walls of static and tortured honks from a heavily processed guitar. Next to him, a wispy, lupine woman in a conservative dress screamed aggressively into a microphone—primal, larynx-shredding shrieks. Behind a table of electronic equipment, a man in a button-down shirt and a thin tie manipulated various knobs and dials, reprocessing the guitar and the screams into a new species of sound that seemed determined to destroy the speakers that brought it into the world. I ordered a beer and began to drink it, but the noise was putting the edge on faster than the beer could take it off, and when the man in the button-down shirt smashed the mesh casing off an old microphone and began to unassumingly and carefully urinate on it, I decided it was time to go.

Lucky. Wander. Boy.

Back on Kiyamachi-dori, the sun was beginning to set. A black Mercedes with tinted windows went by, followed by a group of young men on Harleys who leered at me, looking dangerous. I paid them no mind. Lucky. Wander. Boy.

In front of number 32, I stood before the door meant for me and me alone, unique among all the doors in all the cities in all the world. The journey across the sea had actually been a journey inward, penetrating concentric layers, heading toward a singularity: Japan, Kyoto, S.L.S. . . .

Stage III.

Beneath the brass placard, a doorbell buzzer and speaker grate.

I was ready to cross over.

Lucky. Wander. Boy.

I pushed the button.

inside

● ●

A distorted voice came through the speaker grate. "Hai?"

"Yes, konichiwa, I'm here to see Araki Itachi?"

"Pasuwaado?"

"Uh—I don't know any password—"

"Ainiku."

I looked it up in the phrase section of my guidebook. "Sorry," as in "Sorry, but . . ."

"You don't understand, I've come all the way from America."

"Ainiku." *Click.*

I buzzed again.

"Hai!"

"Look, I just need to talk to her—"

"Ainiku!"

"—about Lucky Wander Boy—"

"Kieus—" He cut himself off mid-vulgarism. There was a silence, followed by a clipped buzz, and the door popped open, revealing a flight of steeply descending stairs.

Everything had a slight blue tint, icy like a bottle of aftershave. Though they could not possibly be a structural necessity, several light blue pillars broke up the space of the room, along with some hot-pink couches arranged around transparent, cube-shaped cocktail tables. The floor was done in small square tiles, mainly white, with a few gray and yellow tiles interspersed in a way that suggested a pattern without delivering one. I stared at the floor for a while and thought about how easy it would be to get sucked in, to believe in the siren-song promise that a crucial signal was hidden amidst the white-tiled noise, and forget all about your initial reason for coming, which for most of the black-suited men present was one of the myriad young lovelies clad in Day-Glo bikinis.

Not all lovelies, actually. Some were homely, some were verging on slightly overweight, some were just plain fat, some were men. An eclectic group, really; all they had in common was their clothing, which for all of them contained the absolute minimum amount of Lycra required for legality in Japanese law, which dictated that no pubic hair could be seen, though many of the employees stretched this regulation to the breaking point by waxing. They sat with their clients on the couches, sipping colorful drinks and making conversation until it was time to lead them by the hand through a set of large green double doors.

The focal point of attention in the room was a thermoplastic reception desk on the far end, manned by a dapper gentleman in a maroon blazer. On the wall behind him, a row of large, red kanji:

And below it, the translation:
SUPER LUCKY SPANK

To the left of this, a smiling cat logo, with smiling eyes that were really small frowns beneath its eyebrows, rosy red patches on its cheeks, and a matching rosy glow on each of its two prominent buttocks, which jutted toward the title. Beneath, a bill of fare. The first few were in Japanese and English, with prices listed in yen:

Straight Spank (give) (woman)	¥4200
Straight Spank (give) (man)	¥4200
Straight Spank (give) (woman, Supermodel class)	¥6000
Straight Spank (give) (woman, chunky sized)	¥7000
Straight Spank (get) (woman)	¥5500
Straight Spank (get) (man)	¥5500
Straight Spank (get) (woman, Supermodel class)	¥7500
Straight Spank (get) (woman, chunky sized)	¥8000
Paddle Spank	×2 for all above
Stinging Nettle Spank	×3 for all above
Spank & Fetish Combo	×4 for all above
Happy Day Spank	¥25,000
Seven Happy Neighbor-Nesting	¥50,000
Scenarios	by appointment; as negotiated

The more exotic varieties that followed were left untranslated, like the fish-head soups and chicken-feet stew on a Chinese restaurant menu, suggesting that if you could not read them, you could not possibly be interested.

When I stepped to the desk, the man in the maroon blazer bowed and smiled. I began to tell him why I'd come, but I was interrupted by a girl who slapped me in the ass hard enough to knock me into the thermoplastic. A free sample. Turning around, I saw her sizing me up, arms folded across her chest, a blonde stripe dyed into her straightedge black hair. With a flip of her head, she walked away. The man in the maroon blazer flashed his teeth and prompted me with eager nods. You like?

"I would like to speak with your boss," I said.

Bowing incomprehension.

"Marufuku?"

A deeper bow, and a brief intercom exchange. Marufuku emerged from behind the green doors, wearing the same gray suit and white gloves, but this time with no attaché case. Recognition blossomed when he saw me. He pumped my hand warmly; through his white glove, I felt his plastic pinky. He pointed at my own attaché case and nodded with vigorous approval:

"Daibu kasen mazakubu inupachi! Unapachi! Una . . . un-uona!"

"Ms. Itachi?" I asked, and he laughed, patting me on the back. He signaled for me to leave my suitcase with the man in the maroon blazer, which I did. With fastidious politeness, he led me back from where he'd come, into a long corridor that, unlike the waiting room, was *very* blue, a deep pulsing blue that lulled me into a state of tremendous calm despite the climactic nature of the moment. All mental rehearsals of the scene to follow ceased. My head was void, empty, clean as a taut bed sheet all the way to the end of the hallway.

The office was pure default-option Japanese, three Shoji screen walls, tatami mat floors, furniture reaching no higher than my knees with simple flower arrangements that somehow bespoke hours of contemplation. Behind me and to either side, the muffled sounds of hands, paddles, switches and more inventive materials slapping against flesh made the rice paper of the screen walls flutter faintly like big square woofers. I tried to ignore the discrepancy between sight and sound. Only the far wall was solid, and it was there that a woman in a Western skirt suit stood with her back to me, next to a wooden door whose rich grain made me want to take a bite out of it. She peered into one of eight spy holes that would have been eye level to a short man.

She turned. It was Araki Itachi.

I tried to determine how old she *looked*, but any age I threw at her only stuck for a few seconds before sliding off and falling to the floor. She was short, but she stood like a tall woman, and wore stiletto heels; though I had at least six inches on her, I felt self-conscious about my height. Her beauty was merciless, sharp as a *wakizashi* blade, and her face was as impossible to read as in her photo.

I felt like a million pounds per square inch of pressure were bearing down on my body, and being met with an equal but opposite pressure from within—a state of perfect calm, yet one in which the potential energies at play were enormous.

She said nothing, so I introduced myself.

Walking past me, she consulted a chart spread on a knee-high table. I peered over her shoulder. At first glance, it appeared to be a schematic electronics diagram. Though I could no longer read one, I had been able to as a kid thanks to my Heath Kit projects, and something about this one did not look right. Upon closer inspection, I found that the wire-coil curlicues, resistor squiggles, capacitor smiles and transistor circles were not labeled with pertinent voltage, watt or ohm information, but with rows of Japanese characters, one of which had my name written beneath it in English. This was one of the divination charts that Tetsu Bush had mentioned in Alamogordo. Various dates were written inside logic-gate diagram shapes, and a profusion of connector lines sprouted between the shapes, bending gratuitously at neat right angles, making the page look like an overly cautious player's game of Qix. An uncovering of the world's secret circuitry, the electric knots of resistance and capacitance that hindered or enabled the flow of possibility. Her first words to me made all my extremities tingle with shock:

"It is good that you've arrived today. If you'd come tomorrow, I would not have been able to speak with you, which would have been a tremendous shame. But today is fortuitous."

She pointed to her divination chart; the line between my own name and the "AND" gate housing today's date was highlighted in orange.

"It is an honor, Ms. Itachi."

"Come," she said. "Come and look. A tour, of sorts."

She led me to the spy-hole wall, and moved aside to allow me access to the spy holes. I inhaled deeply through my nose to try to smell her perfume, but she was odorless. When she touched my arm to put me in front of the right spy hole, I felt as though every nerve in my body had converged upon the skin beneath her fingers, like the indigo lightning in the plasma globes sold at specialty stores.

The clear lens of the spy hole provided a view of a small alcove about a cubic foot in volume, with a black top and bottom and bloodred velvet curtains on either side. On the far end, a sixteen-inch video monitor displayed what appeared to be a live feed of a facsimile Old West saloon, complete with swinging saloon doors and unlabeled bottles of whiskey on the bar top. On a bar stool sat a Japanese man with black suit pants and a white dress shirt. He had removed his suit jacket, however, and replaced it with a brown suede vest, and his dress loafers had been swapped out for a pair of ill-fitting cowboy boots. On his head, a cartoonish cowboy hat. Splayed across his lap, a Japanese woman had her ruffled dress skirt pulled up to give the man a clean shot at her naked buttocks, which he spanked with great intensity, nearly hard enough to unbalance them both and send them tumbling to the floor. The scene unfolded in silence; I tried to match it to one of the sets of muffled slaps coming through the Shoji screens, but the saloon must have been set up in a distant room.

The next peephole had an identical setup, but on its surveillance screen, I absurdly recognized the mock-up of Tom Mura's living room from the Japanese TV show *Space Giants* (1967) that I'd watched every day after school in reruns on channel 44 in Chicago. This time, a male client about my age was himself being spanked while wearing the silver-antennaed helmet of the rocket-boy Gam, by a woman wearing the silver foil costume of Silvar, Gam's mother, who like Gam can change into a rocket at will.

"This is your business venture? This is why you needed the money from the Lucky Wander Boy option?"

It was.

"You've given up on video games? I'd assumed you were doing something—with all the possibilities, the gigahertz, the endless memory, I just thought—you could build a world. You could sculpt a future, a thousand futures—"

"I am the future," she said. "The future is not in silicon or fiber optic cable or a million polygons a second." With a precise, theatrical gesture, she motioned to the line of peepholes, her update of the Enlightenment-era porno conceit. Her conviction was unflinching. "The future is infantile. The future is humiliation. The future is punishment. For me, the future is money. We do extremely well."

Letting this slide, I tried to assume a heroic insouciance, like a samurai returning to his master. "I've solved your Portal problem. No more faking ignorance with Kurt Krickstein, no more dealing with him at all. He's got a whole new set of worries on his hands. He'll let the *Lucky Wander Boy* option lapse."

"Oh, I know," she said.

"You know? How could you know what I did?"

"I'm afraid I don't see what any of it has to do with you."

With pride—it leaked through my words, I could not help it—I explained what I had done, the dismantling I had orchestrated in the Portal Plant. She heard me out with an expression of extreme interest, but when I finished telling her about it, she lost her characteristic control for long enough to let out an explosive chuff of laughter, as if my whole story had been an unexpected joke with a particularly clever punch line. Then she regained her composure, but a faint Gianconda smile remained on her lips as she stepped over to a floor-level bookshelf.

"That was very thoughtful of you." Bending at the knees, she picked a book off the shelf, one with a plain white cover marked by only three or four kanji.

"Tell me," she said, "have you ever read the novella *Leng Tch'e* by Dafei Ji?"

Elation! She had unintentionally vindicated my theory concerning the work's influence on her by bringing it up unprompted. The pieces were falling into place.

"Yes! It's one of my favorite books! If I may say so, I've often thought about it in conjunction with your work."

She flipped through the book and indeed, her copy's pages were extensively annotated. "This is one of my favorite passages. I'll translate from the Japanese translation to English as best I can."

She proceeded to read one of *my* favorite passages from the novella, one with which I was quite familiar. To the best of my memory, her impromptu translation was almost identical to the studied English in my Penguin paperback:

I hold no grudge against the men who scatter my parts to the five directions, because each piece of my body is a hindrance to my immortality; as I shuffle off each part, I become further invested in timelessness . . . yes, my breast is gone, I know this because the whiteness that once was pain has expanded, dislodging a piece of my twice-lived life from itself, the piece falls away like a discarded puppet and where the puppet's shadow was there is now only the white, free to be filled with new shadows, a milky timelessness with room enough inside it to live other lives in other worlds, room enough for all of them as my twice-lived life falls away piece by piece with each stroke of the Head Man's knife, and I lose all that I was but gain all that I was not, which is fitting, for the experience of being cut into pieces makes of all people the same person, and thus are the fragments of my experience as insignificant as the fragments of my body, and the only importance of the web into which these fragments are woven is that by following its strands I have been led to this consummation. . . .

She shut the book.

The other worlds are all real. All configs are a part of the ultimate config of the universe, and they were all within reach. If I could just fuck her, we would both melt away, dissipate into the Ultimate like ink drops in water.

We stood together, saying nothing. Distant slappings the only sounds.

"Do you know the story of how this book came to be published in Japan?" Seeing that I did not, she looked at her watch and continued. "It is late—I will give you the condensed version."

She sat on her knees at the low table and motioned for me to join her, which I did.

"In early 1938, a nineteen-year-old Japanese soldier named Kanchingai Ana took part in the Nanjing . . . expedition. By his own admission, he was a young man of immoderate anger and emotion, and the smallest sip of aggravation was enough to fuel his rage for weeks: an imagined slight, a lazy bow that did not reach the depth he felt he deserved. Under the command of Prince Asaka, Emperor Hirohito's uncle, the worst in Ana's nature was given free reign. I will not detail the atrocities in which Ana took part, although I know of them. They are a matter of public record everywhere but here in Japan, where many refuse to acknowledge the horrors perpetrated by their parents and grandparents. In the course of the systematic destruction of the Nanjing and the massacre of its inhabitants, Ana came upon the home of an old man who surprised him by speaking to him in flawless Japanese, thereby postponing his own death for long enough to speak a few words.

" 'I understand why you have come,' the old Chinese man said. 'I will not try to dissuade you from your course of action. I have myself stood where you stand; I have done the things you have done, and worse, for I did them to my own. In the course of administering a punishment that was my job to administer, I saw something in the face of the woman who was dying at my hands, something I could not forget. Eventually, it led me to write this. Here, take it. It is for you.'

"The old man handed Ana a stack of rice paper pages covered in elegantly written Chinese and bound with two red ribbons. Ana put his bayonet through the old man's windpipe, but he took the pages and put them in his pack, and when he returned to Osaka after the war, thin and exhausted, the pages went with him, though he knew not a word of Chinese. For years, as he slowly buried what he had been under a veneer of civilian life, acquiring a wife, fathering a son, Ana kept this manuscript, which he could not read, and this combination of proximity and impenetrability haunted him. He found himself brooding over the Chinese more and more, wondering what it said, often to the point of distraction—to this day, his left thumb is misshapen from a hammer blow he delivered to himself while thinking about the rice paper pages when he should have been thinking about the nail. When he found his four-year-old son leafing roughly through them one afternoon, he beat him severely enough to warrant a hospital visit. He tried to put the pages out of mind, hiding them in a desk, in a trunk in his attic, going so far as to wrap them in wax paper and bury them under a tree in the park, but it was no use. The more engulfing his obsession with the Chinese pages became, the more reluctant he was to entrust their translation and the knowledge of their contents to anyone else, and thus the less likely he was to learn what they said—

"Unless he learned to read Chinese himself. In postwar Japan, after the rubble had been cleared, the streets repaved and the smoke of confusion blown away, there were far more opportunities available for a common man to acquire this knowledge than previously. Kanchingai Ana devoted himself to the Chinese language for five years in his spare time and during periods of unemployment, but he did not run to the manuscript after each new lesson. He wanted to experience it all at once, without breaking his concentration to consult a dictionary or reference book, or even go to the toilet, so he deferred his fulfillment until he had passed his Advanced Proficiency Exam in written Chinese. Then he unwrapped the old man's manuscript from its wax paper and began to read."

My knees began to hurt. Knees did not seem designed for this kind of sitting.

"After twelve years, for the first time, he learned the name of the man he had murdered: Dafei Ji. The manuscript was a story entitled *Leng Tch'e*, and was written not from Dafei's own point of view but, judging from the old man's brief comments, the point of view of a woman he had executed by the Death of a Hundred Cuts in rural China during the late Qing Dynasty for a murder she herself had committed. Ana read the entire sixty-five pages in one sitting, and the reading transformed him, perhaps in a way similar to that in which the events described therein transformed the writer himself. Ana has never used the word *satori* to describe it, yet those who have undergone this experience never do.

"Less than a week after his first reading, Ana left his wife and child in the care of relatives and took his vows at the Enryaku-ji monastery on Mount Hiei, about ten kilometers from where we now stand. The ordeals of the monks of Mount Hiei are legendary—they involve a nine-day *doiri* fast without water, sleep or food, and extremely arduous athletic feats, culminating in the thousand-day marathon, which is spread out over seven years, and involves walking as many as eighty-four kilometers each day with nothing on their feet but *tabi* socks and straw sandals. After becoming one of the few monks in history to complete two thousand-day marathon cycles, Kanchingai Ana became the Abbot of Enryaku-ji, and it was only then that he sat down to translate *Leng Tch'e* into Japanese, and it was from this translation that all subsequent translations were made. He has released enough of the original manuscript for scholars to verify its veracity and the faithfulness of his translation, but no more. *Leng Tch'e* still has not been published in China.

"Obviously, *Leng Tch'e* has not had the same effect on all those who have read it," and here she paused to indicate herself and me as examples, "as it did on Kanchingai Ana. Perhaps it was situational: Lessons come to those who are ripe to learn them, and not to others. I am sure you have read many Zen koans that end with the phrase, ' . . . and the monk attained enlightenment' without becoming enlightened yourself. Or perhaps in translation, or reproduction, the manuscript lost something essential, that which brought about the change in Ana. In either case, aside from translating *Leng Tch'e*, he has done much for the poor of Kyoto, and the children, including his own son, with whom he reestablished contact when the boy was sixteen. Indeed, if it were not for the conversions of the warlike, Buddhism would have ceased to exist long ago—for it was the Indian Emperor Asoka who initiated the spread of the dharma to China and beyond in the third century BCE, and he only found inner peace after much conquest and bloodshed.

"It is my speculation that the conditions surrounding Ana's

own enlightenment allowed him to endure his son's membership in the Yakuza without complaint. Perhaps there was some causal connection between his early violence and the boy's language problem which, Ana felt, disqualified him from passing judgment on his son, who was named Marufuku, and known to most only through the local Kyoto legends of the Smiling Man. Perhaps Ana felt that the boy's own bodhishattvahood awaited him in the dying faces of one of his many victims. I do not know if it has.

"I had heard the legends of the Smiling Man growing up. He was what I believe you would call the bogeyman to many children in my neighborhood. When I was working at Nintendo as a young woman, Marufuku's arrival to carry out an assassination order on the CEO Hiroshi Yamauchi coincided with my own departure to start Uzumaki. I recognized him from the stories, and when I confronted him, his inability to speak anything but nonsense confirmed my suspicions. It did not take long to convince him to change his career path and come to work for me. I was a very convincing woman. His failure to complete the Yamauchi job led the Yakuza to cut off his little finger, but his life was spared out of respect for his father. Word of this likely reached Yamauchi himself, who settled whatever differences may have led to the initial order. Marufuku's smile remained unaltered during his transition from hit man to vice president of Uzumaki, Inc., and he has obviously said nothing about his enlightenment or lack thereof. Since that time, though, he has killed no one. He did not get to open his briefcase at Nintendo, and of course, there was never any need for him to open it at Portal Entertainment."

"Wait," I said, "he did open it. He opened it and gave me some kind of information sheet."

Itachi seemed momentarily jarred by this. "Hmmm. That is very interesting. The briefcase is usually empty except for the ceramic pistol he keeps beneath the false bottom under an X-ray blind, and the pen that conceals the pistol's firing pin."

"He was sent . . . to kill Krickstein?"

She smiled. "You watch too many movies. Such extremes were hardly necessary. The entire edifice of Mr. Krickstein's business rested precariously on the production of the third *Eviscerator* movie, as anyone could see. Marufuku's father, Abbot Ana, proved very amenable to stringing Mr. Krickstein along with the absurd possibility of blowing up a part of the Mount Hiei monastery until Super Lucky Spank had been firmly established, in exchange for free use of our services for the rest of his life."

"The abbot of a monastery comes here to spank people?"

She rose, and I did as well, although I'd been sitting on my knees so long they almost buckled when I tried. Through the far video peephole, she showed me a feed of an elderly man in the garb of a Buddhist monk, spanking a chunky girl with great relish. I tried to make out the details of the man's face, but the image was too small, and the resolution too low.

"Isn't that an odd thing for a monk to be doing?" I asked.

"If I tried to make my clientele's motivations my business, I would not be in business for long. According to some initial inquiries I've made with one Chad Millman at a company called D,S&A Venture Group, when the monastery explosion deal topples, the whole *Eviscerator III* deal will topple, and when the *Eviscerator III* deal topples, the company will fall with it. Thus the futility of your own efforts, as valiant as they were. The inevitability of this sequence of events is probably becoming clear to Mr. Krickstein right now. He will not find it so easy to pick up the pieces and start over. He is Not Hollywood, after all, and we are all moving into leaner times. All the lame horses are being shot and rendered.

"So," she continued, checking her watch, "now that your old job is no longer available, what are your plans?"

I unsnapped my attaché and removed my unfinished *Lucky Wander Boy* script.

"I've been working on this since our phone conversation. Now that Portal's option is going to lapse, I thought we could do the *Lucky Wander Boy* movie right, the way you wanted. It's only the first two acts, but I think it's a strong start."

She opened to the middle and read a page.

LUCKY crawling wandering lost where to go

                    LUCKY

              I must go on.

staggering falling face to the sands

                    LUCKY (CONT'D)

              I can't go on.

A MEKU APPEARS

                    MEKU

          PERHAPS YOU OUGHT

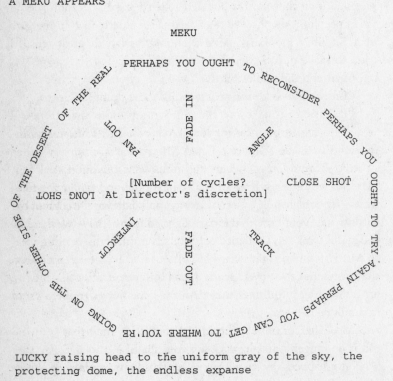

          [Number of cycles?   CLOSE SHOT
          At Director's discretion]

LUCKY raising head to the uniform gray of the sky, the
protecting dome, the endless expanse

                    LUCKY
              I'll go on.

A SHOVEL appears. He pulls himself back to his knees
and begins to dig, down down down

not at all

Itachi folded her hands into prayer position, closing my script.

"That is not what I wanted, not at all. That is not a movie. No one would go see it."

I had not allowed for this reaction, and had no prepared response.

"But—don't you see, as his ego dissolves, as the arbitrary rules governing his behavior dissolve, the arbitrary rules governing the format, the typography—it's a sort of level jumping, where the content of the story begins to reshape the form itself, so that on all levels there is this fluidity and flux, at first it's only about what the character knows, it's epistemological—but it *jumps*, it jumps to the ontological, and what *is* becomes unclear—people won't watch this movie for some pat formal resolution and catharsis, they'll watch it for the same reason they played the game, for the joy of this uh—constant—unfolding—of possibility—I'm imagining this radically uncertain ending—"

"They won't watch it at all," she said. "They did not play the game at all. Lucky Wander Boy was a complete and utter failure. Because the most wildly successful games of the day were somewhat surrealistic and nonsensical, I reasoned that a *completely* surrealistic and nonsensical game would be more successful still. I was wrong, I recognized I was wrong, I moved on. And really, when I see something like this . . ."

She flipped through the pages of my script again before passing final judgment.

"When I see something like this, dissolution of ego is the last thing that comes to mind."

My expectations were decaying before my eyes like the buildings in Double Dragon, crumbling, falling off piece by piece.

"If Lucky Wander Boy was a failure," I said, attempting an offensive, "why would you topple an entire company to get it back?"

"It is important to maintain diversity in one's holdings. Failure or not, Lucky Wander Boy is *mine*, and I did not become a successful businesswoman in a country that frowns upon successful businesswomen by simply giving away things that are mine. Who knows when another such company might take the bait, and provide me with a fresh cash infusion?"

A shudder of recurrence rippled through me, as I experienced the nightmare frisson that came with traveling many miles only to wind up in the same place. An emergency redeployment of hope was imperative. I put all my chips on Lucky Wander Boy.

"If it's yours, you must have a Lucky Wander Boy machine here."

"No," she said. "I do not."

"Somewhere else then. At home."

"Would you display a reminder of your biggest mistake in your living room?"

"Anywhere," I said, "I need—"

Her wristwatch began to chime midnight in twelve small even beeps.

beep beep beep

"I'm sorry," she said, "our conversation is nearly over."

beep beep beep

"Wait," I said, "I don't—what do you want me to do—"

beep beep

"—I came all this way, I lost my job—"

beep beep

She said, "Well. . . ."

beep

"How do you feel about spanking?"

beep

"When can we talk again?" I asked.

She frowned, unsure, and looked at her arcane diagram, the solid state divination chart on which I'd fallen out of alignment. She soon grew tired of it, however, and left the room. I looked at the chart, trying to follow some thread of meaning in its lines and determine when she would speak to me again, but there was really no telling.

replay

● ● ● ● ● ● ● ● ● ● ● ● ● ● ● ● ● ● ● ●

Itachi folded her hands into prayer position, closing my script after
reading the last page.

"Yes," she said. "You understand it perfectly."

I flushed with joy, emboldened by her praise.

"I'm glad you like it. Do you have a Lucky Wander Boy machine here, by any chance?"

"Of course."

She opened the door in her office's far wall.

It was little more than a closet, with black walls, ceiling and
floor that swallowed the light rays from the office and refused to
spit them out again.

The only object in the tiny room was a Lucky Wander Boy
machine.

Only when I ran my hand along its laminate side did I trust its
reality. From beneath my splayed fingers, Lucky's huge left eye
gazed into the blackness. Gargoyle, apple and screwdriver hung on
the illuminated marquee.

"Do you play it?" I asked.

"It is the first Lucky Wander Boy machine. I have never
touched it. That machine is here for the first person who comes
looking for it. It is here only for you. You are the only one who
will ever play it. Go ahead. I'll wait outside."

She shut the door behind her, making the on-screen demo the
only source of light. I pushed "1 Player." The fanfare sounded.

I played. I don't know how long I spent; I played with Zen ease through the zombie-slow Sebiros of the first screen, through the Mega-Sebiro of the second screen. I navigated the disorientation of the final screen and its evil Photo-Sebiro, and was sucked up the pipe right into the Stage II desert. I played and played and played, wandered and acquired and lost and reacquired through day and night and beige and white. I kept the mirror. I dropped the mirror and picked it up again. Many times I thought about jumping off the cliff and starting over, maybe it was like a game of solitaire where only certain initial configurations even presented the potential for a winning game, but I thought better of it and kept playing until it happened.

The mirror floated from my pocket, and I ran toward it as the desert rose up around me, I ran into the tunnel of sand that should have caved in but did not, ran after the mirror when it shot from sight until I found it again, glowing blue green, grown to full size, growing larger as I got closer, larger and larger until I was swimming in it, the whole screen.

Drowning in it. No reflection, no passing through to the other side. The blue green began a retreat, becoming a shrinking, amorphous blob that eventually receded into the black. Not the gray black of an inert CRT screen. Dead black. The joystick was unresponsive. Warp Skip! did nothing.

Like Tim Sczerby after 879,200 points on Donkey Kong, I was killed off without explanation or apology. It all crashed, and my game was over.

replay

● ● ● ● ● ● ● ● ● ● ● ● ● ● ● ● ● ● ● ●

The mirror floated from my pocket, and I ran toward it as the desert rose up around me, I ran into the tunnel of sand that should have caved in but did not, ran after the mirror when it shot from sight until I found it again, glowing blue green, grown to full size, and in the mirror I saw my face, broken down into crisp vector polygons, immaculate and sharp, a caricature of myself so economical and perfect that it was not a caricature at all but a pure distillation of the idea of Adam Pennyman.

And then I stepped through the mirror into Stage III—

And time stopped—

And I was *in the picture*—

In a house—my house, or our house, because Clio was there waiting for me with blonde-and-red vector hair that had all the flowing intricacy of wood grain. Her cheek bones were delicately crosshatched, and she was happy, and so was I, in a vector mirror in the hallway I saw myself smiling—

But it was airy. My smile was a phantasm, insubstantial, between the white lines of my small, neat teeth, and between the sharp pink contours of my lips there was nothing but black absence, a relentless dark Nothing that threatened to swallow all the tenuous, adjacent licks of frozen light like a black hole. The happiness, like the doors and the TV and Clio and myself, had been robbed of something. It was a cheap knockoff, it didn't play like real happiness. When the real was refracted to the ideal through the prism of the screen, something vital was stripped away. Call it an aura. When the ideal became detached from the physical self to which I was still bound like that squirming thorax that refused to let the butterfly's wings fly free, the ideal lost the force that kept it aloft.

And standing there in my too-straight house with my dream of the Girl Who'd Walked Away, I saw for the first time that Clio was a ghost and had been all along. It was a horror-movie moment, right out of one of those Japanese ghost-story films like *Kwaidan* or *Ugetsu*, where easy happiness turns out to be a mere phantasm that cannot hold, and simple love is always the love of ghosts doomed to collapse along with their world. All the key players on my personal stage bore only a tangential relation at best to the creatures they were emblems of; any resemblance to actual persons living or dead was coincidental. The Girl, the Helper, the One Walking Away, the Monkey, the Big Boss, the Mystery Woman, the Samurai, the Moment of Decision, idealizations, demonizations, distillations—

It was the Mario Illusion, all down the line.

replay

● ● ● ● ● ● ● ● ● ● ● ● ● ● ● ● ● ● ● ●

She did not even need to say it, it was written in the lines of hurt and reproach on her forehead as she turned to look at me one last time before leaving—but she did say it, quietly, with quivering lips:

"You're a selfish monster, you know that?"

I wanted to explain to her that I was not, I wanted to make her see. When she ran down the stairs and out the door, I ran after her.

There was something poignant about the ache I felt, standing there on the sidewalk as I watched her approach her car, that made her sexier to me than ever, made her resonate with me all the more. In my mind she was baptized as the One Walking Away and reimbued with all the concomitant mystery.

But as she opened the Jetta's door, I revised this thought. She was not a dream. She was a person. "The One Walking Away" bore only a tangential relation at best to the creature she was an emblem of. My version of Clio was the Mario Illusion, all down the line. In blatant violation of the inverse square law, as she walked away from me, she moved *out* of the realm of the ideal—but still I was over-whelmed by a blinding, white-hot need to be with her and stay with her forever. Canaan was receding, as usual, and if she got into that car and drove away, nothing would ever change. It would be the treadmill for me from then on.

It took a shout that drew some of the neighbors out of their homes to stop Clio from climbing into the Jetta. She turned to look at me, trembling with hurt. I only had one chance.

I took the LAX-Osaka flight coupon from my pocket and tore it into sixteen pieces.

I tried to do the same with Krickstein's passport, but laminated documents are almost impossible to tear.

We had to leave L.A., but the consequences of my actions at Portal did not follow us. Karma took a holiday. We moved to Chicago, because my family lived there and hers lived only three hours away in Iowa. We got married.

We found jobs at an ad agency, I as a copywriter, she as a graphic designer. We did not love our jobs, but it was better than Portal, and we were together, almost. On adjacent floors. On my floor, we found a file storage closet where ancient, unused files were kept, I stole a key, and once a week we'd sneak in there to fuck during lunch.

We had two children whom we named Lawrence and Benjamin, and they in turn had five children between them.

We were happy. There were disappointments, of course, but if I can truly say we were happy, and I can, why dwell on them? Nothing you couldn't imagine for yourself. Rejections, setbacks, emergencies. My hairline marching up and over the ridge of my head, in lockstep with my own march toward the end. The inevitable illnesses.

Breast cancer took her before stomach cancer took me. I will not go into that. I absolutely refuse to go into it. I held out for twenty years after she went, outlasting almost everybody. They were not happy years, but it was only on my deathbed that I was beset by a curious, scraping dissatisfaction. Drug-addled, lying there while grandpa Lawrence forced my little great-granddaughter Tracy to hold great-grandpa's hand—why I don't know, she was only five and I was obviously scaring the shit out of her—when everyone I had ever truly known was finally gone, as my children and grandchildren and great-grandchildren waited for me to stop being me and to become just another thing, an object that could no longer pretend to be otherwise, all I could think of was Lucky Wander Boy.

Strange, isn't it? But there it is. Maybe it was the drugs. Lucky Wander Boy. Nothing else. Not my kids, not my parents, not my grandkids or grandparents, not even Tempest or Peacock Palace. Lucky Wander Boy, Stage III. I had left it behind, I had abandoned the only transcendence I had ever envisioned, and now it was going to happen: I was going to cease. Fuck Buddhism—I did not want to cease. But it was too late. The morphine was not stretching me to infinity, as it did to the narrator of *Leng Tch'e*; it was shutting me down. The door had been out there, somewhere, waiting for me for my entire life, only for me—but now it was being shut. What kind of life would have sprouted from the moment when Clio climbed into the Jetta if I hadn't stopped her, if I hadn't collapsed my possibility wave, if I'd got on the plane and taken the trip, headed off for my plywood-shelled pillar of Hercules? The last thing I knew as the last dropperful of morphine sulfate hit my tongue and shut the door on me was that I would never know.

replay

● ● ● ● ● ● ● ● ● ● ● ● ● ● ● ● ● ● ●

The only object in the room was a Lucky Wander Boy machine.

The fanfare sounded—

I played, I don't know how long I spent—

Many times I thought about jumping off the cliff and starting over—

The mirror floated from my pocket, and I ran toward it as the desert rose up around me—

And in the mirror I saw my face, a pure distillation of the idea of Adam Pennyman that had never been obscured by fat or acne—

And then I stepped through the mirror into Stage III—

And time stopped—

And I was *in the picture*—

And I knew where I was immediately.

The Peacock Palace game room was more beautiful as a set of vectors than it ever was in my world. This was not a simplified representation of the place I had been many times, the place that had burned down and been steamrolled and paved over to make way for a red-brick strip mall. That place had been an imperfect version of this Platonic ideal, fallen into time and allowed to accumulate all the petty details of decay. All the times I had gone there, this was the place I'd been looking for. A cathedral of light.

It was a full house. My mother and father were waiting for me at the door, my father smiling through his gray-stippled beard. And my grandparents, my maternal grandmother standing straighter than her osteoporosis had ever allowed in my lifetime, smoking a vector cigarette, exhaling wisps of French curve smoke. And my childhood friends, and my childhood enemies, and my grade school teachers, and my college professors, and the girls who'd made fun of me, and the few who had not, and the entire Portal staff, and Kurt Krickstein dressed as Ibn Alhrazed, who gave me the thumbs-up as I passed and mouthed the words "Loved the script!" with vector lips. And Mandy Cline. And Anya—all was forgiven—and Clio—all was forgiven—and Marufuku and Itachi herself with an entourage of twenty Super Lucky Spank lovelies, all watching me with admiration, all there for me. All made of light, just like my hands when I held them before my face. Whatever I did was *right*, and wherever I went, they followed. It was all perfect.

They even had a Lucky Wander Boy machine, enshrined in its very own corner. There was nothing I'd rather play.

Everyone gathered around as I stepped to it, and every bit of my being tingled with lightness and hummed a perfect fifth, because this was my haven, right here in front of this cabinet, this was my place. I reached into my pocket for one of an infinite number of quarters and dropped it in the slot, pushed "1 Player." The fanfare sounded, and I played. When I made a narrow escape, everyone cheered. It did not matter how long I spent, because I was no longer wearing the shackles of time, and my arms felt light without them as I played through the first stage, and the second, and this time there was no trial and error, the proper combination of items found and lost and recovered was clear to me from the very beginning, and in no time the mirror floated from my pocket, and I ran toward it as the desert rose up around me—

And in the mirror I saw my face—

And then I stepped through the mirror into Stage III—

And time stopped—

And I was *in the picture*—

And I knew where I was immediately.

Peacock Palace, a new order of beauty higher than the last, a refinement of a refinement—

And mother, and my father—

And my grandparents—

And my friends—

And my enemies—

And the teachers, and the girls, and the coworkers—

And Krickstein—

And Anya—

And Clio—

And Itachi—

And the Lucky Wander Boy machine, enshrined in its very own dark corner. There was nothing I'd rather do.

Everyone gathered around as I stepped to it, and reached into my pocket for one of an infinite number of quarters, and dropped the coin in the slot and played through the stages until the mirror floated from my Lucky's pocket, and I ran toward it as the desert rose up around me—

Mirror. Face.

Stage III. In the picture.

Peacock Palace.

Mother. Father.

Grandparents. Other people, ghosts like me.

Anya.

Clio.

Itachi.

Clio, Itachi.

Clio? Itachi? Clio? Itachi?

No . . . the Lucky Wander Boy machine, enshrined in its very own dark corner, a corner so dark it refused to spit out a single shard of light. I could not think of a single better thing to do, a single better place to be, than right in front of that machine. I wanted to want something else, I tried to want something else, but it was impossible. The Moment had come, and I had chosen. This was what I had come to find.

I reached into my pocket for one of an infinite number of quarters, and I began to feel their weight, I wanted to stop and ponder the meaning of the weight of an infinity of quarters, but I no longer had the luxury of time. I dropped the coin in the slot and pushed "1 Player," though I knew what awaited me behind the screen.

The fanfare sounded, and I played.

CATALOGUE OF OBSOLETE ENTERTAINMENTS
GAME: ADAM PENNYMAN
Format: Person
Manufacturer: Harold and Joanne Pennyman
Year: 1971

The object of this game is—

Slowly, the hemispheres of my eyelids rise, the dried blood around them cracking with the sound of rending rocks, and the whiteness is replaced by the uniform gray of the sky. It is not a dome as I once believed. It is an endless expanse. It goes on forever.

—Dafei Ji, *Leng Tch'e*